The General's Dog

James Garcia Woods

First published in 1999 by Robert Hale Limited.

This edition published in 2019 by Endeavour Media Ltd.

This book is for César, Marisol, Pili and Chus, who are not only my oldest friends in Spain, but are also four of the warmest and most generous people I have ever met.

And for my fellow madrileños, who have made this city we share the greatest in the world.

Table of Contents

Chapter One

The dog – a large German shepherd named Principe – loped down the dark alley with his tail raised high in the air. From behind him came the sound of pounding feet and desperate, heavy breathing, but the animal was not the least bit disconcerted. He knew his pursuer well, and was sure that he, too, was enjoying this new game.

The man, gasping for air, increased his pace. The dog, in response, put on an extra little spurt which widened the gap between them even more.

'Stop, Principe! There's a good boy,' the man called out, in a voice which betrayed his rising panic.

The dog ignored the plea. His day so far had been filled with wonderful new adventures, and he was still far too excited to consider obeying a man who wasn't even his master.

Principe turned the bend in the lane. He was not very far from the Calle Mayor now. Maybe he would abandon this particular game when he reached the main street, he thought. Perhaps, instead of playing 'chase', he would devote his energies to scrounging bits of *chorizo* and morsels of sheep's brains from the uniformed men he was sure to find there.

'Stop, Principe! Please stop!' the man behind him croaked.

But the dog only tossed his head from one side to the other, and kept on running.

He had almost reached the corner of the Calle Mayor when he heard the loud explosion and felt the sudden – terrifying – pain in his left shoulder. He didn't stop moving – his only desire was to run away from whatever was hurting him – but now, instead of travelling in a straight line, he was weaving crazily from one side of the street to the other. With each new stab of agony, the dog howled louder and louder, as if protesting to the whole world that he had been treated unfairly. He was still howling when a second bullet took the top of his head off.

*

There were hundreds of soldiers jostling one another for space around the crowded bars on the Calle Mayor. Some of them were conscripts who had expected to be sent to North Africa, and instead had found themselves less than fifty kilometres from Madrid. Some were professionals, who had seen so much service they could scarcely make a move unless it was preceded by a barked order. And some were recent volunteers, who had received little more than a minimal training while in the Fascist militias. Yet all of them were linked by a common bond. Each and every one had been out on the sierra, heard the angry boom of guns and seen, if only from a distance, the horrors which war can bring. They had experienced the grief of losing comrades in arms, and the almost overwhelming sense of relief that it had been someone else who had died. And now, weighed down with the knowledge that they would have to face it all again the next day, they were determined to get gloriously and forgetfully drunk.

Of the six privates who were drinking together outside the bar closest to the church, it was the small one with a face like that of a cornered rat who was undoubtedly the leader. When he spoke, the others held a respectful silence. When he shook his head doubtfully at what one of his companions was saying, the speaker became so confused that he soon lost track of his argument. Private Pérez, though only a couple of years older than his companions, was a man to be deferred to – a man who had a knowledge of the world outside his own village.

It was Pérez, always on the alert, who heard the first shot, and told the rest of them to shut up and listen. And it was Pérez who started running towards the sound of the second shot, confident, without even looking over his shoulder to check, that his comrades would be right behind him.

There were no lights in the alley which ran alongside the church, and when Pérez first caught sight of the black shape lying awkwardly on the ground, he thought that it was a child. Then, as his eyes gradually grew accustomed to the darkness, he recognised the shape for what it really was. He bent down next to the corpse, and struck a match.

'Somebody's shot a dog,' said Private Jiménez, stupidly, from behind him. 'Now why would anybody want to do that?'

Pérez moved his blazing match closer to what was left of the animal's head. 'I don't know why anybody would want to shoot it,' he said. 'But there's one thing I am sure of – if they ever catch whoever did it, he'll be up before a firing squad in no time at all.'

'Up before a firing squad?' Private Jiménez repeated. 'Just for killing an animal?'

'This is no ordinary animal,' Pérez explained patiently. 'This isn't any old mutt you might kick out at as you're walking down the street. This, my friends, is the *General*'s dog.'

*

From his bedroom window, Paco Ruiz looked down on to the Calle Hortaleza. It was close to one o'clock in the morning, but the street was still crowded with people, as it always was during the stifling hot summer nights. Paco recognized most of the men and women below, but that was hardly surprising, because he'd lived in this fourth-floor apartment ever since his discharge from the army. At first he'd shared it with his wife. Then – when her move back to her parents' house in Valladolid had marked the beginning of their unacknowledged, though undoubtedly permanent, separation – he had carried on living there alone. But he was alone no longer, as the smell of alluring perfume which filled the room only served to remind him.

He continued to observe the scene below his window. His friends and neighbours were going about their business – and their pleasure – just as they had always done, he thought. If anything was different, it was that there seemed to be a little extra touch of gaiety – almost the atmosphere of a fiesta – now that the enemies of the people had fled the city in droves. Yet Madrid had changed in the last few days – changed so profoundly that anyone returning from a short trip would scarcely recognize it.

Only a week earlier it had been a city so conscious of style and appearance that it was an offence for a man who habitually wore a jacket to remove it while on the streets, however hot the weather. But not any more. Since the military had risen in Spanish Morocco, and then rapidly taken control of nearly half the mainland, Madrid had become the city of the people – of the working-class men and women – and to be dressed at all smartly was automatically to attract suspicion. The *mono* – a blue boiler-suit – was now the thing to wear, together with a red-and-black check neck-scarf if you were an Anarchist, or a party button if you belonged to either the Communists or the Socialists.

On the radio earlier that evening, he'd heard an announcer claim that the government was still in control of large parts of the country. Well, maybe it was and maybe it wasn't – who knew what to believe any longer? But it certainly wasn't in control of the capital. The unions, backed up by their armed militias, were running Madrid.

It was they who tracked down the right-wing snipers operating from the roof-tops and attics of the city. They who ran the businesses which had been abandoned by the rich. All the food which came in by rail from the Levant coast was immediately requisitioned by them, and served up in restaurants where the only charge was the possession of the right union membership card. The system which had grown up almost overnight was haphazard and *ad hoc*, but at least for most of the time, it seemed to work.

'Admiring your reflection in the window, aren't you, you handsome devil?' asked a teasing feminine voice behind him.

'No, I was just seeing what was happening out on the street,' Paco replied truthfully.

But now that the idea of his reflection had been put into his head, he did shift his position slightly, so there was another Paco staring back at him – the Paco whom Cindy Walker would see every time she looked at him.

His was not a remarkable face, he thought. His dark, almost coal-black eyes were his best feature, and he knew that when he wanted to, he could make other people feel as if he was looking right down into the depths of their souls. But other than the eyes, what else was there to say? He supposed it was a perfectly acceptable face – a face which some women in the past had perhaps found attractive – but that Cindy Walker should consider it handsome was just one more of the many truly miraculous things about her.

'You're not *just* looking out, are you?' Cindy asked, a hint of mock-accusation in her tone. 'You're not seeing the street as I, or any other normal person, would. You're looking at it through the eyes of a policeman.'

He supposed she was right. Supposed, too, that he would never lose the habit of examining things that way, even though he wasn't a policeman any longer – even though there were no real policemen in the whole country after the chaotic events of the previous few days.

For sixteen years he'd worked devotedly within the criminal justice system. And where was that system now? Gone! Vanished almost overnight! Revolutionary justice was the only justice which counted in the new Madrid. And it was a simpler justice – much more black-and-white – than the one he'd learned to cherish. There was only one real crime – that of having Fascist sympathies – and the punishment imposed by the hastily convened militia tribunals invariably involved a journey out to the scrubby woodland of the Casa del Campo in the dead of night, followed by a bullet through the back of the head.

Yet horrifying as the summary executions were to him, they were nothing compared to the savage acts committed by the other side in the bloody conflict, which was why, with more resignation than hope, he had joined a militia himself that very morning.

He turned away from the window, and towards the woman he had only known for two weeks – but with whom he was already deeply, desperately in love. Cindy Walker was a natural blonde, a common enough occurrence back in her Mid-West hometown, but a rare sight on the streets of Madrid. She had blue eyes, high cheekbones and a generous mouth. She looked as if she were in her early twenties, though she was closer to thirty, and was wearing a man's shirt and a disturbingly short skirt which barely covered her knees. Paco marvelled all over again that any of this could be actually happening – that she could actually have fallen for him as he had fallen for her.

'What are you thinking about?' Cindy asked.

'A lot of things,' Paco replied. 'I'm thinking that from the way people are behaving outside, you'd never guess the rebel army was only fifty kilometres from the city. I'm thinking that only yesterday afternoon, I was a detective inspector arresting a murderer, and now I'm a militiaman. I'm thinking about . . .'

'About tomorrow?'

'That too,' Paco said – and suddenly, he was. How could he not think about it? Tomorrow meant a trip up to the sierra in the back of an open lorry, surrounded by his new comrades. And when he reached the mountains? Then it was his job to seek out the enemy – proper soldiers who at least had some idea of what they were doing – and do his best to kill them.

'I thought when I finally handed in my rifle at the end of my military service, I'd never have to touch one again,' he said.

A worried frown crossed Cindy's brow. 'You don't have to go, you know,' she pointed out. 'You've got influence.'

'Influence!' Paco scoffed.

'I mean it,' Cindy said earnestly. 'Your old friend Bernardo is a union secretary, which, these days, makes him an important man. If you asked him to find you a job in the city, I'm sure he'd do it. And who's to say you wouldn't be of more use here than you'd be in the mountains? Don't you think it's at least worth considering the possibility?'

Paco shook his head. 'I'd be of no value behind a desk. I never was. But out there on the sierra, there is a part I can play. We need people up in the mountains who've actually seen real action, and who won't treat this war as some kind of glorified day-trip.'

Cindy ran her right hand through her silky blonde hair, and Paco found himself falling in love with her all over again. 'I know we all like to think that we're indispensable,' she said, 'but I'm sure that the union militias aren't half as useless as you claim they are.'

'They take picnics with them, for God's sake!' Paco exploded, 'Not military rations, you understand, but omelettes and stews and goatskins of red wine. And, of course, there's always a bottle of brandy to help their meals go down. Did you know that most of them come back home in the evenings, because they don't like the idea of spending a night away from their wives and girlfriends? You can't fight a war like that!'

Cindy frowned again. 'From what you've just said, am I to take it that *you* won't be coming home to me at night?' she asked.

'Damned right I won't be coming home. If nothing else, I can at least try to lead by example.'

Cindy's frown slowly changed into a warm smile, as it often did when he got so serious. She reached her slim hand up to the top button of her shirt and lazily – sensuously – began to unfasten it. 'Well, then, if I won't be seeing you for quite some time, I suppose I'd better give you something really spectacular to remember me by,' she said.

'Soldier's comfort,' Paco muttered, almost to himself.

Cindy's smile widened. 'Oh, you think it's no more than pity, do you?' she asked. 'Does that mean you're not interested?'

Paco grinned. 'You know damn well it doesn't,' he said, starting to unbutton his own shirt.

12

Chapter Two

Even at just after six o'clock in the morning, the air on Calle Hortaleza was starting to warm up, and as Paco entered his local bar, the Cabo de Trafalgar, he found himself almost looking forward to the cooler temperatures which would greet him in the mountains.

There was much about the bar that had remained unchanged in all the years Paco had been drinking in it. The two large wine barrels, for example, had always stood in the corner. The zinc counter, on which Nacho the barman rested his huge stomach, seemed so solid and permanent that it was almost possible to believe the building had been constructed around it. Even the tables, their surfaces worn away by the endless shuffling of dominoes, were reassuringly familiar.

Yet though the war was still only a few days old, it was starting to affect life in the Cabo. Bernardo and Ramón, Paco's oldest friends, who would normally have been there at that hour, were absent – Bernardo because he now had important duties in helping to run the city, and Ramón because the fact that he carried a briefcase to work had been enough to ensure that he disappeared once the militias had started making their arrests. Nor was there a glorious display of sea food, crabs and oysters, mussels and shrimps, lying on the counter in a bed of crushed ice – the famous *marisco* trains which kept Madrid supplied with the delicacies of the coasts had now been requisitioned to carry more basic supplies.

But perhaps the biggest change of all was in the men who were standing in the bar at that moment. They were people Paco had known for years – Eugenio the postman, Luis the tailor, Pepe the street-sweeper, and little Alfredo, who had polished gentlemen's shoes on the corner of the Gran Via. Just days earlier, they had been ordinary folk going about their ordinary lives. Now they had cartridge belts slung across their chests, and could scarcely walk without seeming to adopt a military swagger.

Nacho the barman set up a row of brandy glasses on the bar, half-filled each one with rich brown brandy from Jerez, then topped them up with a pale anis. 'Sun and Shade', the locals called the drink, and for most working men in Madrid, it was the only proper way to start the morning.

Paco took a sip from the glass that the barman slid towards him, and was not in the least surprised when, a couple of seconds later, a bomb exploded in his stomach and it felt as if someone had hit him on the back of the neck with a shovel.

'I've made some lunch for you chaps to take with you,' Nacho said. 'There's no bread, but I've cooked you up some meat and rice. It'll have gone cold by the time you get to the mountains, but I expect you'll manage to light a fire somewhere and heat it up.'

'No bread?' little Alfredo said, sounding aggrieved. 'Why isn't there any bread?'

Nacho shrugged, sending a ripple through the flab of his huge stomach. 'The baker's was closed,' he said. 'There was a sign outside saying they hadn't got any flour.'

Of course they wouldn't have flour, Paco thought. Most of the wheat-growing areas of the country were already under enemy control. And if the rebels also managed to seize part of the railway between Madrid and the coast? Well then, all they'd have to do to bring Madrid to its knees was sit outside it while the people starved to death.

Nacho reached under the bar and produced a large goatskin bag. 'Full of red wine,' he announced grandly. 'Whatever else happens up there in the mountains, you won't go thirsty.'

'You're a real pal,' Luis told him, raising his glass of Sun and Shade. 'One of the best.'

Nacho simpered. 'It's the least I can do for a bunch of heroes like you chaps,' he said.

But that's the trouble, we're not heroes yet, Paco told himself. And even if we ever do earn the title, it'll probably be as *dead* heroes.

Through the window, they saw a red double-decker bus pull up outside the bar. 'There's your transport, comrades,' Nacho said. 'It's time for you to get out there and start killing Fascists.'

And Luis the tailor, Eugenio the postman, Pepe the street-sweeper and all the rest of them – left through the front door of the Cabo de Trafalgar swearing to do just that.

The new militiamen eagerly clambered on board the bus. A bus! Paco thought. They were not even going out to the battlefront in an open lorry. They were using public transport, as if, instead of being involved in a desperate struggle for survival, they were merely setting off on a holiday excursion. As he took his seat, he half expected a conductor to come to him and ask him for his fare.

The whole thing was a farce, he told himself but then he supposed that it was no more farcical than many of the things which had happened in the previous couple of days. And along with the farce, there had also been the incredible bravery of the men who had stormed the Montaña barracks – men who had exposed themselves to heavy fire in their efforts to capture the rifle bolts they needed for the guns which the government had finally, and reluctantly, issued them with. Maybe that was what all wars were like, he decided, remembering his experience in Morocco – a mixture of incredible courage and downright stupidity.

The bus was already three-quarters full. The only thing which identified most of the men as belonging to a militia were their blue boiler-suits and party badges, though a few of them had managed to scrounge steel helmets or forage caps from somewhere, and now wore their new military headgear with an air of bravado. There were regular soldiers on the bus, too, wearing red armbands to show that though much of the army had deserted the Republic, they, at least, had remembered the oath of loyalty they had sworn.

And there were women! Some of them were dressed much as the men were, wearing cartridge belts across their chests and expressions on their faces which defied anyone to question their right to make the journey. Others, in conventional summer dresses, sat close to young men who could only have been their husbands, pinching their arms affectionately and occasionally whispering in their ears.

A third group of women sat huddled together at the back of the bus. They, too, were dressed in a uniform of sorts. Their frocks were cut daringly low over their heavy bosoms, and the thick makeup they had applied to their faces did little to disguise the fact that they were all well past their prime. Whores! Of the lowest kind! The ones who were not considered attractive enough to work in brothels on the Calle Echagay, and so had to earn whatever pitiful living they could out on the streets. And now they were going to war, seizing the opportunity to make a few pesetas during any lull which might occur in the fighting.

Paco lit up a Celtas and sucked the smoke into his lungs. Whores of the lowest kind! he repeated to himself. It did not bother him that the women should have wanted to come along – who could blame them for seeing their chance? – but it did bother him that on a serious mission like this

15

there had been no one with the authority, or the foresight, to prevent them. It was just one more example of the amateur way the whole defence of the Republic was being conducted.

The few people who were out on the streets at that early hour of the morning gave clenched-fist salutes to the red bus which was on its way to stop the Fascists, and the militiamen on board responded enthusiastically. Wine bottles were passed round, and some of the boiler-suited would-be heroes were already starting to tuck into the food they had packed for lunch-time.

The bus had soon left the old part of the city, and was passing through the Arguelles district. There were no greetings from the pavement here. This *barrio* was firmly behind the military revolt, and stood out on the political map of Madrid as one of the few patches of pure blue surrounded by a sea of red.

*

The road which led to the sierra was busier than it had ever been before. It seemed as if every available vehicle was being used to transport the eager young militiamen to the heart of the fighting. Trucks which had been hauling vegetables or coal a couple of days earlier were now crammed with men waving their rifles in the air. Private cars, with the initials of one of the trade unions hastily painted on them, vied with each other to get to the head of the queue. There were motor bikes with sidecars, horses pulling ancient, creaking carts, and even men on donkeys, all itching to get a crack at the enemy.

It was nearly three hours before the bus finally came to a halt, half-way up a steep mountain road. Pepe the street-sweeper, who had been sitting at the front of the bus, now stood up and faced the rest of the passengers.

'When I was here yesterday, the Fascist bastards were dug in over there,' he said, pointing out of the window into the pinewoods. 'So what are we waiting for, comrades? Let's go and get the sons-of-bitches.'

'Wait a minute,' Paco said. 'Before we start out, we should form ourselves into units.'

'Units!' Pepe echoed him scornfully. 'What the hell do we need units for? We each have a rifle, don't we? All we have to do is point them at the enemy and pull the trigger.'

A roar of approval greeted his remark. Paco shrugged, fatalistically. He had known it would be useless to make the suggestion from the start. These men were so fired up that it would take some considerable losses before they realized the value of organization and military discipline. He could only pray that they came to their senses before it was too late.

*

The ragged line of blue–boiler-suited men moved noisily through the conifer woods, coughing and spitting, laughing at each others' crude jokes, cursing when they almost tripped over a tree-root. They could hear the sounds of battle in the distance – the crack of rifle-shots, the boom of light artillery – but after almost an hour of walking steadily uphill, they had still to meet any of the enemy they fondly imagined it would be so easy to vanquish.

Tempers began to wear thin. Some of the militiamen argued that they should be heading in another direction entirely. Others complained loudly that they were carrying more than their fair share of the food. Only when Luis the tailor suggested that they take a short break was there general agreement.

They sat in a circle in a small clearing, broke open some of their supplies and passed around the goatskin bag which contained the wine.

'We need to be much better organized than we are now,' Paco, said, making one last attempt to talk some sense into his hotheaded comrades. 'We should have two scouts, one on our left flank and one on our right. That's how we did things in Morocco.'

'Don't try to lecture us, Paco,' Eugenio the postman said. 'We've all been in the army. We've all served our time in Morocco, just like you have.'

'You haven't all seen the same kind of action that I have,' Paco pointed out. 'During the retreat to Melilla . . .'

'You know what he's after, don't you?' little Alfredo the shoeblack asked the rest of the group. 'He fancies being our leader.' He turned to Paco. 'Well, let me tell you something. We didn't win our liberty from the capitalists only to start taking orders from you.'

*

It was just after eleven o'clock, when the sun was already high in the sky, that the militiamen found the action they thought they'd been looking for. They had left the shelter of the woods, and were crossing an area of fire-blackened tree stumps, when the machine-gun opened fire. Luis the tailor was the first one to be hit. In an instant, he was transformed from a trudging militiaman into a demented puppet which jerked first one way then the other, as the heavy bullets slammed into his frail flesh. For a

17

second his comrades just stood there – frozen to the spot, hardly able to believe what was happening – and then they flung themselves to the ground, getting what protection they could from the tree stumps.

Paco, already flat on his stomach, fired a couple of rapid rounds into the trees. But even as he pulled the trigger, he knew he was doing no more than wasting ammunition. The machine-gun was probably positioned in a shallow dug-out, he guessed, and though it was possible that the gunner might be hit by a lucky shot, it wasn't really likely. He and his comrades, on the other hand, while not quite sitting targets, could be picked off by simple attrition.

The other militiamen had recovered enough from the shock to be able to return fire, and their rifles cracked all around Paco, filling the clear mountain air with the stink of cordite. A fountain of earth spurted up just in front of him, as one of the machine-gun's bullets buried itself in the ground centimetres from his nose. The machine-gunner was getting the range, he told himself. It was only a matter of time before they would all be dead. He twisted round, and, crawling on his belly, started to make his way back towards the edge of the clearing.

It could not have been more than twenty metres to the safety of the woods, yet it felt like the longest journey he had ever taken. As he snaked his body over the rough ground, every stone, every twig, seemed to take a malevolent pleasure in digging itself into him.

The firing continued behind him, and there was the occasional scream as a bullet found its target. Someone – it may have been little Alfredo – called out, 'Look at Paco! He wanted to be our leader, and now he's running out on us. The louse!'

And if he was killed before he reached the woods, that was how he would be remembered, he realized. The louse! The man who had abandoned his comrades to their fate in order to save his own miserable skin. Except that if he didn't make it to the woods, none of them would be alive to tell that particular tale.

His elbows and knees were rubbed raw, his ribs and spine ached, but finally he felt his left hand touch the base of a tree. He crawled a little further, then quickly clambered to his feet. Paco glanced back at the clearing. Some of the others were still firing in the general direction of the machine-gun, but many of them lay in the awkward, twisted positions which said, more clearly than words, that they would never again brag in the Cabo de Trafalgar about how many Fascists they were intending to kill.

18

A bullet embedded itself with an angry thud in the tree-trunk just above his head. Paco plunged into the deeper safety of the woods.

*

He decided to take a circuitous route to his destination, swinging in a wide arc around the clearing. He was aware, even as he took that decision, that it would mean more of his comrades would die. But better that should happen than that he should run into enemy look-outs and lose his own life – because then all of the trapped men would be doomed.

It took him fifteen minutes to work his way around to a point from which he had a clear view of the shallow dug-out. There were only two men in it – one was firing the machine-gun, the other feeding the belt through. From the piecemeal nature of their uniforms – mismatched jackets and pants – he could tell they were not regular soldiers at all, but Fascist militiamen who, just like his own compañeros, had probably been doing perfectly ordinary jobs a few days earlier. Amateurs! he thought. They had not even gone to the trouble of posting guards on their flank.

He went down on one knee, raised his rifle to his shoulder, and took careful aim. Yet even with his finger on the trigger, he hesitated. He had killed before. There had been at least a dozen Moroccan warriors he'd accounted for. And during the course of his career in the police, he'd shot several men who'd decided they had more chance of remaining free with him out of the way. But this was different. These men weren't foreign warriors or homegrown criminals. He couldn't even say, with absolute certainty, that they were fighting on the wrong side and he on the right one. Even the fact that they'd been so careless made it difficult for him – it seemed almost unfair to take advantage of their incompetence.

A fresh burst of machine gun fire on his trapped comrades quelled his misgivings. He closed one eye, and pulled the trigger. The machine-gunner leapt backwards, as though he were on a long piece of tightly stretched elastic and could fight against its pull no longer. The gunner's mate immediately grabbed the gun, and swung it round in the direction of the new, unexpected danger. But before he'd even had time to take proper aim, Paco flicked back the bolt of his rifle, fired a second time, and put a bullet through his forehead.

For perhaps another half a minute, the militiamen in the clearing continued to fire into the trees. Then, as they began to understand what must have happened, an eerie silence fell, soon to be followed by a loud, triumphant cheer.

Paco did not feel triumphant. He had done what had to be done, and that was all that could be said of it. He stood up and stretched his legs. Perhaps his surviving comrades would believe him now, when he said that war was more than just an adventure, and that without discipline, the risks were multiplied beyond calculation. He was just about to break cover when he heard the sound of a twig snapping behind him. He turned around – but not quickly enough. The rifle butt caught him a heavy blow on the side of the head. And then everything went black.

Chapter Three

In his first few conscious moments, the only thing that mattered to him was the pain. His brain felt as if it were being stabbed by thousands of tiny red-hot needles, and the left side of his head throbbed with a continuous and agonizing rhythm. But then, as he began to fight to get these pains under his control, he became aware of the voices.

He had only been to the theatre once in his life, and, as luck would have it, there had been a power cut. The management had been unwilling to refund the ticket-money, and so the actors had continued to play their roles in almost complete darkness. And it was like that now with him, he thought, lying on the floor with his eyes closed, and listening to a little drama unfolding.

'What do you think they're going to do with us, Pepe?' asked a very frightened voice which he recognized immediately as belonging to little Alfredo the shoeblack.

'Do with us?' the street-sweeper replied, contemptuously. 'Isn't it obvious what they're going to do? As soon as they can find time to get around to it, they're going to shoot us.'

'But they brought us food!' Alfredo said desperately. 'Why would they have brought us food if they were going to kill us?'

'Who knows the way the bastards' minds work?' Pepe answered. 'But mark my words, we'll all be dead before morning. What were all those shots we heard earlier, if they weren't executions?'

Paco opened his eyes. He was lying on a dirt floor, and from the quality of light which was filtering in through the barred window in the wall opposite, he guessed it was close to dusk. He tried to move, and the pain came back so sharply that he let out an involuntary groan.

'Paco's come round at long last,' Pepe said. He knelt down and looked into his comrade's eyes. 'How are you feeling, old chap?'

'Not good,' Paco admitted. 'What happened?'

'There was a Fascist patrol out there in the woods. Twenty or thirty of them, there were. They must have been drawn towards the clearing by the sound of gunfire. They appeared just after you shot the machine gunners, and told us to drop our weapons. It would have been suicide to do anything else – not that it will make any difference in the long run.'

'They made us carry Paco all the way back here. Why would they have done that if they been planning to kill him?' said little Alfredo, who was still clutching at straws.

'You're a fool,' Pepe told him. He turned his attention back to Paco. 'Is there, anything I can do for you, old chap?'

'You could help me get to my feet.'

Pepe put his hands under Paco's armpits, and very gently began to lift him up. Moving caused more needles of pain to stab Paco's brain, but now he was more concerned about his legs, which seemed to have turned into rubber.

'Do you think you'll be able to stand up on your own?' Pepe asked solicitously.

'Lean me against the wall,' Paco gasped. 'I'll be all right in another minute or two.'

His vision was blurred, but not enough to prevent him from seeing he was in some kind of storeroom, and that, in addition to Pepe and Alfredo, it also held three other men – strangers to him – who were dressed in *monos*.

A sound drifted in from the street, a dull heavy sound which could only have been marching feet. 'Soldiers,' Pepe said. 'It seems you've come round just in time to be shot, Paco.'

'Don't say that,' Alfredo begged. '*Please* don't say that.'

The soldiers had come to a halt, and someone was drawing back the bolt on the outside of the door.

'They've probably come to ask what you'd like to eat for dinner, Alfredo,' Pepe said sourly.

The door swung open, and Paco saw there were at least half a dozen soldiers standing outside, each with a rifle in his hand. Their sergeant, who had greying hair and bad teeth, stepped forward, but stopped just outside the doorway.

'Now listen very carefully, you Communist scum,' he said. 'We're all going for a nice little stroll. I want you to walk out of here in single file. Stay close to the man in front of you, and don't try to run away, or you'll be shot.'

'Where are you taking us?' Alfredo moaned.

'You'll find that out soon enough, you piece of shit,' the sergeant told him. He turned his attention to Paco. 'You! You're the one who was unconscious, aren't you?'

'Yes.'

'Can you manage to walk a few hundred metres, or will you need some of these other bastards to help you?'

'I can walk,' Paco said, and he was thinking, I have to walk, because no one's going to drag me to my death.

'Right, well let's have you then,' the sergeant said. He pointed to Alfredo. 'You first, little man.'

They stepped out into a narrow cobbled street with a gutter running down the centre of it. The soldiers had already taken up their positions, three slightly ahead, to lead the column, three holding back to guard the rear. It was all very professional, Paco thought. They had obviously done this kind of thing before – probably many times before.

'Move it!' the sergeant barked. 'And remember what I told you. No funny business!'

Paco felt he had more control over his legs now, and his vision was almost back to normal. He looked around him. The plaque on one of the houses said that this street was the Calle de Segovia, but someone had crossed out the name with black paint, and written underneath it Calle de Jose Antonio. So this village had already renamed one of its streets after the leader of the Falange. That showed where the villagers' sympathy lay. Or perhaps not. Perhaps they were not right-wing, but merely prudent.

As they marched along the street, Paco noticed that they were being observed from the narrow iron balconies which jutted out from the first floors of the houses. Most of the watchers were women and children. There was no excitement in their eyes. There was not even much curiosity. The war was in its first few days, and already watching men being marched to their deaths had become nothing more than a dull habit.

He remembered the executions he had seen in Morocco, the way the condemned men – mostly deserters and black-marketeers – had marched on to the parade ground to the sound of a relentlessly beating military drum. He would have appreciated a drum at that moment, he thought, not so much to help him keep in step as to assure him that his death was of some significance – a positive act of war, rather than an exercise in vermin reduction. Yes, he told himself, a drum would have given the whole thing much more solemnity.

23

There were two soldiers on guard at the edge of the Plaza Mayor – the main square – and they stood aside to let the column pass. The plaza itself was typical of the plazas in such villages as this. The rows of buildings formed a rough rectangle with an entrance road at each corner. The upper storeys of all the houses stuck out much further than the lower and were supported by stone pillars, thus creating an arcade in which the villagers could shelter from the summer heat or the winter rain. In the centre of the plaza was a fountain, gushing forth water even in dry July.

During the fiestas, the plaza would be used to stage the village bullfight and the late-night dance which always followed it. But it was hosting a very different kind of function that day. At the far end of the square was a whitewashed wall, glinting in the late afternoon sun. Just beyond the wall was an open army truck – and on the ground next to its tailboard lay a jumbled heap of bodies, all of them dressed in blue *monos*.

The sight of the dead militiamen was too much for Alfredo to take. He stopped walking and sank to his knees, his hands clasped tightly in front of him. Behind him, the other prisoners came to an awkward halt.

'Please don't kill me!' the little shoeblack begged. 'I'm not what you think I am. The others only brought me along to cook for them!'

The sergeant with the bad teeth grasped the collar of Alfredo's shirt, and tore it roughly to reveal the quaking man's skin. 'You got a wedge-shaped bruise on your right shoulder,' he shouted. 'Do you want to tell me where that came from?'

'I don't know,' Alfred blubbered hysterically. 'I swear to you that I really don't know.'

The sergeant stepped back, as if he found the idea of being close to the little man repulsive. 'You're a lying son of a bitch,' he said. 'That bruise comes from your rifle stock. You're just as guilty as the rest of this scum.'

Alfredo turned his head frantically, and his eyes rested on Paco. 'Shoot him!' he sobbed. 'He was the one who killed your men. I saw him with my own eyes. I don't deserve to die.'

A major, who had been standing some distance away, approached the grovelling man. He was, Paco noted automatically with his policeman's eye, in his early thirties, and of slightly less than average height. His brown eyes suggested a quick mind – or at least a cunning nature. His uniform was immaculately maintained, though a little shabby, and his highly polished boots could certainly have done with reheeling.

24

The major came to a halt a few centimetres from Alfredo. 'Get up!' he said disgustedly. 'You people are always saying that it's better to die on your feet than live on your knees. Well, now's the time to prove it.'

'I can't move,' Alfredo sobbed. 'I just can't.'

The officer took his pistol out of its leather holster, and jammed the barrel against the back of the little shoeblack's head. 'This is your last chance to act like a man,' he said.

'Please!' Alfredo implored.

The major shrugged, then pulled the trigger. There was a muffled explosion, and Alfredo juddered slightly, then slumped forward.

'Oh my God!' said the militiaman just behind Paco, as if it were only now that he had finally realized what fate lay in store for all of them.

'See where I'm pointing?' the sergeant bellowed, holding out his arm and indicating the whitewashed wall. 'I want you all lined up against that pretty damn quick. So jump to it!'

The five remaining prisoners stepped around Alfredo's lifeless body, taking care to avoid the blood which had already begun to seep out of his head on to the packed clay ground. Paco forced his eyes to focus on the wall which would be the backcloth for his execution, as – on the evidence of the number of holes in it – it had been the backcloth for so many others.

As he was the head of the column now that Alfredo had gone, he was the first of the militiamen to reach the wall. He stopped, and turned round so that he was facing the centre of the square.

'*Right* up against the wall, you bastard,' the sergeant screamed.

Paco took a step backwards, and felt the rough brickwork pressing against his shoulder blades. Why was he making things so easy for them, he asked himself, and supposed it was because this was the only way he could meet his death with a little of his dignity intact.

The other four prisoners had now joined him against the wall. So this was it, Paco thought. The man next to him – the one who had said 'Oh my God!' as Alfredo died – was now mumbling the rosary to himself, but Paco had lost his own faith long ago, and could not recapture it even as he faced death. Instead, he intended to spend his last few moments on earth thinking about Cindy. He wished he could have met her earlier – so he would have gone to his grave with even more happy memories. But then, he told himself, he had been incredibly lucky to have found her at all.

The men who were to compose the firing squad had all dropped down on to one knee. A few more seconds and it would be all over. Paco hoped that the man assigned to kill him would make a clean job of it.

'Ready,' the sergeant shouted.

'My life was never up to very much anyway,' said Pepe the road-sweeper. 'At least now I'm worth a bullet.'

'Aim . . .'

'I helped burn down a church,' mumbled the man who had been saying the rosary. 'Oh, dear, merciful Señor, please forgive me.'

'F . . .'

'Wait!' the major commanded, even as the soldiers' fingers were beginning to tighten on their triggers.

The officer strode up to the wall and stopped directly in front of Paco. 'I've been trying to work out since I first saw you why you looked so familiar,' he said. 'And now I think I know. What's your name?'

Could there be any harm in telling him now? None whatsoever. 'Francisco Ruiz,' Paco said.

'And what did you do for a living before you threw in your lot with this Communist rabble?'

'I was a policeman.'

'A detective?'

'Yes.'

The major nodded. 'I thought I recognized you. I've seen your picture in the papers. You're the Paco Ruiz who solved the case of the headless corpse in Atocha station, aren't you?'

What was all this leading-up to? Paco wondered. 'Yes, that was me,' he admitted.

The major signalled for two of the soldiers standing by the lorry and guarding the corpses, to approach him. 'Take this man back to the lock-up on Calle Jose Antonio,' he said. 'I shall want to talk to him later.'

The soldiers stepped forward, and each grabbed one of Paco's arms. 'Don't try any tricks,' said the one on his left, as they frog-marched him away from the wall. 'You wouldn't get more than ten metres without being cut down like a dog.' He laughed. 'Now *that's* bloody funny. Or it would be, if the dog had belonged to anybody else.'

'What are you talking about?' Paco asked.

'Never you mind. Just don't give us any trouble.'

As if he could, Paco thought. He had been steeling himself up for his own execution, and now it was to be postponed, he felt completely drained – as weak as a newborn baby.

The soldiers continued to keep a tight grip on him as they marched him across the plaza. They had almost reached the fountain when they heard the sergeant with the bad teeth give his order, and the rifles bark out their messages of death.

Chapter Four

The thick bands of black shadow which lay across the floor grew longer and longer, before finally vanishing as the sun sank below the horizon and night began to fall. Paco sat in the corner of the storeroom turned prison, his last cigarette burning slowly away in the corner of his mouth. In some strange way, he felt cheated. If he'd been shot earlier, on the main square, he would at least have died next to Pepe, a man who, with only seconds to live, had still had the spirit to make a bitter joke about it. Now, the chances were that when he died, he would die alone.

The survivor in Paco rose to the surface. He was still alive and as long as there was life, there was hope. But the real question was, *why* was he still alive? It had to be because he was a policeman – because, with only a headless corpse discovered in the left-luggage office at the Atocha railway station to work on, he had uncovered a high level conspiracy and ensured that several important government functionaries had gone to gaol. But what use were his detection skills now, he asked himself, when evidence was often nothing more than an anonymous written accusation, the trial was usually over in a matter of minutes, and the punishment dished out was invariably a bullet to the head?

He was not aware of having dozed off in the middle of his speculations, but if he hadn't, the sound of the bolt on the door being drawn back would not have come as such a shock. Paco sat upright, and wondered if his moment had come. All he could see at first was the oil-lamp, hanging about a metre above the ground, but as his eyes became accustomed to the light and shade, he managed to distinguish the shape of a man standing behind the lamp.

'Get on your feet, prisoner,' the man barked. 'Major Gómez wants to see you.'

Paco rose to a standing position. 'So, the major wants to see me, does he?' he asked. 'And what if I don't want to see him?'

The man with the lantern chuckled unpleasantly. 'That's right,' he said. 'You make it difficult for us. Make it so we have to use force. After what some of your friends have done to some of my friends out in the mountains today, I'd really like that.'

It was tempting to take a swing at him, but only a fool gets into a fight he has no chance of winning. 'I won't cause any trouble,' Paco promised.

'I didn't think you would,' the man with the lantern sneered. 'You Reds are all the same – full of brave talk while you're sitting around in the bars, but completely gutless when you actually see some real action.' He stepped back into the street. 'Follow me.'

There were two more soldiers on the Calle Jose Antonio, both armed with rifles. 'It's all right, lads,' said the man with a lantern, who Paco could now see was a corporal. 'I've had a word with the prisoner, and he's promised not to cause us any trouble.'

They took the same route as Paco and his dead comrades had followed earlier in the day, up Jose Antonio towards the Plaza Mayor. The square had been transformed in the hours Paco had been away from it. Though it was night, the place was lit up by countless oil-lamps. Each created a small circle of illumination around itself, but some of the lamps were so close together that the circles merged, seeming to form a magic path across the dark ground. The death wagon and the corpses of the late afternoon were gone, and in their place were hundreds of soldiers in khaki uniforms, dozens of *guardias civiles* in their green uniforms and three-cornered hats, and scores of Fascist militiamen in whatever battledress they'd been able to cobble together. Some of the men appeared to be happy to stay at one of the dozen or so new bars which had come into existence since the military had taken over the village, others were so restless that they'd rapidly knock back a wine at one and then move on to another. But whichever method they chose, it was still an impressive display of men working hard at getting drunk.

Prisoner and escort crossed the square, and turned on to a road which was just as busy and lively as the Plaza Mayor had been. 'This is the Calle Mayor,' the corporal said.

'So the main street runs off the main square, does it?' Paco replied. 'How surprising.'

'You have a very big mouth on you for someone in your position,' the corporal snarled.

'Why shouldn't I have?' Paco asked. 'A man under sentence of death doesn't have a lot to lose.'

The church loomed up ahead, a massive stone building which dwarfed all the dwellings around it. Paco wondered how much further they had to go, and what this Major Gómez would want to talk about when they got there.

'We turn right here,' said the corporal, indicating a dark alley framed on one side by the church, and on the other by a high wall. 'This is the Calle Belén.'

'Why are you giving me a guided tour?' asked Paco, who, despite himself, was becoming intrigued by the strange turn of events.

'I'm giving you a guided tour, as you call it, because those are my instructions,' the corporal replied coldly. 'Major Gómez wants you to be familiar with the geography of the village.' He stopped a few yards down the alley and lowered his lamp over a patch of ground which was darker than the dirt surrounding it. 'This is where it happened.'

'Where *what* happened?' Paco asked, exasperatedly,

'The major says he'll tell you everything that you need to know.'

The Calle Belén ran straight for fifty metres, then bent round to the left. Another fifty metres and they had reached a square which, because of the oil-lamps hung outside each house, was almost as well illuminated as the Plaza Mayor. It had a number of pleasant dwellings around its edge, and a fountain in the middle.

'This is the Plaza de Santa Teresa,' said the corporal, still playing the role of reluctant tour-guide. 'Most of the officers are billeted here.'

An armed sentry stood in front of one of the houses. He watched them pass without interest.

'Is that where the commanding officer lives?' Paco asked.

The corporal gave a superior laugh. 'No, the general has done much better for himself than that. Those are Colonel Valera's quarters.'

They stopped at a house two doors beyond the colonel's. The corporal knocked on the door, then, without waiting for a reply, turned the handle. Paco was led into what must once have been a reception room, but had now been turned into an office. Sitting at the table was the major who had shot Alfredo in cold blood, yet had chosen to spare Paco. He had a stack of official documents in front of him, and just beyond them – within easy reach – was his pistol.

'Do sit down, Inspector Ruiz,' he said genially. He turned to the escort. 'You can wait outside.'

Paco sat, and studied the other man. The initial impression he had gained on the square that afternoon was confirmed. Gómez was somewhere around thirty, which was young – but not exceptionally so – to hold his present rank, and the quick, opportunistic brown eyes suggested he was more of a politician than a straightforward soldier.

'It's a pleasure to see you again, Inspector,' the major said. 'You may not yet realize it, but we are colleagues in a way.'

'Is that right?'

'Certainly it is. You are a policeman, and I am General Castro's head of security. You'll have heard of the general, I expect.'

'Oh yes, I've heard of him,' Paco replied. Who had not heard of the man who, even more than General Franco, had been responsible for the bloody suppression of the Asturian miners' revolt only four years earlier? 'But you're wrong to think of us as colleagues. I'm no longer a policeman, and your title doesn't make you one, either. All head of security means to me is that you do the dirty work for the Butcher of Asturias.'

Gómez threw back his head, and laughed heartily. 'The Butcher of Asturias,' he said. 'Very good. Very good indeed.'

'Have I said something funny?' Paco asked, puzzled.

'It always amuses me when people fail to create the effect they intended. You've been working out ways to insult me since you entered the room, and have finally decided that your best approach would be to attack my commanding officer. And how did you expect me to react? Did you think I'd go purple with rage, and give you a long speech on how the general is nothing more than a servant of Spain and God?'

'Perhaps,' Paco confessed.

'Only a fool would waste his time trying to convert a man with your obvious stubbornness,' the major said. 'So if it makes you happy to keep on thinking of the general as a butcher, please feel free to do so. That will not, in any way, interfere with the task I have set for you.'

'What task?'

'The general has – or rather *had* – two dogs, Principe and Reina. Last night, on the Calle Belén, someone shot Principe. The general was very fond of the dog, and so was the general's lady, who had bought it a collar encrusted with semi-precious stones. That collar has disappeared. So we are not only looking for a murderer. We are also looking for a thief.'

Paco found it hard to believe what he was hearing. 'A murderer?' he repeated. 'This afternoon I saw you shoot a man through the back of the head, and now you have the nerve to call someone who shot a *dog* a murderer?'

'I was just doing my duty,' the major said, unperturbed. 'We have no facilities for keeping large numbers of prisoners here, and it would clearly be insane to release them – they would only immediately rejoin their militias and give us more trouble in the future. So what choice do we have but to execute them? Besides, can you honestly say that the same thing isn't going on on your side of the front line?'

'No,' Paco admitted. 'I can't. I wish I could, but I can't.'

'So, let us get back to the dog,' the major continued. 'Whether I consider its death a murder or not is irrelevant. That is how the general sees it, and he is the one who decides what is important and what isn't. He wants the killer caught and punished – and I think you are the man to track him down.'

All the clues had been there, and Paco should have seen it coming. But he hadn't, and now, as the realization of what was expected of him finally hit home, he was filled first with incredulity, and then with rage.

'I won't do it!' he exploded.

Major Gómez smiled. 'I think you will. The alternative, after all, is the firing squad.'

'I don't care,' Paco said hotly. 'When all around me human life is being treated as if it means nothing, I refuse to glorify the death of a dog by treating it as a serious crime.'

'So you are quite prepared to be shot?'

Paco slammed his fist down hard on the table. 'You remember what you said to Alfredo just before you put a bullet in his head?' he demanded. 'You said we should live up to our boast that it was better to die on our feet than live on our knees. What else could you possibly call the job you've offered me than a chance to live on my knees?'

Major Gómez casually picked up his pistol, and aimed it at the centre of Paco's chest. 'I could shoot you now, you know,' he said. 'It would make a bit of a mess, but I have a batman to clear up my messes for me. So I'll ask you one last time, Inspector Ruiz. Will you work for me?'

'Go ahead and pull the trigger,' Paco said defiantly.

The major placed his pistol back on the table, and smiled again. 'You are no good to me dead,' he said.

'And no good to you alive, either,' Paco pointed out.

'There's more than one way to skin a cat,' the major told him.

'And what exactly do you mean by that?'

32

'You should find out some time tomorrow.' The major turned his head towards the door. 'You can take your prisoner back to his cell now, corporal,' he shouted.

Chapter Five

The heat was already building up in the centre of Madrid, as it did early every morning during the long, stifling summers. Nacho the barman watched the water cart trundle slowly past the Cabo de Trafalgar, spraying the street as it went. A new coolness wafted into the bar's doorway, but it was a coolness which would last only as long as it took the sun to climb over the high buildings and start to beat mercilessly down on the Calle Hortaleza.

Nacho retreated back into the empty bar. He sighed. Only the morning before the Cabo had been filled with eager militiamen, drinking their *sol y sombras*, bragging about what they were going to do once they were up in the mountains, and thanking him for the meals he'd made up for them. He would have been glad to do the same thing that morning, too, had there been anyone to serve or cook for. But there wasn't. He'd watched eagerly as the bus had pulled up in front of the bar that evening, but none of the men who'd got off had been patrons of his. He wondered what had happened to Pepe the street-cleaner and little Alfredo the shoeblack, and hoped that wherever they were, they were safe.

The door opened and two young men entered the bar. One of them was tall and skinny, the other shorter and a little podgy, but both were wearing the boiler suits that identified them as workers, and had Anarchist black-and-red handkerchiefs around their necks.

'Good morning, comrades. What can I get you to drink?' Nacho said. 'A coffee? Or a brandy? Perhaps one of each?'

'We don't want anything to drink,' the taller of the two men replied. 'But we would certainly appreciate a little information.'

'You've come to arrest someone?' Nacha asked suspiciously, wondering which of his customers would disappear next.

The taller Anarchist shook his head. 'That's a job we leave to others,' he said. 'We've been up in the sierra, fighting the Fascists.'

'Then perhaps you might know what's happened to some of my cust . . .' Nacho began.

'That's why we're here,' the shorter Anarchist interrupted. 'For most of yesterday, we were fighting side by side with a comrade who went by the name of Francisco Ruiz.'

'Paco!' Nacho exclaimed. 'Do you know where he is, or what's happened to him?'

The taller Anarchist nodded his head gravely. 'I'm afraid that I do know. I'm sorry to have to tell you that Comrade Ruiz is dead.'

'What about the others?' Nacho asked. 'Luis the tailor, little Alfredo the boot-boy . . .?'

'We know nothing of them,' the taller Anarchist said.

'But they left on the same bus as Paco.'

'Perhaps he was separated from them. That's the kind of thing which happens in war. At any rate, we got to know Comrade Ruiz. He fought well and hard, and died bravely.'

'I'm sure he did,' Nacho said solemnly. 'That would be just like Paco.'

'And now our business is with Comrade Ruiz's widow,' the tall man told him. 'You see, we consider it our duty to tell her that he died fighting as a true hero of the Republic.'

'But his wife – his widow I should say – is behind enemy lines. In Valladolid,' Nacho told him.

'Valladolid, you say.' A smile flashed briefly across the man's mouth, and then was gone.

'That's right,' Nacho agreed. 'So there's no possible way you can contact her.'

'Oh, I wouldn't be too sure about that,' said the tall man, turning towards the door.

'What about his girlfriend?' Nacho asked. 'Who's going to tell her that he's dead?'

The tall man stopped in his tracks. 'His girlfriend?' he repeated.

'That's right. She lives upstairs. Well, actually, she started out living on a different floor to Paco, though now she's virtually moved in with him.'

'They have been living in sin?' asked the shorter man, as if the thought outraged him.

The taller man coughed nervously. 'Don't make jokes like that, Raul,' he said to his partner. 'I know you're only having your bit of fun, but other people might think that you really believe in the bourgeois morality which the Revolution has all but swept away.'

'Of course, you're right,' said the shorter man, looking suitably chastened. 'My strange sense of humour's got me into trouble before now.'

The taller man turned his attention back to Nacho. 'This girlfriend?' he said. 'Was Comrade Ruiz just having a fling with her, or was he really very keen on her?'

Nacho laughed, then remembered he was talking about a dead man and was instantly sombre again. 'If you ask me, he was a lot keener on her than he was on his wife,' he said. 'To tell you the truth, if we had such a thing as divorce in this country, it's my opinion he'd have got rid of Pilar a long time ago.'

The two Anarchists exchanged glances. 'Perhaps we *should* go and see her,' the taller man said. 'After all, someone has to break the news to her, and she would probably appreciate the words of comfort we have to deliver.'

'That's true,' Nacho agreed gravely.

'So if you'll just tell us exactly where she lives . . .' the shorter man suggested.

Nacho gave them the address, and the two Anarchists left the bar. They were an odd couple, the barman thought, as he watched them walk out on to the street, and not just because, physically, they were such a contrasting pair. There was something about their manner which wasn't quite right, and though he couldn't exactly put his finger on what that something was, it left him with a vague feeling of unease. And there was the fact that they didn't know what had happened to Luis and Alfredo the shoeblack. How was it possible that they'd managed to get split up from Paco? But, then, as the militiamen had said themselves, strange things happen in a war, and he supposed this was only one of them. Pushing his doubts to one side, he picked up a glass and began to polish it.

*

Cindy Walker looked down at the letter she had just written to her parents – a letter she was not even sure, given the state of things since the army revolt, would ever get delivered.

Dear Mom and Dad, she read, *I expect you'll have been reading in the newspapers all about the war which has broken out over here, and I imagine it seems like pretty scary stuff. But it's not like that at all – at least, not where I am. I'm perfectly safe here in Madrid.*

And so she was, she thought. For the moment. But what would happen if the Nationalists started bombing the centre of town from the air? Worse, what would happen if, as Paco had said it might, the rebel army swept into the city?

There were loads of demonstrations out on the streets when first I arrived here, the letter continued, *but now the militias have taken over order has been restored.*

It sounded all wrong, she decided. Yet it was almost impossible for her to make it sound right. Her parents were country people. They'd seemed lost when they'd visited her in the middle-sized town where she'd done her bachelor's degree. So how could she even begin to describe to them the complex life in a big city – and a foreign big city at that?

She remembered how bewildered they'd been when she'd announced her intention to go to college. But nobody from their town ever went to college, they'd pointed out. It just wasn't done. And as for her telling them she was going on after her degree to study for a doctorate – well, the only doctors they could understand were the ones who delivered babies and fixed broken legs.

She read the next section of the letter – the one she had found most difficult to write.

I have to tell you something very important. I've fallen in love. I know what you're going to say. I've only been in Spain for two weeks. How could I possibly have fallen in love in such a short time? Well, all I can tell you, is that I have. He's . . .

She had run out of words at that point. What could she tell them about Paco? That he was the most wonderful man she'd ever met? That he had absurd ideas on the nature of honour – ideas that were more in keeping with a romantic medieval knight than with a police inspector who had seen so many brutal murders – but that she wouldn't wish him to change one iota? That he was still married, but shared his bed nightly with their darling daughter?

The knock on the door shook her out of her musings, and when she opened it she found two young men in boiler suits standing there.

'Señorita Walker?' the taller of the two asked.

'Yes, that's me.'

'We have brought you a message from Paco Ruiz. He would like you to join him in the mountains.'

Cindy felt her heart start to beat faster. Paco had said that the fighting in the mountains would be a serious business – that it would be no place for a woman. And he was not the kind of man to change his attitude on things like that overnight. 'Did you speak to him yourselves?' she asked.

'Of course. We're friends of his. That's why he asked us to take you to him personally.'

That didn't sound like Paco. It didn't sound like him at all. Cindy forced a smile to her lips. 'And is he keeping his moustache trimmed now that I'm not there to nag him?' she asked. 'I'm always telling him not to let it get too straggly, but I know he never pays any attention to me when he's away from home.'

The taller Anarchist returned her smile. 'Then the sooner you have him under your thumb again, the better. But I must say that when I saw him yesterday, his moustache looked fine.'

Cindy moved quickly, but the tall man was even quicker. As she tried to slam the door, he pushed hard in the opposite direction, and she was sent sprawling backwards on to the floor. She struggled to get to her feet again, but the Anarchist was already on top of her, pinning her arms down with his knees, and clamping his hands firmly over her mouth.

'If you scream when I take my hands away, I will, with great regret, be forced to kill you,' he growled, and now he sounded like one of the rich young men who lived in the barrio de Salamanca, rather than the working man he'd just pretended to be. 'If you understand what I'm saying, nod your head,' he continued, no less menacingly.

Cindy nodded her head as far as it would go, and the taller Anarchist climbed off her. She looked around, and saw that the smaller man was also in the apartment now, and had a pistol pointing right at her.

'Paco Ruiz doesn't really have a moustache, does he?' the taller man demanded.

'No,' Cindy agreed.

'You're a smart girl,' the tall man told her. 'And if you carry on being smart no harm will come to you. On the other hand, if you start acting stupidly, you're as good as dead.'

'What is it you want?' Cindy asked, doing her best to fight back a growing feeling of panic.

The tall man smiled again, but this time it was not at all a pleasant smile. 'We told you just a few moments ago what we want,' he said. 'We want to take you to see your boyfriend.'

*

From the angle of the sunshine which was streaming in through the small barred window, Paco estimated it was two o'clock in the afternoon, which meant that he had been locked up in the storeroom for at least fourteen hours – fourteen hours which had seemed like an eternity. He had been served two basic meals by a stony-faced private who plainly thought the food was wasted on him, and had been allowed to empty his toilet bucket into the street drain once. For the rest of the time, there had been nothing to do but think. Think about Cindy, how much he loved her and how much he already missed her. Think about the fact that he had been a complete bloody fool to turn down Major Gómez's offer – which would at least have bought him a little more time – and yet at the same moment be sure that he had been absolutely right to reject it.

He heard the tramp of soldiers' boots outside, then the door swung open and Major Gómez entered with two very large private soldiers. Someone else, on the outside, bolted the door behind them.

'What's going on?' Paco demanded. 'Have you brought these thugs to beat the crap out of me? Because if you have, you're wasting your time. Whatever you do to me, I'm not going to work for you.'

The major shook his head, almost as if Paco's comments had saddened him. 'You disappoint me,' he said.

'Really?' Paco answered. 'I'm mortified to hear that.'

'Do you want to know *why* I'm disappointed in you?' the major asked, ignoring the sarcasm.

Paco shrugged. 'Why not? I have no pressing appointments to keep.'

'I am disappointed that you could imagine, even for a second, that I would attempt to gain your co-operation by having you beaten up. I'm a good enough judge of men to know what will, and will not, work – and I had hoped that *you* were a good enough judge of men to appreciate that fact about me.'

'So maybe I'm not the hot-shot policeman you thought I was,' Paco suggested.

'Or perhaps you're so outraged at the idea of investigating the death of a dog that your usual instincts have been clouded,' the major said. 'But once you're on the case, all that will change.'

'You never give up, do you?' Paco asked. 'Even when it should be obvious to you that you're not going to get what you want, you never give up.'

Instead of answering the question, the major walked across to the far end of the storeroom. The moment he had taken up his new position, the two big privates stepped into the centre of the room, creating an effective barrier between the officer and the prisoner.

It looked like an orchestrated, pre-planned move, Paco thought. It looked, in fact, as if the major was in fear for his safety. Yet Gómez did not appear in the least bit frightened. He was smiling, and that smile seemed to be one of triumphant amusement. 'I told you last night there was more than one way to skin a cat,' he said.

'And what's that supposed to mean?'

'Why don't you go and have a look out of the window?' the major suggested. 'See what's happening on the street?'

Paco walked over to the window. On the opposite side of the street were two more private soldiers – and standing between them was a blonde woman wearing a grey skirt which only just covered her knees and a white sweatshirt with the number 18 on it.

An anger colder than any he had ever experienced before gushed through Paco's blood. He slowly turned to face the major, who was still protected by his wall of flesh and muscle. 'You're a real son of a bitch, aren't you?' he said.

'Perhaps,' Gómez replied. 'But you have to admit, I'm a *clever* son of a bitch.'

Flinging himself at the two bodyguards in an attempt to claw his way through to the major might give him momentary satisfaction, Paco thought, but it would be a pointless exercise at a time when he should make every action count.

'You can dispense with your thugs now,' he said.

'How can I be sure of that?' Gómez countered.

'I thought you were a good judge of men,' Paco said. 'Or was that nothing more than bullshit?'

The major hesitated for a second, then shouted out instructions to the man on the other side of the door, and ordered his escort to leave. Prisoner and officer stood glaring at each other for a few seconds, then Paco took a couple of steps forward. 'If you've hurt her . . .' he said menacingly. 'If you've so much as harmed one hair on her head . . .'

'She has not been hurt, and she will not be hurt. Once you've uncovered the murderer of the general's dog, you will both be released.'

'I want a cigarette,' Paco said.

40

'Of course,' the major agreed, first holding out his packet and then striking a match.

Paco inhaled the smoke and let it snake its way around his lungs. 'You do realize it's going to be almost impossible to find out who killed the dog, don't you?' he asked.

'I don't see why. For the policeman who managed to solve the Atocha decapitation case, it should not prove to be too difficult a task.'

Paco sighed. 'How many men would you estimate were in the village the night the dog was killed?'

The major shrugged. 'There are some soldiers who go back to their camp instead of blowing their pay on drink, but they are in a small minority. So if I had to make a guess, I would say that there were roughly three thousand soldiers in the village that night.'

'And any of them could have been the killer.'

'No,' Gómez corrected him. 'Only *one* man was the killer – and you will find out who that one man is.'

Paco took another drag of his cigarette. 'Before I even start my investigation, I shall need to speak to the general,' he said.

Gómez shook his head. 'That is neither necessary nor possible.'

Paco sighed again. 'You want me on this case because I am an experienced investigator,' he said. 'Is that correct?'

'Certainly.'

'Yet at the same time, you're refusing to let me use the methods of investigation which have worked for me in the past? Do you really think I'd have been able to solve the Atocha case if I'd been denied access to any of the people I needed to talk to?'

Gómez was silent for several seconds, as if he were weighing up his options in his mind. 'I will talk to the general myself, and see if I can persuade him to agree to see you,' he said finally.

Chapter Six

Paco had once read in a magazine that aristocrats in other countries lived in splendid isolation, well away from the noise and bustle, and especially away from the *hoi polloi*. But in this, as in so many other things, Spain was different. When the Marquis of This or Count of That was deciding where to build his *palacio*, it would never occur to him to site it out in the wilds. Perhaps it would be built to overlook the Plaza Mayor. Perhaps it would be down one of the broader streets, towering over the humble dwellings on either side of it. But whatever the exact location, it would be in the village – where it belonged.

The palace in the village of San Fernando de la Sierra was no exception to the rule. It stood on the Calle Mayor, half way between the main square and the church. It was a storey higher than the buildings which surrounded it, and at least three times as long. There were crenellations running along the edge of the roof. Its windows were much larger than those of the other houses. And in case anyone should doubt that this was the home of a member of the nobility, a stone coat of arms had been carved above main double doors.

The two soldiers on guard outside the doors saluted Major Gómez, but glared at Paco's blue boiler-suit.

'We have an appointment to see the general,' Gómez said.

'Yes, sir,' one of the sentries said, leaving his post and pushing the heavy oak door open.

Paco and the major stepped into an internal courtyard, which was so full of heavy expensive chairs, tables, cabinets and bric-a-brac that it resembled an auction room.

'We requisitioned this place from one of the local aristos,' Major Gómez said dryly. 'The general finds the *palacio* itself perfectly acceptable, but he didn't like the Count's taste in furniture, so he's had his own shipped down from Burgos.'

Paco examined the cabinet closest to him. It was inlaid with mother-of-pearl. 'The general must be a very rich man,' he said.

'He is,' Major Gómez agreed, with just a touch of envy and bitterness in his voice.

A door to their left opened, and a man stepped into the courtyard. He was tall and well built, with slicked-down black hair, quick brown eyes, a smart military moustache and a wide, sensuous mouth. He was around thirty-five years old, and instantly reminded Paco of all those strong, silent men – those matinée idols – who performed heroic deeds on the cinema screen.

'This is the prisoner Ruiz, my Colonel,' Gómez said.

The colonel shot Paco a look of deep loathing. 'Is it really necessary for us to waste the general's time with this guttersnipe, Gómez?' he asked.

'Yes, sir,' the major replied. 'If we want the criminal brought to justice, then I believe it is.'

The colonel snorted. 'Very well,' he said. He turned on his heel. 'Follow me, the pair of you.'

The room into which the colonel led them was dominated by a large oak table covered with maps. Sitting behind the table was a short bald man with a round head. He had to be General Castro, Paco thought. He'd been expecting someone more prepossessing than this almost comical figure. The man who had helped General Franco to put down the Asturian miners' revolt in such a bloody manner – and had been, if the stories were to be believed, even more ruthless than Franco himself – should have had much more of an air of menace about him.

There was one other occupant of the room. Lying contentedly on a rug in front of the stone fireplace was a large German shepherd dog.

'Is this dog the . . .' Paco began.

'Silence!' the colonel bellowed. 'You will speak when you are given permission, and at no other time!'

'What were you going to say, Ruiz?' Major Gómez asked.

'I was wondering if this was the sister of the dog which was killed.'

'Yes it is,' the general said in a squeaky voice. 'And you miss your brother, don't you, my poor little Reina?'

At the mention of her name, the dog turned her head. Rays of sunshine were streaming in through the window, and Paco noted how they played on the jewels which were encrusted in her collar.

'Was the dog that was killed wearing a collar like this one?' he asked the general.

'Stand to the left side of the table, one metre from the edge, and when you speak to the general, call him "sir", you Bolshevik son of a bitch!' the colonel shouted.

Paco shrugged, but did as he'd been ordered. 'Was the dead dog wearing a collar like the one Reina's wearing, *sir*?' he asked.

'Almost identical,' the general told him.

'Wasn't it rather unwise to let the dogs loose wearing such valuable trinkets . . . sir?'

'My men have too much respect – and fear – to ever attempt to steal from *me*,' the general said.

'Then where's the collar?' Paco asked.

The general rubbed his bald head with his right hand. 'You're right,' he admitted. 'Somewhere in this village there is one foolish man who thinks he can defy me. I want that man found and made an example of. Do you think that you can find him?'

'It's possible, sir,' Paco said cautiously. 'But first I will need to know much more about the circumstances surrounding the killing. Are your dogs normally free to run wherever they choose?'

'Of course not! They are expensive animals. Do you think I want them mixing with mangy strays and picking up all kinds of filthy diseases?'

'So they don't usually leave the house?'

'When they require exercise, as they do two or three times a day, one of my men takes them out for a walk on the lead.'

'Then how did Principe come to be on the street alone?'

'He escaped. A servant was foolish enough to leave the door open for a few seconds, and Principe made a dash for it. The man in question has already been disciplined.'

There was a distant rumble, which quickly grew into a louder roar. The window frame rattled as an army truck passed by, soon followed by another, and another.

'It seems that the convoy from Burgos has finally arrived,' the colonel said, unnecessarily.

Paco watched the seemingly endless stream of lorries, all carrying military equipment, and thought of his comrades with their old rifles and their packed lunches. What an unequal fight this war looked like being.

'Do you have any more questions, Ruiz?' the general asked, squeaking loudly, to avoid his voice being drowned out by the noise outside.

'Was the dog in the habit of escaping whenever he had the opportunity?' Paco said.

'Sir!' the colonel bawled.

'Sir,' Paco echoed.

'No, he wasn't,' the general said. 'He was not used to running wild at all. In fact, he liked being in the house, and was often reluctant to go out on one of his walks.'

'Then what do you think could have made him run away on this occasion, sir?'

'Probably a bitch on heat,' the general said, with some emotion. 'If I could find her, I'd have her shot, too.'

There was a knock on the door, and a sergeant entered the room. He was carrying a newspaper in his hand, but instead of advancing towards the table with it, he stopped on the threshold, rolled it up – and whistled.

Reina sprang to her feet and, tail held high and ears pointed, padded across the room and sat down at the sergeant's feet. The soldier held out the newspaper. The dog took it her mouth, walked around the table, and deposited it on her master's lap. The general himself was beaming with pleasure.

Castro flattened out the paper and spread it on the desk. 'She hardly got it wet at all,' he said with obvious pride.

'You are as skilful in handling dogs as you are in handling men,' the colonel said ingratiatingly.

The general slowly read the front-page of the newspaper, his lips moving in time with his eyes. Everyone else in the room waited in an awkward silence for him to finish. At last Castro looked up. 'It is just as I predicted to you, Valera,' he said. 'The Communists and Anarchists are no fighters, and we are rapidly gaining ground everywhere.'

'With wise leadership from our generals and God on our side, we cannot fail,' Colonel Valera replied, and Paco could almost see him saying the same line in one of those flickery historical dramas, which he sometimes used to watch to kill a wet winter afternoon.

Paco coughed discreetly. 'You have still *more* questions?' the general snapped.

'Yes, sir.'

'Then ask them.'

'Who found the dead dog?'

Castro turned to Valera. 'Colonel?'

'The first people to reach the spot were a group of six private soldiers, who were drinking at the bar nearest to the corner of the Calle Belén when they heard the shots,' Valera said, speaking directly to his commanding officer in preference to addressing the guttersnipe from Madrid in the blue boiler-suit. 'Principe was still twitching when they found him. He couldn't have been dead for more than a few seconds.'

'And was the dog's collar already missing when they got there, sir?' Paco asked.

'It was certainly missing by the time the first officer – which happened – to be me, arrived on the scene,' Valera told Castro.

'That's not the same thing,' Paco pointed out.

'Whoever shot my poor little Principe must also have stolen the collar,' the general said. 'There can be no other motive for the murder.'

That wasn't necessarily true, Paco thought. In fact, after what he'd just seen, he'd have been willing to bet his life on the fact that the two incidents – the shooting and the robbery – had absolutely nothing to do with each other. 'Did you institute a search for the missing collar, sir?' he asked.

'As you know, General, the whole village was gone over with a fine-toothed comb,' Valera said, 'as was the military camp. All the men's equipment was checked, every nook and cranny was looked into.'

'And how long after the dog's death did this extensive search begin?' Paco asked.

The general nodded at Major Gómez. 'About half an hour,' the head of security supplied.

'Yes, you were very slow to get organized there, Major Gómez,' Valera said, with an edge of dislike, bordering on hatred, in his voice. 'By the time you finally started your search, the thief had been given ample opportunity to take the collar well away from the village.'

So he had, Paco thought. But unless the man was a complete fool, he was very unlikely to have done so.

The office door banged loudly open, and a woman swept dramatically into the room. And what a woman! She was tall – perhaps twenty-five centimetres taller than the general. She had long black hair which shone as if she oiled it every single day, a wide mouth, haughty cheekbones and flashing green eyes. She was wearing a dress of purest silk which not only matched her eyes, but also revealed much of her firm bosom. She was about twenty-five, Paco decided – and she was an absolute stunner.

46

The dog rushed towards her, but a dismissive gesture of her hand soon made it retreat again. The general and the colonel had risen to their feet.

'What are you doing here, my dear?' the general asked, slightly shakily. 'I thought that you had decided to remain in Burgos until Madrid fell to our forces.'

'And have you lose another one of my poor pets through your wanton neglect?' the woman demanded.

'You've heard,' the general said miserably.

'Would I have endured the uncomfortable journey with the convoy if I *hadn't* heard?' the woman asked. 'Why didn't you tell me, Federico? Was it too much effort to make a simple phone call? How could you even dream of keeping me in the dark for so long?'

The general shrugged his shoulders. 'I . . . I know how attached you were to Principe,' he said. 'I thought it would be better to tell you of his tragic death face to face.'

The woman threw back her head scornfully, 'Better!' she repeated. 'Was that what was really in your mind? I don't believe you for a minute, Federico. I think it's much more likely you were afraid to admit to me that you'd failed to protect my little puppy dog.'

'Please, my dear . . .' the general said, indicating the presence in the room of the man in the boiler-suit.

The woman seemed to notice Paco for the first time. 'And who is this?' she demanded, her voice becoming almost a screech.

'His name is Francisco Ruiz, and he's a . . .'

'He's what they're calling "a militiaman" on the other side of the line, which is another way of saying that he's a godless Communist who burns down our churches and rapes our nuns. Why are you wasting your time talking to a piece of scum like him when you should be finding out who is responsible for murdering my poor little Principe?'

'But that's precisely why he's here,' the general protested. 'He's a famous police detective from Madrid. He's solved a score of important cases in his time. You remember the headless corpse in the Atocha station, my dear? Well, it was Inspector Ruiz who . . .'

'You call this traitor "inspector"?' the woman demanded angrily. 'Even dressed as he is, you grant him the courtesy of using the title – no doubt unfairly obtained – which he once had?'

'Perhaps all you say is true – I mean, I'm sure it is,' the general replied weakly. 'Nevertheless, Ruiz is an expert and . . .'

'I don't want him investigating the case,' his wife said emphatically. 'I would rather have your valet or my maid investigate it than put my trust in this spawn of Satan.'

The general looked down at his hands, as if unsure what to do or say next. 'Have the prisoner taken back to his cell, Major Gómez,' he mumbled finally. 'I will decide what to do with him later.'

'Decide later?' the woman repeated, incredulously. 'But there is nothing to decide. He should be shot as soon as possible.'

'It will probably come to that in the end,' the general half-promised.

'You are no sort of man,' his wife told him. 'A man – a real man – would already have issued the order.'

Gómez tapped Paco on the shoulder, and pointed towards the door. As the two men left the room, Colonel Valera moved from behind the table and rapidly followed them out into the courtyard. Once he had closed the office door behind him, Valera said, 'I'd like a word with the prisoner.'

'With *my* prisoner, you mean?' Gómez asked. 'Certainly, Colonel. Be my guest.'

Valera shot him a hostile glare. 'As far as I am aware, he's no more your prisoner than anyone else's,' he said. 'You didn't capture him personally, did you, Major?'

'No,' Gómez admitted. 'But if it hadn't been for me he'd have been dead now. Still, as I said a moment ago, if you want to talk to him, be my guest.'

The hostility in the, Colonel's eyes intensified 'I would like to speak to Ruiz *alone!*' he said.

For a second, it seemed as if Gómez would say something else, then he shrugged his shoulders and negotiated his way through the stacks of furniture to the front door. Valera waited until he was out of earshot, then said, 'You probably consider yourself under Major Gómez's protection, and maybe you are – though you'd be a fool to believe any promise he makes to you. But whether you are or not isn't really important, because *I* am the one who matters in this village – *I* am the one whom you should be careful not to cross.'

'Are you just trying to scare me, or is there some point to all this?' Paco asked.

'What you have just witnessed in the office was rather unfortunate,' the colonel said through clenched teeth. 'And not at all typical. No doubt you thought the general's lady was a little offhand with her husband, but that was only because she is upset over the death of her beloved dog. Under normal circumstances, she treats the general with the greatest of respect.'

I'll bet she does, Paco thought. A beautiful young woman like her, married to a tubby middle-aged man like him? She must be able to wrap him around her little finger any time she feels like it.

And now, because of the scene in the office, Colonel Valera, whose job it was to insulate the general from the outside world, found himself forced to talk to the man he had studiously ignored during the interview – and he was hating every second of it.

'The point I am making is that you should not discuss anything you have heard with anyone else,' the colonel continued, 'because if you do, steps will have to be taken.'

'Steps?' Paco repeated.

'I have already told you that Major Gómez's protection means very little, and perhaps by tomorrow it will mean nothing at all. So just remember this – the loosest tongue can be stopped by a bullet to the head.'

Chapter Seven

Paco paced the storeroom prison where his comrades had spent their last few hours on earth. Why did he have to be Paco Ruiz, the famous detective? he asked himself over and over again. Why couldn't he have been a street-sweeper like Pepe, or a boot-boy like little Alfredo? True, if he had been, he would now be dead. But at least Cindy would still be safely in Madrid, instead of a prisoner several kilometres behind enemy lines!

No one could help falling in love, he argued to himself. It wasn't his fault that he and Cindy had done just that, thus giving the cunning Major Gómez the weapon he needed. And yet, though he could absolve himself of all blame on a purely intellectual level, he still felt incredibly guilty. When all was said and done, he had got Cindy into this mess, and whatever else happened to him or anyone else, he was determined that he was going to get her out of it again.

He heard the sound of the bolt sliding open, and Major Gómez stepped into the storeroom. 'The general's lady appears to have taken a marked dislike to you, Inspector,' he said. 'But then that's not really very surprising. I've heard her views on the Communists and the Socialists at dinner parties, and next to her, even her husband sounds like a dangerous left-winger.'

'Does that mean I'm no longer on the case?' Paco asked.

The major shook his head. 'I get the impression that as long as she keeps him happy in the bedroom, the general will let his wife have her own way in most other areas. But this is different. The death of the dog has caused him to lose face with his men. If he is ever to regain it, the killer must be caught – and he still thinks you are the best man to do that. Don't prove him wrong.'

'But if the general's wife is so against me . . .' Paco said.

'As long as you are discreet and don't flaunt your presence in the village, the general should be able to keep her at bay.' He ran his eyes up and down Paco's blue *mono*. 'For a start, that boiler-suit will simply have to go. It makes you far too conspicuous.'

'I won't wear a rebel uniform,' Paco said firmly.

Gómez's eyes flashed briefly with anger. 'Most of my brother officers would shoot you on the spot if they heard you calling us rebels,' he said.

'It's what you are, though,' Paco told him. 'And because it's what you are, I won't wear your uniform.'

Gómez nodded. 'All right,' he said. 'We'll find you a suit, like you used to wear when you were a real policeman back in Madrid.'

'And I'll need an office,' Paco pointed out. 'Somewhere I can interview people, and organize my notes.'

'That shouldn't be too difficult. Anything else?'

'Money,' Paco said.

'Money?' the major repeated. 'What in God's name would you possibly want money for?'

'So I can drink at the bars, and listen to what the soldiers are saying. So I can stand a round of drinks when I think I might learn something from it. I have to feel the pulse of a place where I'm carrying out my investigation. It's the way I've always worked.'

'I suppose I can let you have a few pesetas out of the intelligence fund,' Gómez said grudgingly, as Paco noticed, not for the first time, that the major's boots could use a visit to the cobbler's. 'And once you've got all that, you'll be willing to start your investigation?'

Paco looked around the bare storeroom. 'No,' he said. 'I'll need somewhere better than this to sleep.'

'Naturally.'

'And I won't be sleeping alone. I'll be wanting Cindy Walker to keep me company.'

'But you're not married!' Gómez exclaimed.

Paco grinned. 'This village is full of prostitutes from Burgos, and you're shocked that I should want to make love to the woman I hope will be my wife one day?'

'I don't think it will possible,' Gómez said.

'Make it possible,' Paco told him firmly.

Gómez ground his teeth. 'Do I have to remind you that you're a prisoner here?' he asked.

'Maybe I am,' Paco agreed. 'But I'm no ordinary prisoner. I'm one that the general thinks might be so useful that he's keeping me alive, despite his wife's formidable objections. Besides, if I do manage to solve this case, who do you think is going to get the credit for it? A godless Red from Madrid? Or the head of the general's security?'

The point hit its target. 'I will see what I can do,' Gómez promised, as he turned and headed for the door.

*

The black suit was a little tight under the armpits, but otherwise was a reasonable fit. The office Gómez had provided him with in the Calle Mayor was nothing more than the living-room of one of the humbler houses, but that would serve his purpose well enough, too. The only things missing, Paco thought as he sat at the table, were the police regulation pistol which had almost become an extension of his body over the years, and his partner, Constable Fernández.

Fernández – or Fat Felipe, as he was universally known – had worked with Paco for a long time. To some people, both inside and outside the Madrid police, Felipe seemed to be nothing more than a bumbling clown, but Paco valued his plodding, common sense and the habit he had of sticking a pin into the bubble of his boss's more fanciful theories. Without Felipe at his side on a case, he felt oddly incomplete. But then, he forcibly reminded himself, this case was different from all the others he had ever handled. This case was one which, even if the evidence fell on to his lap, he had no intention of solving.

There was the sound of marching feet outside, and a middle-aged corporal opened the door.

'The men who you asked to see have just got back from the front line,' he said.

Only a few days earlier, he would have used the polite form address, calling Paco *usted*, as befitted a man of his rank. But so much had changed in such a short time, and now he used the more familiar *tu*, a reminder, if the ex-inspector needed one, that he, despite his suit and his privileges, was still no more than a common prisoner.

'Do you want to see them all together, or shall I send them in one at a time?' the corporal asked.

'I'll see them all together.'

'You lot! In here! Now!' the corporal shouted.

The six private soldiers marched clumsily into the room, and lined up in front of the table as if they'd been summoned to attend a punishment parade. Paco ran his eyes along the line. The men were dressed – as every private soldier in the history of warfare had been – in cheap, rough uniforms. From their passive round faces and blank eyes he guessed that they were all country boys. With one exception! The man standing at the end of the line – as if he had deliberately positioned himself as far on the edge of Paco's line of vision as possible – had a thin rat-like face and quick, cunning eyes. Looking at him was like being on familiar territory for Paco – like moving among the pimps who worked in the area on the bank of the River Manzanares.

'So you six were the first ones to discover the dead dog, were you?' Paco asked.

The privates all nodded, but none of them spoke. The country boys would be keeping quiet because that was what they did when confronted by anyone who smelled of authority. It was different in the case of Rat-face on the end of the line. His kind were rarely intimidated, but would never volunteer anything unless they could see there was something in it for themselves.

Paco leant back in his chair and wondered which of the privates to question first. For a moment, he was tempted to start with Rat-face, then he decided it might be more interesting to wait and see at which point the sly young man felt the need to intervene.

'You!' he said, pointing to a tall, thick-set boy who, if anything, looked even more confused and uncomfortable than his companions. 'What's your name?'

'I'm Private Jiménez, señor,' the boy answered in a strong Extremaduran accent.

Paco had to force himself not to grin. To the corporal on guard outside, he was one of the enemy, but to this simple boy he was a man wearing a suit, and therefore to be given his due respect. 'Why don't you tell me what happened that night, Private Jiménez?' he said.

Jiménez's mouth opened and closed several times in the panic of being the one selected to speak. He looked, Paco thought, just like a fish which has been landed and is gasping for air.

'I . . . Um . . . I . . . I mean all of us. . . .' the young peasant stammered.

'Take your time,' Paco said encouragingly.

'We . . . we were all having a drink outside this bar near the corner of Calle Mayor and the Calle Belén.' Jiménez blushed as if he'd already been deliberately misleading. 'It's . . . it's not really a bar at all. Before we arrived, it was a fruit and vegetable shop, but it got some barrels of wine and some glasses and. . . .'

'I understand,' Paco said. 'Carry on.'

'We heard shots. Well, only Pérez heard the first one, but we all heard the second.'

'Who's Pérez?' Paco interrupted, and was not at all surprised when the rat-faced man said, 'I am.'

'We went to see what was happening, and that's when we found the dog,' Jiménez continued. 'When we got there, he was still twitching. But that's no more than most animals do after they've been killed. He was dead as a doornail – there's no doubt about that.'

'Did you see anyone else?'

'No. Well, what I mean to say is, we did hear someone running away down the Calle Belén, but . . .'

'But whoever it was had already turned the corner by the time you got there?' Paco supplied.

'That's right.'

'And none of you thought to follow, to find out who it was who was running away?'

Private Jiménez looked blank. 'No, señor,' he admitted. 'We . . . we were all looking at the dog.'

Paco nodded understandingly. He had been on enough murder cases to know that a dead body – even a dog's dead body – is infinitely more interesting to the average person than anything around it which is still living. 'So you were looking down at the dog,' he said. 'Did you happen to notice whether or not it was still wearing its collar?'

'There wasn't any collar on the animal,' said a firm voice from the end of the line.

'How can you be so sure, Private Pérez?' Paco asked, turning to the rat-faced soldier.

Pérez shrugged. 'Half the dog's head was blown away. That's where we were all looking. At the wound. If there'd been a collar, we couldn't have failed to have noticed it.'

'So you're saying that whoever shot the dog must also have taken the collar?' Paco asked.

But Pérez was too wily a bird to give a direct answer to a question like that. 'I couldn't say,' he replied. 'All I know is, the collar wasn't round the dog's neck by the time we arrived.'

Paco turned his attention back to the big, slow Private Jiménez. 'What happened next?'

'A lot of other lads turned, up. There was quite a crowd of us by the time the officer arrived.'

'And that officer was, in fact, none other than Colonel Valera, wasn't he?' Paco asked.

'He . . . I . . . I'm not sure,' Jiménez confessed. 'They all have nice uniforms and . . .'

'It was Valera,' Pérez said.

'You're certain you recognized him?'

'Oh yes. I know him when I see him. He's the one who tries so hard to look like Clark Gable.'

Paco nodded. 'So how much time was there between you lot finding the dog, and the other lads turning up?' he asked Jiménez.

The private wrinkled his brow. 'Not long.'

'A minute? Less than that?'

'I don't know.'

Of course he didn't. Country boys could tell you exactly how many furrows they could plough between sunrise and sunset, but on matters of pure time they were useless. 'How long do *you* think it was, Pérez?' Paco asked the rat-faced man.

'Couldn't have been more than fifteen or twenty seconds, I should say,' Pérez replied.

'But that would have been long enough for you to slip the collar off the dog, wouldn't it?'

'I suppose so,' Pérez admitted. 'But if we'd taken the collar, what did we do with it? We were all searched. The whole village was turned upside down. The camp as well. The collar wasn't anywhere to be found.'

'You could have hidden it outside the village,' Paco said, even though he'd already practically dismissed from his mind the idea that the collar was anywhere but in San Fernando.

Pérez sneered. 'We never left the village and we can prove it. After we'd given our names to one of Colonel Valera's aides, we went straight back to the bar we'd been drinking in earlier – and we've got at least a dozen witnesses who'll swear to that.'

'*All* of you went back to the bar?' Paco asked.

Pérez's sneer widened. 'Well, all of us apart from old Jiménez here.'

'What did he do?'

'The sight of a dog with half its head missing seemed to have knocked the stuffing out of him, and he went to the church. To *pray*!'

Paco turned to the big peasant boy. 'Is that true, Jiménez?' he asked. 'Did you go to pray?'

'Yes, señor,' the boy admitted, 'I used to go to church a lot at home. My mother's very religious.'

'And you've always been a mummy's boy, haven't you, Tomas?' Pérez said nastily.

Jiménez turned towards the rat-faced private, the expression on his dull face probably the closest he ever got to anger. 'My mother is a saint,' he said.

'Of course she is,' Pérez readily agreed. 'This country is full of saints – and most of them live in shitty little villages in the back of beyond.'

Jiménez bunched his ham-like fists. 'You take that back,' he growled menacingly.

'That's enough!' Paco said. 'If you're going to fight, do it in your own time.' He ran his eyes up and down the line once more. 'Does any of you have anything to add to what's already been said?' The privates all shook their heads. 'All right, you can go now – but I may want to talk to you again.'

'That'd be a complete waste of energy,' Pérez said. 'We've already told you all we know.'

The privates trooped out of the door. Paco gave them a few seconds, then stepped over to the window. Four of the soldiers were heading for the nearest bar, but Pérez and Jiménez were still standing in the street. The big peasant's stance was still aggressive, the rat-faced private's much more conciliatory. Paco watched as Pérez gestured with his hands, obviously trying to explain some simple point to his companion. It was a full two minutes before the country boy started to relax, and another two before Pérez felt confident enough to put his arm on Jiménez's shoulder as a sign of friendship. Then, their reconciliation complete, they, too, set off for one of the bars.

Paco lit a cigarette. What had all that been about? he wondered. Had Pérez been deliberately goading Jiménez a few minutes early, and if he had, for what purpose?

He remembered Pérez's parting words: *We've already told you all we know.*

Like hell you have! Paco said softly to himself.

Chapter Eight

It was a little after eight o'clock in the evening when the door of Paco's new office opened, and Major Gómez stepped inside.

'Don't you ever knock?' Paco demanded instinctively, without even looking up from the notes he was making.

Gómez chuckled. 'Old habits are hard to break, aren't they?' he said. 'But it's time you realized that we are not in Madrid, and you are no longer an inspector of police, Prisoner Ruiz.'

Paco sighed and put his pencil down on the table. 'What can I do for you, Major?' he asked.

'I've come to escort you to your quarters,' Gómez said.

'You mean, you've come to see I'm safely locked up for the night,' Paco corrected him.

The major shrugged. 'Perhaps that is what I mean, but there are those, including myself, who would consider being locked up with a beautiful woman not too much of a hardship to bear.'

Paco felt his heart suddenly start to beat a little faster. His threats had worked, and he was going to be allowed to spend time with his beloved Cindy. Even more important than that, he had proved to himself that even with all the cards stacked against him, he could still win one small victory. And that fact gave him at least a little hope for the future.

'Shall we go?' the major asked. 'Or is seeing your woman of so little interest to you that you'd prefer to stay here and do some more work?'

'We'll go,' Paco said, standing up and reaching for his jacket.

They stepped out on to the street. The two sentries on duty looked quizzically at the major. 'Will you be needing an escort, sir?' one of them asked.

Gómez shook his head. 'Go and get yourselves a couple of drinks while the bars are still open.'

The Calle Mayor seemed to be one enormous bar. Every shop had been converted into a drinking establishment, as had the parlours of half the private houses. Even this was not enough to cope with the demand, and some of the villagers were running businesses which consisted of nothing more than trestle tables set out in the street.

There were soldiers everywhere. Soldiers demonstrating their *machismo* by downing large glasses of brandy in a single gulp. Soldiers drinking a mixture of Asturian cider and cheap red wine. Soldiers being sick. Soldiers pissing in the street. And, of course, there were the whores. Like the ones who'd travelled out on Paco's bus from Madrid, they were mostly a bunch of raddled hags, but in the atmosphere of desperation and drunkenness which co-existed side by side on the street that night, even they found themselves a steady trade.

'I consider myself a sociable sort of chap,' Gómez said, as they weaved their way around the knots of young soldiers, 'I'm popular in the officers' mess, and very much in demand at regimental balls. Yet you don't seem to like me. Now why should that be?'

'I saw you kill a man yesterday afternoon,' Paco reminded him.

'And just before I executed him, I heard him scream out that you had killed two of our soldiers that very morning. So what right do you have to feel superior to me?'

'That was completely different,' Paco said, slightly uneasily. 'I killed them out on the battlefield.'

The major laughed. 'This whole country is a battlefield, my friend, I'm afraid if you're going to dislike me, you'll have to come up with a better reason for it than shooting a man who was already in the process of betraying you.'

'You also arranged for Cindy Walker to be kidnapped,' Paco said. 'If I didn't think it would make the situation worse than it already is, I'd kill you for that right now.'

'If you'd agreed to co-operate with me in the first place, the kidnapping would not have been necessary,' Gómez said, as if Paco's last comment had completely washed over him. 'And can you honestly say that in my position you would have acted any differently?'

'I'm not in your position.'

'True,' Gómez agreed. 'And you should probably thank your lucky stars for it. Mine is not an easy tightrope to walk. But let's talk about the case. This afternoon, the general said he was convinced that whoever shot the dog did it because he wished to steal the collar. I was watching you closely at the time, and I didn't think that you looked very convinced by that particular line of reasoning. Did I read your expression correctly?'

'Yes, you did,' Paco agreed, making a note to remember to be very circumspect with his expressions when the major was around.

'So explain to me why you don't think the dog was killed for its collar,' Gómez said.

'I saw the way the other dog – Reina – took the newspaper off the corporal this afternoon,' Paco explained.

'What did that tell you?' Gómez asked, intrigued.

'That she's soft – and spoiled half to death. And I see no reason why Principe should have been any different.'

'He wasn't,' Gómez confirmed. 'If anything, he was even softer. But you still haven't answered my question.'

'If I'd wanted to steal the dog's collar, the first thing I'd have done would have been to get him to beg,' Paco explained. 'Then, while he was sitting down, I'd simply have unfastened the collar and slipped it into my pocket. If he'd resisted – which is unlikely – I'd have slit his throat. What I wouldn't have done is take the risk of shooting him near a very busy street, where there were any number of people who might see me.'

They had reached the Plaza Mayor. It was almost dark now, and scores of hurricane lamps had been lit, filling the whole square with an eerie glow. In one corner, a guitarist was playing Galician folk songs. In the space in front of the water fountain, an attractive gypsy woman was dancing to a flamenco guitar, while a ragged child with a large upturned cap in his hands was collecting small coins from those who were watching the performance.

'So what *did* happen to the collar?' Gómez asked.

'The chances are, it's still in the village.'

'It can't be!' the major protested. 'I had my men carry out a thorough search. If it had been here, they'd almost certainly have found it. So isn't it far more likely the thief – whether or not he's also the murderer – has hidden the collar somewhere in the countryside?'

Paco shook his head. 'No, it isn't, as you'd realize if you thought things through clearly.'

'Why don't you give me some help in that direction?' the major suggested.

'All right,' Paco agreed. 'As you know yourself, there's a battle going on out there – and the front line is changing every day.'

'So what?'

'So if the Socialist militias make any advances in tomorrow's fighting, the collar could end up behind enemy lines by nightfall.'

'Perhaps the thief is confident that a well-trained army will prevail over a disorganized rabble of plumbers and carpenters,' Major Gómez said. 'I know that I am.'

'Even if the militias don't advance, there are still so many other things which could go wrong,' Paco told him.

'For example?'

'Say he's hidden it up a tree. What guarantee does he have that a stray artillery shell won't blow that particular tree to hell? Or perhaps he's buried the collar – with armoured cars churning up the ground as they are, there's a good chance the jewels will be ground to powder. And riskiest of all for him, with thousands of men fighting out there, there's a very strong possibility that one of them will accidentally come across it.'

'So you're saying that while the collar may not be very safe in the village, the thief still knows that this is the safest place there is?' Gómez asked.

'Exactly,' Paco said, beaming with pleasure that the major had followed his logic.

And then, a sudden, disturbing thought hit him! This conversation he was having with the major could just have easily have been taking place between himself and his partner, Fat Felipe. He recognized this for the danger sign it was. The case might only concern the death of a dog, but he was already starting to become as obsessed with its solution as he'd been with all his other cases. And given the perilous situation he and Cindy were in, he simply couldn't allow that to happen.

'So if the dog was not killed for its collar, why was it killed?' Major Gómez asked.

Paco shrugged. 'If I knew why it was killed, then I'd probably also know who'd killed it.'

They turned on to the Calle Jose Antonio, and Paco gave an involuntary shudder as they passed the storeroom which had been his condemned cell. A little further up the street, they reached a modest house with two soldiers standing on guard outside it.

'These will be your quarters from now on,' Major Gómez said. 'Your woman is already inside, waiting for you. I will have supper sent over to you in half an hour. Eat, drink and be merry.'

'For tomorrow I die?'

Gómez shrugged again. 'Perhaps tomorrow we all die,' he said. 'It certainly increases our chances when we have a general who values the life of his pets over those of the men serving under him.'

*

Cindy fell into his arms the moment he walked through the door. 'Thank God you're safe!' she gasped. 'They swore to me that you were all right, but until I saw you for myself, I could never quite believe it.'

'How about you?' Paco, asked, hugging her body tightly to his. 'Have they harmed you?'

Cindy shook her head. 'They were a little rough at first, but once they'd managed to convince me that they really were bringing me to you, they could see I wasn't going to cause them any trouble.'

'You wanted to come here?' Paco asked incredulously.

'Of course not. Why would anyone want to be taken behind enemy lines? But I did want to be with you – and this is where you were.'

What had he ever done to deserve a woman as magnificent as this, Paco asked himself. Had he, at some time in the past, carried out some virtuous deed which he could no longer remember? Or was his luck as random as the fall of the dice or the turn of a card? He didn't know – and he didn't care, either. But one thing he did care about. Passionately! He had sworn a solemn oath that he would protect Cindy – and he would, even if it cost him his own life.

'So, Don Francisco, are you going to tell me what this is all about?' Cindy asked.

Paco looked around the room for the first time. There was a small table and two chairs in the centre of it, and next to the fireplace was a large sofa which not only looked very comfortable, but gave him an idea of how the two of them could put it to use.

'Explanations can wait until the food comes,' he said.

'But I want to know now,' Cindy said.

Paco cupped her chin in his hands and kissed her passionately on the lips. 'We can eat and talk at the same time,' he said, when he finally forced himself to break away from her, 'but there are other things we could be doing which would demand our complete attention.'

*

Paco answered the loud knocking on the door wearing only an old overcoat which he'd found in the closet. The soldier who was standing there, holding a tray, was perhaps the same age as he was, but had the

61

pinched face of a man who goes through life collecting resentments as some men collect stamps.

The soldier glanced down at the tray – though he must already have known what was on it – and scowled. 'You're one of the enemy, yet you live better than we do,' he complained as he handed it over.

Paco examined the tray himself, and decided that the disgruntled private was probably right. Major Gómez had sent his prisoners *albóndigas* – hot, spicy meatballs – and *riñones al jerez* – kidneys cooked in sherry. He'd even been thoughtful enough to include a couple of bottles – one containing a young red wine from La Mancha, the other a bottle of Catalan brandy.

Paco closed the door, placed the tray on the table and shrugged off the overcoat. Then, sitting opposite each other and completely naked, he and Cindy polished the food and wine off with gusto. Only when they had finished eating and were sipping their *copas* of brandy, did Paco start to tell Cindy about the general's dog.

'So you're going to find the killer, are you, just like you always do?' Cindy said when he'd finished his story.

Paco shook his head. 'Not this time.'

'Why not?'

'Major Gómez is in a fix,' he explained. 'As head of security, it's his job to find the killer, so, for the moment at least, he needs me. Which is why he's treating us so well. But the second I've given him what he wants, I become superfluous. Which is another way of saying that I'll be as good as dead.'

'What about me?' Cindy asked. 'And don't lie to me, Paco. I'm a big girl now, and I won't stand for it.'

'I won't lie to you,' Paco promised. 'I don't ever want to lie to you about anything.'

'Well, then?'

'If countries like the United States of America continue to stay neutral, then the rebels will probably win this war,' Paco said. 'And the military know that just as well as I do.'

'So?'

'So they will want to avoid any incidents which might help to tip the balance of sympathy of the general public in these neutral countries towards the democratically elected government.'

'An incident like me complaining to my embassy that I've been kidnapped?' Cindy asked.

'Exactly.'

'And since no one knows that I'm here, the easiest solution for them might be to see that I never get back to the city to kick up trouble?'

'I'm afraid so.'

Cindy took a generous slug of her brandy. 'You have a plan,' she said. 'I know you. You always have a plan.'

'Yes, I do,' Paco confessed. 'But I'm afraid that it's not really a very good one.'

Cindy held her left hand up in front of her, and examined it closely. It was shaking, but not as much as she feared it might be. 'Tell me what this plan of yours is, anyway,' she said.

'As long as we're alive, there's always a chance of us escaping,' Paco told her. 'So the trick is *staying* alive. I will pretend to be investigating the death of the general's bloody dog – I might even have to do some real investigating to make it seem genuine – but all the time what I'll actually be doing is looking for an opportunity to get us away from here.'

Cindy shook her head in a half-comic, half-tragic, way. 'You're right,' she said. 'It isn't a very good plan.' She looked down first at his empty glass, and then at hers. 'Wanna another slug of hooch, Ruiz?'

'More than anything else in the world,' Paco confessed.

Chapter Nine

Even deep in his sleep, Paco was becoming aware of a loud rattling sound. At first, it worked its way into his dream, and he was once again one of the thousands of men storming the Montaña barracks under the hail of heavy machine-gun fire. It was so real that he could sense the fear and desperation all around him, and could feel his own heart beating ever faster. Then some corner of his brain which had not been taken over by the nightmare whispered that he was not back on the grassy slope at all – that the blood and gore of the savage encounter had already retreated into history.

He groaned, and opened his eyes to see the small bedroom over the small living-room which made up most of his and Cindy's small prison. Paco climbed out of bed carefully, so as not to disturb his lover, whose shallow breathing told him she was still asleep. The barred window which overlooked the street was shaking furiously. Paco padded across the room and looked down on to the street. An army lorry, almost as wide as the calle itself, was edging its way towards the Plaza Mayor. It passed, and a few seconds later, another followed.

These streets had not been designed for military transport, Paco thought. The men who had planned and built the village had never imagined that it would one day be the headquarters of an army whose sole function was to wage war on its fellow Spaniards. His country was tearing itself apart, and he, a lone voice crying in the wilderness, could do nothing about it, and so had finally joined in the destruction himself.

His clothes were lying on the chair where he'd left them. As silently as he could, Paco dressed. Once he had his shirt on, he reached to the back of the chair for his shoulder holster, then laughed mockingly when he realized it wasn't there. It was years since he'd been without a weapon, and now, when everyone except the whores and the shopkeepers had guns, he was completely unarmed. And that was a dangerous situation to be in, because whilst he had no intention of ever finding the killer of the general's dog, the killer himself didn't know that – and was probably already jittery at the thought of having a trained investigator on his trail.

Paco finished dressing and looked down at Cindy. A beautiful woman, he told himself – a really beautiful woman. And an exceptional one, too. She hadn't blamed him for her predicament – hadn't reminded him that but for his own outdated ideas of honour and responsibility, they'd never have been in the mess they were in now. Eat, drink and be merry, Major Gómez had said, and they'd certainly done plenty of that the night before. But how many more nights like that would they have? How long would it be before the general grew tired of waiting for him to unmask Principe's killer? Or before the general's wife, by denying him her sexual favours, got him to agree it would be a mistake to keep the godless police inspector alive any longer?

Paco tiptoed over to the bed, and placed a gentle, almost featherlike kiss on Cindy's forehead. 'I'll get you out of here, my darling,' he whispered. 'I promise you I will.'

But even as he spoke, he was considering the odds against that happening, and though he meant every word he'd said, it still sounded like nothing more than a vain boast.

There were two new guards standing outside the door. They were both younger than the one who had brought Paco the food the previous evening, but from the expressions on their faces, they were no less hostile to the policeman from Madrid than the older soldier had been.

'I need to go and see Major Gómez,' Paco told them.

The taller of the two guards shrugged. 'So go and see him, then. I expect he'll be in his quarters at this hour of the morning.'

'Just like that?' Paco asked. 'Go and see him? No escort?'

'No escort. The major left orders that you were to be allowed to come and go as you pleased.'

'And Miss Walker?'

The sentry grinned unpleasantly. 'You mean your *Yanqui* whore? She stays here.'

Paco leant forward, so that his face was almost touching the other man's. 'You have a weapon, and I don't,' he said, in a low, menacing growl. 'So it will not be easy, but if you ever call Miss Walker that name again, I swear I'll find *some* way to kill you.'

The sentry visibly paled. 'You can't threaten me like that,' he said in a shaky voice.

'I just have,' Paco said, stepping into the street.

He walked up the Calle Jose Antonio towards the Plaza Mayor. It was a strange sensation to be out on the street alone. Though he had been a prisoner for less than two days, he had already got used to having armed men at either side of him, and without them he felt curiously naked.

He crossed the main square where, the night before, there had been so much drinking and music. Now, apart from the prostitutes sleeping off their evening's work under the arcades, the square was deserted.

Paco turned on to the Calle Mayor. Looking down the straight street, he could see the wooded mountains looming majestically in the near distance. The mountains offered escape – at least *some* chance of survival. But to reach those mountains, it was first necessary to get past the checkpoint which had been thrown up at the end of the street, and probably – Paco thought gloomily – at the end of every other street in the village.

He stopped in front of a small shop which had the words **G. Robles and Son, Fruit and Vegetables** painted crudely over the door. This must have been the temporary bar where the six privates were drinking when they heard the shots, Paco decided. Or rather, where they were drinking when the rat-faced Private Pérez heard the *first* shot, he corrected himself.

Even at a steady walking pace, it took him less than half a minute to reach the church at the corner of the Calle Belén. If the soldiers had been running, as they claimed, it would have taken them a considerably shorter time to get to the spot. But the killer had already gone by then – dashing down the street and disappearing around the sharp bend.

Paco stopped again, and looked down at the dark, almost star-shaped stain in the beaten clay. Principe's blood! But why had the killer shot the dog? That was the question. Had it been a personal act of revenge against the general? Or had the killer a pathological hatred of all dogs, and just happened to choose this one to take it out on?

'It doesn't matter,' Paco said aloud. 'You're not interested in solving this case. You *can't* be interested in solving this case.'

Whether the motive for the murder had been specific or general, the killer should have waited for a more opportune moment, he thought. The man had been a fool to shoot Principe so close to a crowded street, where there was every chance he would be spotted. Unless. . . . Unless he had no choice, because there was a compelling reason for killing the dog right then! But what the hell could that compelling reason possibly be?

He started walking again, turned the sharp bend at the corner of the church, and saw the pleasant Plaza de Santa Teresa ahead of him. There was a sentry standing in front of the house where Colonel Valera – the matinée idol – was billeted, just as there'd been one at the same post the last time he'd visited the square. Paco came to a halt in front of the man.

'Were you on duty the night that the general's dog was killed?' he asked.

The sentry scowled. 'I know who you are,' he said. 'You're that detective from Madrid.'

'That's right,' Paco agreed.

'I don't want to talk to you,' the sentry said.

Paco sighed. 'Major Gómez has put me in charge of the investigation into the dog's death,' he said. 'He will have no objection to you talking to me. What he *will* object to is my dragging him away from his breakfast so he can order you to co-operate.'

The sentry considered what Paco had said. 'No, I wasn't on duty,' he admitted finally.

'So who was?'

'Nobody.'

'Nobody?' Paco repeated.

'There are three of us on permanent assignment to this post,' the sentry explained. 'We each of us do an eight-hour stint of duty. Except that sometimes we don't.'

'And what exactly do you mean by that?'

'Sometimes, Major Gómez comes along and tells us we won't be required that day.'

'Let me get this straight,' Paco said. 'You're saying that Major Gómez comes along personally and says that you won't be needed?'

'Yes.'

'That doesn't make a lot of sense,' Paco, pointed out. 'Either a building is worth guarding, or it isn't. Wouldn't you say that's true?'

The sentry shrugged. 'It's not my place to make sense out of things,' he said. 'I'm told to stand guard somewhere, and I stand guard. I'm told I can go away and have a drink, and that's exactly what I do. I've given up trying to figure out the way officers' minds work.'

Paco nodded as if in agreement, turned, and walked across the square towards the house where Major Gómez was billeted. Of course there wasn't a sentry on duty that night, he thought. He should have been able to work that out for himself, without even speaking to the guard.

He stopped in his tracks, and shook his head in self-disgust. He was thinking about the bloody case again – not just pretending to, but actually applying all his brain-power to getting to the bottom of it. Idiot!

He reached Gómez's house, knocked on the door, and was admitted by a valet who looked at him as if he were dirt.

The major was sitting at the table in a reception room, drinking coffee and smoking a cigarette. 'One of the few advantages of being the head of security is that I don't have to make an early start, like most of my brother officers,' he said.

'And another one is that you don't have people shooting at you every day,' Paco said dryly.

Gómez grinned, as if he were genuinely amused. 'Take a seat, Inspector,' he said. 'Would you care for a cup of coffee?'

Paco nodded, and sat down. 'I'll have it black,' he said.

Gómez clicked his fingers, and the valet placed a cup in front of Paco and filled it with strong, black coffee. 'I trust the food I had sent over to you last night was satisfactory,' the major said.

'Why wasn't there a sentry on duty outside Colonel Valera's house, the night that the dog was killed?' Paco asked.

Gómez studied the glowing end of his cigarette as if it had acquired a sudden fascination for him. 'Wasn't there a sentry on duty?' he asked.

'You know there wasn't.'

'I have posted scores of guards all around the village perimeter,' Gómez said. 'There is no real need for sentries within the village itself, but the colonel likes to have one because that shows what an important man he is. And sometimes I like to withdraw his sentry – to remind him that he is not quite *as* important as he would sometimes wish.'

'Just like that?' Paco asked incredulously.

'No, not just like that,' Gómez replied. 'I spin him some line about needing the men for other duties, and he pretends to believe me. But we both know what is really going on.'

'Aren't you afraid he'll complain to the general about you?'

'That would be as good as saying that he cannot control one of his subordinates. It's not a position he wants to find himself in.'

'Let's get back to the night the dog was killed,' Paco said. 'Are you now admitting that there was no sentry on duty?'

Gómez frowned. 'Do I *admit* it?' he asked. 'I think you're forgetting your position again, Ruiz. I am the head of security here, and you are my prisoner. I will *not* be interrogated by you.' His face relaxed a little. 'But I see no harm in answering that particular question. Withdrawing or maintaining the sentries is a matter of whim, rather than policy. Sometimes I feel like insulting Valera, sometimes I don't. But since there is no system, there is also no record. There may, or may not, have been a sentry on duty that night. I simply can't remember.'

Paco shook his head. 'That's not true, and you know it,' he said. 'The private soldiers I talked to yesterday heard the killer running off down the Calle Belén. If there had been a sentry posted outside Colonel Valera's house, he couldn't have failed to see the man as he entered the square. Which would mean that you'd have no need of me now.'

For a second, Major Gómez was silent, then he threw back his head and roared with uncontrolled laughter. 'I somehow keep forgetting that I'm not dealing with one of those bloody idiots from the military intelligence unit, but with the man who was capable of solving the Atocha station murder case,' he said, when he'd finally calmed down. 'It's obvious to me now that I'll have to give you more rope than I'm usually prepared to give them. But . . .' his voice was suddenly serious again – almost, in fact, threatening, '. . . but do be careful that you don't use all this extra rope I'm giving you to hang yourself with.'

He still hadn't explained why he'd decided to lie about not knowing for sure whether there'd been a sentry on duty that night, Paco thought. But there was only so far you could push a man like Gómez, so that line of questioning was closed to him at least for the moment.

'Why did you decide that I didn't need an escort any more?' he asked.

'I thought over what you said about needing the same freedom to carry out your investigation as you had in Madrid. It soon became obvious to me that having two soldiers following you about would impede that freedom. So I issued instructions that you were to be allowed to move around alone.'

'Aren't you afraid that I'll take it as a golden opportunity to make a run for it?'

The major shook his head. 'Oh no, my friend. Not at all. As long as we have your *Yanqui* lady-friend safely under guard, you wouldn't even dream of leaving this village.'

'You really are absolutely sure I won't decide to abandon her, are you?' Paco asked.

'Absolutely,' the major confirmed. 'As I've told you before, I can read men very well. And I know that you would not desert her – even if your life depended on it.' He took a sip of his coffee, and lit up another cigarette. 'The general has had the dog buried,' he continued, going off at a tangent. 'But if you wish, I am sure I can persuade him to let us dig the animal up again.'

'Why should we want to do that?' Paco asked.

The major's eyes narrowed. 'I am not a policeman like you, so perhaps I'm wrong, but isn't it normal in homicide investigations for the detective in charge to want to see the corpse?' he asked suspiciously.

Paco cursed his own stupidity. He felt as if he were sitting on some kind of mental see-saw, first becoming far too involved in the case, and then going in exactly the opposite direction – and making it obvious to Gómez in the process that he had absolutely no interest in it at all.

'You're quite right, major,' he said. 'I do always want to see the corpse.'

'Then why didn't you request permission to view it this time?' Gómez asked, with the hint of suspicion still in his voice.

'Perhaps it's because the victim is a dog,' Paco replied, making his explanation up as he went along. 'Somehow, I've been treating it differently from the way I treat other murders. But it isn't different at all. The killer is human, just as all the other killers I've dealt with have been human. And the body may indeed give us some clue as to who this killer is.'

'That's just what I was thinking,' Major Gómez said.

'Where is the dog buried?'

'In the garden behind the *palacio*.'

Paco drained the last of his coffee, and stood up. 'Then, by all means, let's go and disinter it,' he said.

Chapter Ten

The walled garden behind the *palacio* was a pleasant retreat from the hustle and bustle of the village. It was criss-crossed by paved paths, and there were several stone benches, each of which caught the sun at a different time of day. Almond and apple trees were flourishing, and it was plain that though there was a war going on, the flower-beds had suffered from no lack of attention.

Major Gómez led Paco and the two enlisted soldiers to the fig-tree which was growing up against the back wall. 'A couple of days more and we'd have been too late,' he said to Paco. 'The general's lady has ordered a marble tombstone from Burgos, and once that's in place, I don't think the general himself would ever have agreed to us digging up the corpse.'

A marble tombstone! Paco repeated to himself. A bloody marble tombstone! For a dog! He watched as the soldiers began to dig. It was not nearly as hot up in the sierra as it would be down on the plains around Madrid, but it was still hot enough, and by the time one of the diggers' spades hit something solid, both men's vests were drenched in sweat.

'Be careful!' Major Gómez said hastily. 'Don't damage the coffin. Dig around it.'

'The *coffin*?' Paco said.

Major Gómez shrugged. 'As far as the general and his lady are concerned, nothing is too good for Principe.'

The soldiers knelt down, and began to scoop soil out of the hole with their hands. It was a slow, awkward process, but eventually they had cleared enough earth away to pull the casket free. It was made of polished walnut, Paco noted, with a beautifully crafted curved lid, on which there was a brass plate which read:

Principe, dear friend and loyal companion.
We will never forget you.
Your loving master and mistress.

A sudden thought struck Paco. 'Did the general's wife really care about the dog?' he said to Gómez.

'Why do you say that?'

'I'm not sure,' Paco admitted. 'Perhaps it's because when she got back from Burgos she was making such a fuss about Principe being dead, but she almost completely ignored Reina.'

Major Gómez nodded thoughtfully. 'It's probably true that the general has greater affection for the animals,' he said. 'But it's also undoubtedly true that Principe was devoted to the general's lady.'

That was often the way with dogs, Paco thought. It was the love they really had to work for that they cherished the most. 'Open the coffin up,' he said to one of the diggers.

The soldier lifted the lid, and the air was instantly filled with a foul smell. Paco looked down into the coffin. Principe had been placed in it in such a way as to conceal most of his injuries, and had probably looked quite peaceful when he'd been laid to rest – but nothing looks peaceful after the maggots have been working on it for a couple of days.

'Take the dog out of the coffin, and put it out on the ground,' Paco told the soldiers.

Gingerly, the two men lifted the decaying body out of the box and placed it beside the fig tree. Paco bent down over the corpse, and Gómez, a handkerchief to his nose, did the same.

'How can you stand the stench?' the major mumbled, almost gagging after every word.

Paco chuckled. 'When you've examined corpses which have been bobbing up and down in the River Manzanares for a couple of weeks, this is nothing,' he said cheerfully. 'Now let's just see what we can learn from this particular stiff.'

He ran his finger along the dog's side, and when he reached the dead animal's shoulder, he let out a short whoop of triumph.

'Have you found something?' Major Gómez asked.

'Yes. The entry wound.'

'But the dog was shot in the head.'

'Private Pérez is certain that he heard two shots,' Paco said. 'It was the second one that blew half the animal's head off.'

'How can you be so sure?'

'Because if the first shot had been the fatal one, there would have been no need for a second. So what happened with that first shot? Well, it could have missed its target completely, or it could merely have wounded Principe. We now know that it was the latter case.' Paco looked up at the two soldiers, who were standing some distance away. 'Has either of you lads got a knife on him?'

One of the privates handed him a big clasp knife of the type which peasants use for everything from splicing pieces of rope to cutting up pieces of spicy *chorizo* sausage for their lunch. Paco opened the knife and gouged into the flesh of the dead dog.

'I'm looking for the bullet,' he explained to Major Gómez. 'It won't be as much use to me as it would be if I had all the resources of the forensics lab in Madrid at my disposal – we won't, for example, be able to prove it was fired by any particular gun – but at least it will establish the type of weapon that was used.'

He dug a little more with the knife, then extracted the bullet from the rotting corpse. He held it in the flat of his hand for Major Gómez to examine. 'What do you make of that, señor head of security?' he asked.

'It's a thirty-two calibre bullet,' the major said confidently. 'There's no doubt about it.'

'And what calibre does your pistol fire?'

'Thirty-two.'

'And that, of course, is true of all the other officers, too.'

Gómez suddenly looked very disturbed indeed. 'This is not good,' he told Paco.

'Isn't it? I would have thought it was very good. There are thousands of enlisted men in the village, but many fewer officers. We've narrowed down our list of suspects considerably.'

'Perhaps we have,' Gómez agreed. 'The problem is, we've narrowed it down to the wrong list of suspects.'

'The wrong list?' Paco repeated.

'The general intends to have whoever killed his dog executed. If it's an enlisted man, then there's no problem. It will serve as a good example to the rest of the men of what happens if they ever dare to step out of line. But it's an entirely different matter if the killer turns out to be an officer. Officers are gentlemen. You do not shoot one of them like a dog, even if he has shot a treasured dog himself.'

'Are you saying that the general won't want to hear the truth?' Paco demanded.

'I am saying that he will want a truth which suits him,' Gómez replied. He brightened, as if a new idea had come into his mind. 'Who is to say that it was an officer's gun which did the shooting, anyway? After all, there are many thirty-two calibre pistols in Spain.'

'But how many are there in this village which are not in the hands of army officers?'

'Perhaps a few. Perhaps more than a few.'

'You don't sound very convinced,' Paco told him.

Gómez's face darkened again. 'Be careful, my friend,' he warned. 'If you let your investigation proceed along this path, you will be treading on very dangerous ground indeed.'

Paco stood up and wiped his hands on the trunk of the fig tree. 'You can bury the animal again,' he told the two soldiers.

He felt a prickling at the back of his neck, and knew that he was being watched. He turned round quickly, and directed his gaze at the upper windows of the *palacia*. The beautiful, angry woman he had seen for the first time the day before was staring down at him. And even at that distance, he could read the look of pure hatred on her face.

She wanted her beloved dog's killer found he thought – but not as much as she wanted to see the ex-policeman who was investigating the crime safely in his grave. What was it that Gómez had said about her? That he'd heard her talk at dinner parties, and her views made even her husband seem like a dangerous left-winger. That wasn't hard to believe. Though her eyes were alluring, they were also the eyes of a fanatic.

The general's wife continued to watch them for a few seconds more, then, after giving Paco a final, contemptuous flick of the head, she disappeared from the window. Beside him, Paco heard Major Gómez let out a deep sigh, and turning saw that he, too, had been looking up at the window.

'There are those who contend that the general's lady is the most beautiful woman in the whole of Spain,' the major said wistfully. 'And sometimes I think that perhaps they are right.'

'Tell me about her,' Paco said.

'About the general's lady?'

'That's right.'

Gómez glanced at the soldiers, who had placed the walnut coffin back in the shallow grave and were now covering it with soil. 'We've been standing still long enough,' he said. 'Why don't we stretch our legs a little?'

Paco followed him up the garden. Gómez came to a halt at a point midway between the fig-tree and the house, then looked quickly at both, as if checking that it would be safe to have a private conversation. Apparently satisfied that no one could overhear them, the major placed his right foot on one of the stone benches, and took out his cigarettes.

'So you want to know about the general's lady,' he said, striking a match. 'What exactly would you like me to tell you about her? And more importantly, how could it possibly be of any value to your investigation?'

'A policeman automatically collects all kinds of information from all kinds of sources,' Paco told him. 'Most of it never turns out to be of any use, but occasionally, he'll find he has a tiny sliver of knowledge which just fits into the pattern and makes the picture complete.'

Gómez nodded, as if accepting the point. 'Where would you like me to start?' he asked.

'Let's begin with her background,' Paco suggested. 'Is her family as rich as her husband's so obviously is?'

Gómez shook his head. 'She comes, I believe, from relatively humble circumstances.'

They were often the worst, Paco thought. The ones who had climbed the mountain themselves were usually the people who did their best to ensure that nobody else scaled the same heights. The ones who had once been the victims of snobbery turned into the greatest snobs of all once they had it in their power to be so. 'How did the general meet her?' he asked.

'She was an actress,' Major Gómez replied. 'And by that,' he added hastily, in case there should be any misunderstanding, 'I don't mean to suggest that she was a music-hall performer.'

Paco grinned. 'Of course you don't. How could a general's wife ever have been anything but an actress in the truly classical sense?'

'She has appeared in all the great plays of the Golden Age of Spain,' Gómez said sharply, as if he had taken it on himself to defend her honour from a suspected slight. 'Molina's *The Prudence of a Woman*, Vega's *Pedro Carbonero* – any masterpiece you care to mention.'

'And was she any good?' Paco asked.

Gómez looked vaguely uncomfortable. 'I went to see one of her performances once. I couldn't take my eyes off her for a second. And I was not alone in that. She had all the men in the audience in the palm of her hand.'

'That doesn't answer my question,' Paco, pointed out. 'I didn't ask you if she was beautiful – I can see for myself that she is. What I wanted to know was if she had any talent.'

'She was not a naturally gifted actress,' Major Gómez conceded. 'But, you see, that really didn't matter. Her name alone was enough to fill any theatre she appeared in. And anyone who saw her perform came away adoring her. I expect that's how it was for the general. No doubt he saw her on stage one night, and fell in love with her. Flowers would have followed, and finally they would have got to meet each other.'

'And when they did meet, she saw his bald head and stumpy little legs, and she couldn't help throwing herself at him?' Paco suggested.

'A little scepticism is a useful quality in a criminal investigator,' Gómez said, with a warning edge creeping into his voice. 'But if you take that scepticism too far – or let the wrong people hear you expressing it – then even I can't protect you from the consequences.'

'I'm sorry,' Paco said, trying his best to appear to express the contrition he didn't actually feel. 'Let me ask you one more question. Has the general's wife, as far as you know, ever . . .?'

Major Gómez put up his hand to silence him. 'I think I have already said enough,' he told Paco. 'Possibly more than enough.' He looked back towards the fig tree at the bottom of the garden. The soldiers had finished refilling Principe's grave, and were now patting the earth down with their shovels. 'It is time for me to get back to my other duties,' he continued, throwing his cigarette on to the path and grinding it with the sole of his boot. 'Perhaps when we've had a few drinks together one night, I may be willing to answer more questions about the general's lady, but for the moment, the matter is closed.'

Chapter Eleven

Paco and Cindy sat at the table in their homely gaol on the Calle Jose Antonio, the remains of a superb paella on their plates in front of them, the bottle containing the dry Rueda wine almost empty.

'Your Major Gómez certainly knows how to look after his prisoners,' Cindy said contentedly.

'Hmm,' Paco answered, absently.

'What's on your mind, Ruiz?' Cindy asked.

'Gómez. I've no idea what game he's playing. Part of the time I think he really wants me to work on this case of his, and part of the time I'm almost sure he doesn't.'

Cindy looked puzzled. 'I don't see what possible motive he could have for *not* wanting you on it,' she said.

'Neither do I,' Paco admitted. 'Unless, of course, he himself is involved in some way with the death of the dog, and so doesn't want it solving.'

'If he didn't want the case solving, why did he rescue you from the firing squad?' Cindy asked. 'He didn't have to do that, did he? Nobody else had any idea who you were, and in another few seconds you'd have been just one more unidentified dead body.'

'True,' Paco agreed.

'And then, of course, there's the fact that he had me kidnapped,' Cindy continued. 'He risked sending his men into enemy territory just so they could bring little Cindy back to this village. And for what reason? To make sure you'd co-operate with him.'

'I know all that,' Paco said. 'And the theory that he *does* want to get to the bottom of the mystery is supported by the fact that it was him, not me, who suggested that we dig up the dog to see if we could find any clues.'

'So what's your problem with him?' Cindy asked.

'My problem is that there are a couple of things he's said which might suggest that the last thing he wants is for the truth to come out.'

'And what might they be?'

'The first one is that he lied to me when he said he couldn't remember whether or not he'd posted a sentry outside Colonel Valera's house the night the dog was killed. Why did he lie? Perhaps because removing the guard was far from the random act he claimed it was.'

'What are you saying, Paco?'

'That it's possible he knew exactly what was going to happen, and didn't want anyone there to witness the killer running into the square.'

Cindy poured the last of the wine into their glasses. 'That doesn't make any kind of sense,' she said. 'The basis of your whole theory so far is that shooting the dog was unplanned – nothing more than a measure of desperation. Now you're contradicting yourself completely and saying that Major Gómez had anticipated the whole thing.'

'I know,' Paco groaned. 'But there has to be some reason why the major lied about the guards.'

'What was your second point?'

'If he really wants the killer brought to justice, why did he tell me to disregard the most vital piece of evidence we've uncovered so far?'

'The bullet?'

'Yes, the bloody bullet. It was almost definitely fired from a pistol belonging to one of the officers, yet Gómez warned me in no uncertain terms to stay well away from them.'

'And he also explained why,' Cindy pointed out. 'The general doesn't want to know if one of his officers is involved.'

'That's what Gómez *said*,' Paco agreed, 'but I'm not sure that I believe him. You have to remember that the general has suffered a tremendous loss of prestige over the dog, and if it means shooting one of his officers to regain it, I don't think he'd hesitate for a second.'

'You might be wrong about that, and Gómez may be right,' Cindy said. 'After all, he does know the general much better than you do.'

'You're missing the point,' Paco told her. 'It's not what I believe which is important here. It's what the major believes. And I don't think Gómez really believes that the general would refuse to accept the fact that one of his officers is the dog's killer.'

'So why did he feed you that particular line of bullshit?'

'I don't know,' Paco admitted.

A rueful grin appeared on Cindy's face. 'You know what you're doing, don't you, Ruiz?' she said. 'You're talking about the case. And not only that, but you've got me interested in it, too. I thought we'd agreed this was one murder which you had no intention of solving.'

78

'I have to talk about the case,' Paco said in his own defence. 'I made the big mistake this morning of not being the one who suggested we exhume the dog. The only reason we're still alive is because I've got a job to do, and if I'm to convince Gómez that I'm really serious about finding a solution, I have to devote at least a part of my mind to the investigation.'

He was telling the truth – but not all of it. It was necessary to appear to be working on the killing, but he was also in the grip of his investigator's instinct, and he wanted to solve the case – if only for his own satisfaction.

'What about the other part of your mind?' Cindy asked, cutting into his thoughts.

'I'm sorry. I don't quite understand.'

Cindy smiled indulgently. 'The part of your mind which is supposed to be trying to find a way to get us out of here.'

'Not much luck there,' Paco said, shaking his head. 'Major Gómez seems to have done a very good job of sealing this place off. There's a checkpoint on every road out of the village. And there are motorized patrols scouring the area for any Socialist militiamen who have strayed beyond their own lines. Even if we could find a way to get rid of the guards outside this house, and then somehow managed to sneak through the village undetected, we wouldn't get more than half a kilometre as things stand at the moment.'

'At the moment?' Cindy repeated.

Paco shrugged. 'The situation may change. The militia might overrun the village at any time, and we'd be free again.'

'But that's not likely, is it?'

'Not from what I've seen of the way the two sides are conducting the fighting,' Paco confessed. 'It's much more likely that it will be the rebels who advance.'

'Well, then?'

'That might also present us with opportunities. The rebels are concentrated around this village now. Once they start to spread out, we might see a loophole we can slip through.' Paco looked at his watch. 'It was a good lunch, and now I'd better get back to pretending to be an investigator,' he said.

Cindy raised a questioning eyebrow. 'Pretending?' she said.

*

Towards dusk the heavy trucks began to rumble back into the village, followed by the tramp, tramp, tramp of thousands of pairs of weary feet.

Lamps were lit in the bars on the Calle Mayor and the main square. From out of the shadows came the prostitutes, heavily painted and ready to ply their trade once more. The army had returned from its day's fighting in the sierra, and after a brief rest it would be ready for its night's drinking and whoring.

Paco walked towards the Calle Belén, the two parts of his mind working simultaneously on his two separate problems. If he knew why the dog had been killed, he argued for the hundredth time, it should be obvious who had killed it. If he could find some way of getting out of the village, he could save his darling Cindy. And suddenly, the two problems fused together, and became only one. If he could track down the killer, he could use the offer of silence to blackmail the man into helping them make their escape!

'Sometimes I'm so smart I even surprise myself,' he said aloud.

And sometimes you can be so stupid that you can overlook the most obvious clues and go off on a wild-goose chase, a tiny, nagging voice at the back of his brain reminded him. He wished he had Fat Felipe with him at that moment. He could imagine his overweight partner lumbering along at his side, belching, scratching his armpits and occasionally asking just the right question to put his boss back on track.

The church door was open, and, on a whim, Paco stepped inside. It was like most country churches – plain in the style of its outer construction, but elaborate in its internal decoration. Feeling as if plaster saints were watching him disapprovingly from every alcove, Paco advanced down the aisle towards the statue of the Virgin. On feast days she would be dressed in a rich cloak and a gold crown, then paraded through the streets high above the crowd, on a pallet which it took ten strong men to lift. But even without the extra trappings she acquired for the fiestas, she was still impressive enough.

Paco ran his gaze over the wooden cloak which had been carved so skilfully that it looked as if it were swirling in the wind. He let his eyes rest on the face, which almost seemed alive, and on the wooden jewellery which had been painted so cunningly that it actually seemed to glitter. The statue was a labour of love – a combination of art and devotion – but he did not think the simple Nazarene woman who had given birth to Jesus Christ would have been able to recognize herself at all in this representation.

He took a further step forward. Even the carved tears cascading down her wooden cheeks appeared to be real. It had been a statue of the Virgin in another village, far to the south of this one, which had helped to solve his last case, he remembered – but he didn't anticipate this particular Virgin getting him any nearer to the truth about who had killed the general's dog.

He heard a muted cough, and realized he was not alone in the church. He turned, and saw a soldier – a private – on his knees behind one of the pews. The man had his hands clasped together, and his head bent reverently in prayer. Then he lifted his head, and Paco saw it was Jiménez, one of the group of soldiers who had discovered the dead dog.

'Good evening, señor,' the private said.

'Good evening to you,' Paco replied, and then, perhaps because of the proximity of the statue, he suddenly remembered an amusing joke which had been going round the bars in Madrid, and chuckled to himself.

'Is something funny, señor?' the boy asked.

'Yes, as a matter of fact, there is,' Paco replied. 'Do you know how you can prove, beyond a shadow of a doubt, that Jesus Christ was a Spaniard and not a Palestinian?'

'No, señor,' the young soldier replied, a blank expression, which was probably habitual, on his dull face.

Paco took up the same attention-grabbing stance he would have adopted if he'd been telling the joke to some of his cronies in the Cabo de Trafalgar. 'There are three ways you can prove it,' he said. 'Firstly,' he held up one finger, 'Jesus didn't leave home until he was thirty-three.'

The regulars of the bar would already have started to chuckle, but Jiménez looked at him as if he were speaking a foreign language.

'Secondly,' Paco pressed on, holding up another finger, 'we know he was Spanish because his mother thought he was God.'

The men in the bar would have been punching each other on the arm by now, but Jiménez still gazed at him uncomprehendingly. Still, Paco thought, he'd gone too far with the joke to stop.

'And the last proof,' he said, raising a third finger, 'is that *Jesus* thought his mother was a *virgin*!'

The blank expression remained on the young soldier's face. 'I don't understand, señor,' he said.

No, of course he didn't, Paco thought, cursing himself for being as insensitive as Private Pérez had been when he'd goaded poor, slow Jiménez the day before. The young soldier was a country boy, not one of the pampered middle-class professional students who lived in the city, sponging off their parents until long after the time they should have started

81

supporting themselves. He couldn't even begin to imagine their leisurely existence – and hence was lost even at the start of the joke. His life before joining the army would have been entirely different. He would have been working in the fields from the time he was ten, and probably knew the land far better than any professor of agriculture.

An idea struck Paco – a way he could use the knowledge that this young *campesino* had acquired through years of backbreaking work.

'You remember the day that the general's dog was killed, don't you?' Paco asked.

'Yes, señor.'

'Could you tell me whether or not there were any bitches in the village on heat on that day?'

'No, señor, there weren't,' the young soldier replied, without a second's thought.

'Are you sure about that?'

The boy laughed, as if this time Paco had made a joke which he could understand. 'Of course I'm sure.'

'Explain your reasoning.'

'Excuse me, señor?'

'How do you know there were no bitches on heat?'

Jiménez frowned, and Paco could almost trace his slow mental processes. These kinds of things were not something you thought about, the country boy was telling himself – they were something you just *knew*.

'The male dogs who are allowed the free run of the village lay in the shade as they usually do,' Jiménez said finally. 'And the ones which were chained up did not howl.'

Of course, Paco thought. It was simple once it was explained. There had been a time when he would not even have needed to ask Jiménez the reason for his certainty, because as a village boy himself, he'd already have known the answer. But after over twenty years of being away from the land, he'd lost all the country instincts he'd once possessed.

'Is there anything else you want to ask me, señor?' Jiménez asked.

'Yes, as a matter of fact, there is,' Paco replied. 'Yesterday, when I was questioning you, Private Pérez said some nasty things, didn't he?'

'Yes, he did,' Jiménez admitted. 'But he didn't mean them.'

'How do you know?' Paco asked. 'Because that's what he told you when you were back on the street again?'

'Yes, señor. He said that he was sorry, and promised that he'd never do it again.'

'He doesn't seem the kind of man to say he's sorry that easily,' Paco said, 'and, to me, he didn't look as if he was just apologizing. If anything, I'd guess that what he was doing was explaining something very complicated to you. Now isn't that what was really happening?'

'No, it wasn't,' Jiménez said stubbornly. 'He was telling me he was sorry. Can I please go now, señor?'

'Yes, you can go,' Paco said.

He watched the country boy make his way down the aisle, moving awkwardly yet far more at home in a church than he felt himself. In answering the question, the young soldier had posed another, far more complex, one, Paco thought. The general's dogs were always taken out on the lead by a member of his staff. They never left the house alone. Yet, if what the general's servant had said was to be believed, something had caused Principe to decide to make a bolt for it on that particular day. And if that something hadn't been a bitch on heat, then what the hell *had* it been?

Chapter Twelve

Though he could see paraffin lamps glowing in most of the windows of the houses where the rebel officers were billeted, the square on to which those houses looked was completely deserted. And that was wrong, Paco thought, as he stopped by the fountain to light a Celtas. There should have been one man, at least, on the Plaza de Santa Teresa that night – the sentry on guard outside Colonel Valera's house.

What had happened to the bloody man? Had Major Gómez dismissed him to demonstrate to Valera, yet again, that holding a higher rank did not necessarily mean having greater power? Or was there a more sinister reason behind his absence? Was he missing because – as on the night when the General's dog was killed – something dramatic was just about to happen?

Despite the fact that it was a warm night, Paco felt a shiver run through his entire body. You're being fanciful, he told himself angrily. You're building monstrous conspiracies out of simple coincidences.

He crossed the square and headed up the Calle Belén. The church loomed ominously to his right, the high brick wall to his left. As on the previous occasions he'd walked along this street at night, there were no lamps to guide him, but there was enough light from the moon to enable him to avoid twisting his ankle in any of the small potholes which pitted the ground.

The general's dog had made this same journey three nights earlier, he thought. Where had the animal been going? Back to the general's house, perhaps? But that was not the really important question. It would be much more interesting to know where had he been – and why had he been there. Paco had a nagging feeling that he already had part of the answer somewhere in the back of his mind – but try as he might, he couldn't drag it out.

He heard the sound of footsteps behind him just as he turned the sharp bend. Was he being followed? Or was whoever was behind him out on some errand of his own? He strained his ears to hear more. The man – and he was sure it was a man – was not walking normally, but instead taking soft steps, as if he wanted to avoid making too much noise.

Paco stopped and turned on his heel. The other man rounded the bend, and also came to a halt. He was still too far enough away to be anything more than a black shape, but the way that he stood – relaxed yet disciplined – marked him out as a soldier.

'Are you following me?' Paco asked.

The black shape made no answer, yet somehow still seemed to generate menace.

'What do you want?' Paco demanded. 'Do you have something to tell me about the death of the dog? Some information which you can only give me when we're alone?'

In one smooth movement, the other man reached down to his side; then, hands clenched together, raised his arms until they were pointing directly towards the ex-policeman.

No, that wasn't it at all, Paco realized with horror. The hands weren't clenched together, they were clenched *around* something. And that something could only be a gun! He instinctively felt for his own pistol, but his hand found no reassuring butt to take hold of. He looked around desperately for cover, even though he already knew that there was none to be had on this empty street.

The black shape had not moved a millimetre since he'd aimed the gun. Perhaps he was enjoying all this – taking pleasure from the fear he knew he must be generating in his victim.

Paco's mouth was dry, and his heart was thumping furiously against his chest. He wondered – briefly – why he'd been so sanguine when facing death in front of the firing squad, yet was so frightened of it now. 'There's no need for any of this,' he said in a cracked voice. 'I'm no threat to you. Even if you're the one who killed the dog, I'm never going to find out your identity unless you do something stupid.'

As he spoke, he moved a little to the left. The black shape countered it with a slight, but perceptible, change in stance, which told Paco that he was a trained marksman. He wasn't going to be panicked if his intended target charged him. Nor was he going to have any difficulty picking off that target if it ran away, whatever diversionary tactics it tried.

Paco sensed that the moment had nearly arrived – that the gunman had got tired of playing games and was about to finish the job. Only amateurs go for the head, he thought. This would be a chest shot. He listened for the slight click which would tell him that the trigger was being pulled, and when he heard it, he flung himself to the ground.

The bullet whizzed over him, and Paco came up in a roll. He had bought himself a few extra seconds of life – but no more. He knew that to be true, yet he still could not bring himself to give in to the inevitable. He wished the assassin would speak to him – would at least tell him why it was that he had to die. But as the man calmly lined up his second shot, he was as silent as he had been since he first rounded the bend.

There was a second click, louder and uglier than the first. The pistol's jammed, Paco thought – the bloody pistol's jammed! And even before his brain had had time to formulate a plan, his legs were carrying him in a rush towards his would-be killer.

If the other man had taken to his heels immediately he might have made a clean getaway, but instead he wasted time trying to unjam his pistol, and had only just started to make a run for it when Paco hit him with a flying tackle.

The two of them crashed to the ground, but it was Paco's opponent who took most of the impact, and he groaned loudly as the wind was knocked out of him, then lay perfectly still.

Could it be this easy? Paco asked himself. Did he only have to turn this man over, and then strike a match, to discover the killer of the general's dog?

The man beneath him twisted suddenly, and in a second, their positions were reversed. Paco felt the pressure of two knees pressing down on his chest and a pair of strong hands tightening around his throat. Even as he fought for air, he cursed himself for falling for such an old trick.

Why wasn't anyone coming to his aid, he wondered. Surely someone must have heard the shot, and even now be running towards it to find out what had happened, as Pérez and his gang had done only a few nights earlier? But none of the soldiers on the Calle Mayor that night seemed to have Pérez's sharp ears, and apart from the sounds of the two men engaged in mortal combat, the alley was as silent as the grave.

Breathing was becoming harder, and black dots were beginning to appear before Paco's eyes. It wouldn't be long before he lost consciousness, and once that happened, he was as good as dead.

The strong hands continued to press down relentlessly on his larynx. His opponent was breathing hard too, gasping from the effort of choking the life out of him. Paco forced his right arm into the air, groping for the other man's face. His attacker tried to twist his head out of the way, but Paco had already found what he was searching for. The nose. He stuck one finger up each nostril, and twisted as hard as he could.

His would-be assassin screamed, and released his grip. With what little strength he had left, Paco pushed against his chest, and felt the other man fall backwards.

Climbing to his feet was an almost Herculean task. When he reached the kneeling position, he was sure he was about to faint. On standing up, he realized that the alley was spinning around him like some grotesquely reversed carousel. He turned, shakily, to face his enemy, but the other man had had enough, and was running towards the Plaza de Santa Teresa.

Paco tried to follow, but his burning lungs refused to take in the air which he needed, and he was forced to lean heavily against the wall while he coughed up bile and spittle.

'I was so close,' he gasped. 'I was so damn close, and I let him get away from me.'

He turned, slowly, to walk back up the Calle Belén to the Calle Mayor. And that was when his foot kicked the heavy piece of metal lying on the ground.

*

Major Gómez was sitting alone at a table outside one of the bars on the Calle Mayor – a place which charged a few centimos more for each glass of wine than most of the other establishments, and hence was used exclusively by officers. He looked cool and relaxed, Paco thought, but then he'd looked much the same way just after he'd put a bullet in the back of poor Alfredo's head.

Gómez signalled Paco to sit down. 'Look at these men,' he said, indicating the soldiers who were staggering up and down the street, or else leaning drunkenly against the old whores who were trying to talk them into parting with their day's pay. 'They are behaving little better than animals. And yet who can really blame them? It is a rare man indeed who goes into battle completely sober.'

Paco was in no mood for philosophical discussions. 'Someone has just tried to kill me,' he said.

'Kill you?' Gómez repeated. 'Are you sure?'

'It's not really something I'd be likely to make a mistake over,' Paco replied. He reached into the waistband of his trousers, pulled out the pistol, and slammed it on the marble table-top. 'This was the weapon he used. It's my guess that it was also the pistol which killed the dog.'

Gómez frowned. 'I warned you yesterday about uncovering anything which might seem to implicate one of the officers,' he said.

'You're missing the point,' Paco told him. 'You're like a man pressed right up against a picture in the museum. You only see a tiny fragment of it. What you need to do is take a few steps backwards, so that you can look at the whole sweep of the canvas.'

The major took a thoughtful sip of his wine. 'And what does the whole canvas look like?' he asked.

'I don't know,' Paco admitted. 'But at least I'm sure that it's there now. Can I ask you a question?'

Gómez smiled. 'As long as it doesn't turn into an interrogation again, I don't see why not.'

'Did you ever, honestly, think that I had a chance of finding out who killed the general's dog?'

The major hesitated for a second. 'No, not much of one,' he admitted. 'But I knew you certainly had a better chance than I did, and with Colonel Valera constantly pointing out to the general what a failure I was as head of security, I was prepared to try anything.'

'You knew the killer was safe, and I knew he was safe,' Paco said. 'So how likely is it that he couldn't work out the same thing himself?'

'He had a great deal to lose if you did manage to track him down,' Gómez said.

'That's not what I asked you,' Paco pointed out. 'And you bloody well know it isn't.'

The major lit a cigarette, took a drag, and blew the smoke out through his nose. 'All right,' he conceded. 'Let us accept the fact that, unless he is a remarkably stupid man, the killer knows there is little chance of him being detected. Where's this leading to?'

'It's leading to another question. If he knew he was safe, why did he run the risk of trying to kill me?'

Gómez tapped the ash off his cigarette on to the ground. 'I'm sure you have a theory about that,' he said.

'This whole affair has to be about much more than the death of the dog,' Paco said. 'Principe wasn't shot for his collar, and he wasn't shot out of some twisted notion of revenge. He was shot to conceal something else –

and it's that something else which the killer is so worried I might find out about.'

A wry grin played on Major Gómez's lips. 'And what exactly is this "something else" he wishes to conceal?' he asked.

'I don't know,' Paco confessed. 'But whatever it is, it has to be important enough for the general to want to know about it – even if one of his officers *is* involved.'

'Perhaps you're right,' Gómez said reluctantly. 'Perhaps, after all, we must pursue the investigation wherever it takes us.' He looked down at the pistol lying on the table between them. 'Do you think this will help you find what your "something else" is?'

'It will go some of the way towards it – because it will tell me who it was who tried to kill me.'

'Ah yes,' Gómez said, seeing the way in which Paco's mind was moving. 'Each pistol has its own individual number, and there is a record of which officer it was issued to.'

'Exactly,' Paco agreed.

'And where, in this centralist country of ours, do you imagine those records will be kept?'

Paco felt a sinking feeling in the pit of his stomach. 'They're kept in Madrid?' he guessed.

An ironic smile played briefly on Gómez's lips. 'In Madrid,' he agreed. 'In the central offices of the Ministry of Defence, just off the Plaza Cibeles. Do you really think the Republicans who are running the ministry now will be willing to co-operate with our investigation?'

Why did he always seem to find it so amusing to point out the obstacles in the way? Paco wondered. And what right had he to call it 'our' investigation, like that? How long had the two of them been partners? And didn't he yet understand that, as far as Paco was concerned, he himself was a long, long way from being ruled out as a suspect?

'How long would you say you have been sitting here at this bar, Major?' he asked.

'I would guess I wasn't here for more than about five minutes before you arrived. Why do you ask?'

Because it had been at least fifteen minutes since the fight, which left plenty of time for Gómez to cross to the Plaza de Santa Teresa, cut up the Calle Cristo Rey, and be back on the Calle Mayor by the time Paco found him.

'I asked why you were so interested in how long I'd been here,' the major repeated.

'No particular reason,' Paco lied. 'But let's get back to the pistol. I've just realized that it doesn't matter whether we have the serial numbers or not.'

'Doesn't it?'

'No. All we have to do is to call all the officers together, and ask them to show us their weapons. But one of them won't be able to do that – because we have his gun right here.'

Gómez nodded thoughtfully. 'That might work,' he said. 'And in view of the suspicious nature of your question a few moments ago, I suppose I'd better show you something.' He unstrapped his holster and took out his gun. 'I, you see, still have my weapon.'

A young lieutenant, looking very red in the face, came running up to the table. 'Major Gómez, sir,' he gasped. 'I've been looking for you everywhere. Colonel Valera wants to see you in the Plaza de Santa Teresa right away.'

'Right away, you say?' the major repeated. 'Why? Has something serious happened?'

The young officer sucked in some more air. 'The colonel ordered me not to say anything, sir. He said he'd give you all the details himself.'

'I see,' Gómez said, rising to his feet. He turned towards Paco. 'In that case, Ruiz, you stay here, and we'll continue our most illuminating conversation when I get back.'

'I'm sorry, sir, I don't seem to have made myself clear,' the young lieutenant said. 'The colonel doesn't want to see just *you*. He told me to bring the detective from Madrid along as well.'

Chapter Thirteen

A man should not have to pass the spot where, only half an hour earlier, someone had tried to kill him, Paco thought as he and Major Gómez approached the bend in the Calle Belén. Nor should he be walking beside the man who might well turn out to be his would-be assassin.

You're not thinking clearly, Paco, he told himself. You're perfectly safe with Major Gómez. He can't possibly be the man who fired at you – because he still has his pistol in his holster.

They turned the bend, and Paco got his first view of the square. It had been empty when he'd visited it earlier, but now at least a couple of dozen portable paraffin lanterns were dancing around in the darkness like demented fireflies. At the edge of the plaza stood two soldiers with rifles in their hands. One of them lifted his lantern, shone it into Gómez's face and said, 'Carry on, sir.'

'If the general's lost his other dog, I'm really going to be in the shit,' the major said to Paco.

But it wasn't a dog this time. The ex-policeman was sure of that. He could smell the atmosphere – an uneasy mixture of shock, disgust and disbelief – and knew that, finally, he was back on familiar territory.

There were officers milling around all over the square, but the biggest group had formed a rough half circle about two metres away from the fountain.

'What do you think has happened?' Major Gómez asked.

'Isn't it obvious?' Paco replied. 'Somebody's died.'

The officers close to the fountain stepped to one side to let them pass, and in so doing revealed Colonel Valera. He was standing by the very base of the fountain itself, and at his feet lay what was obviously a dead body.

'*Joder!*' Major Gómez said to Paco. 'You were right.'

The colonel glared at both of them in turn. 'This is – or rather was – Lieutenant Anton,' he said, pointing to the corpse. 'One of his brother officers came across his body only a few minutes ago.'

'May I examine him?' Paco asked.

'Why the hell do you think I wanted you here, if not to examine him?' Colonel Valera demanded. 'See what clues you can find, then meet me in my office in precisely ten minutes.'

And with that, he stormed off angrily in the direction of his quarters.

Paco knelt down next to the body, being careful to avoid the sticky lake of blood around the dead man's head. 'I'll need some more light if I'm to do a proper job,' he said.

One of the young officers stepped forward, and held a paraffin lantern over the corpse. In life, Lieutenant Anton had probably been a fresh-faced boy with a pleasing smile, Paco guessed. But death changes everything – and the expression of panic and horror which was frozen on his face now only belonged in the deepest, darkest nightmares.

The wide gash across his throat was clearly the cause of his death. His murderer had probably crept up behind him, thrown one arm across his chest to restrain him, and wielded the knife with the other. Paco felt Lieutenant Anton's skin with the back of his hand. It was still warm. He lifted the dead man's arm, then let it fall lifelessly back to his side. There was no sign of even the start of rigor mortis.

'From the condition of the body, I'd say he's not been dead for more than an hour,' Paco said looking up at Gómez. 'But, of course, we both know it's been a much shorter time than that, don't we?'

'I have no idea what you're talking about,' the major told him.

Paco sighed. 'Why do you think he was killed?' he asked. 'Because he'd made enemies? Because he had gambling debts? Or maybe you think a group of bloodthirsty Socialist militiamen sneaked into the village, murdered this one man, and then slipped out again unnoticed.'

'You're beginning to irritate me,' Gómez told him.

'He was killed for no other reason than that he was unlucky enough to be in the wrong place at the wrong time,' Paco said. He straightened up. 'I think it's about time we went to see the colonel.'

*

Colonel Valera sat behind his desk, a long black cigarette holder in his hand. He looked like a very angry matinée idol, thought Paco, who, like Major Gómez, was standing the approved metre away from the desk.

Valera lit his cigarette, and inhaled. 'Lieutenant Julio Anton was a most promising young officer who'd been mentioned twice in dispatches,' he said. 'Now he's dead, slaughtered like a pig out on the street – and I hold the two of you personally responsible.'

92

'Us?' Major Gómez said. 'But all we did was—'

'Shut up!' the colonel barked. 'You, Ruiz! What have you discovered so far about the dog's murder?'

'It's still very early in the case, Colonel,' Paco said. 'At this stage we don't really have—'

'In other words, you've discovered nothing at all!' the colonel interrupted. 'Now I don't know how in God's name poor Lieutenant Anton's death could be connected with the dog's, but since they happened in the same general area only three days apart, I'm sure there has to be some kind of connection. Wouldn't you agree, Ruiz?'

'It's possible,' Paco said cautiously.

'Possible!' Valera snorted. 'I said a few moments ago that the pair of you were responsible for Anton's death. Now I'm going to tell you why. You, Gómez, must bear the responsibility for saving this great detective of yours from the firing squad, and so setting off the whole chain of events.'

'We don't know that Inspector Ruiz's being on the case had anything to do with . . .'

'Shut your mouth!' the colonel screamed. 'Next we come to you, Ruiz. You must take the blame for not solving the case of the general's dog before matters got completely out of hand. As far as I'm concerned, neither of you is worth a bucket of shit. So now we know where we all stand, don't we, Major?'

Gómez nodded.

'I said, now we all know where we stand, don't we, Major?' the colonel repeated.

'Yes, Colonel,' Gómez said through gritted teeth. 'Yes, we do.'

'I understand exactly how that devious mind of yours works, Major,' the colonel said. 'You want my job so much that it's eating your insides out, and you thought that presenting the general with the dog's killer would go a long way towards getting it for you. But it hasn't worked out that way, has it?'

'My only interest,' Gómez protested, 'was in seeing whoever killed the dog brought to just—'

'Don't give me that crap!' the colonel interrupted. 'I could probably have you shot for incompetence, Major, if I really put my mind to it. As for you, Ruiz, it would take me less effort to have you executed than it would to order a cup of coffee.' He stubbed his cigarette viciously into the ashtray. 'But if I did that, who would be left to investigate Lieutenant Anton's murder?' he asked rhetorically. 'No one! So even though you've proved to be completely bloody useless so far, I'm going to have to keep you on in hope that you accidentally stumble over something which helps to crack the case.'

He paused, as if he were expecting one of them to speak. After perhaps five seconds of silence, Major Gómez said, 'Thank you, sir,' though he appeared to be almost choking on the words.

'The only thanks I want is a successful conclusion to the investigation,' the colonel said. 'But let's get one thing perfectly clear. There are going to be some changes in the way you conduct yourselves. Your days of having a completely free hand are over. From now on, everything you discover will be reported to me the very moment it is discovered.' He pulled the stub of the cigarette out of its holder, and inserted a new one. 'That's all I have to say for the present. Now get the hell out of here!'

Paco and Gómez stepped into the hallway, the major leading. They were almost at the front door when Paco felt the familiar tingle at the back of his neck which told him someone was watching him. He turned round quickly – but not quickly enough to catch more than a glimpse of a woman's naked foot disappearing around the bend in the stairs.

*

The corpse of the lieutenant had been removed to the mortuary, the officers who had been milling around had finally left, and the Plaza de Santa Teresa was as deserted as it had been when Paco had visited it an hour before.

'There's no sentry,' he said to Gómez, as they walked across the square towards the Calle Belén.

'What?'

'There isn't a guard on duty outside the colonel's house.'

'I've explained all that,' Major Gómez said irritably. 'I withdraw them periodically just to show that bastard Valera that he isn't quite as important as he likes to—'

'It's the second time there hasn't been a sentry there when something significant happened.'

They had reached the fountain. Gómez stopped dead in his tracks. 'Just what are you suggesting!' he said, growing angry now. 'That I killed the dog? That I took a shot at you and slit Lieutenant Anton's throat?'

'It's possible,' Paco told him.

'But for God's sake, man, the killer lost his pistol, and you know I've still got mine.'

'I know you've got *a* pistol,' Paco said. 'Whether it's yours or not is quite a different matter.'

'So what did I do? Conjure a new one up out of thin air?'

'No, but what you could have done is killed Lieutenant Anton, and taken his. I said earlier he was unlucky to be in the wrong place at the wrong time. And that's exactly what he was. While I was examining him, I took the opportunity to pat his holster. It was empty.'

'So he was killed for his gun?'

'It looks that way.'

'And I'm a suspect?'

'I can't see any reason why you shouldn't be.'

'If I'd killed the dog, why would I have saved you from the firing squad?' the major demanded. 'Why wouldn't I have let you die, and then just pretended to investigate the case myself?'

'Because then, if the investigation failed – as it would be bound to do, since you had no intention of turning yourself in – it would have been your failure. This way, it's mine.'

Gómez laughed hollowly. 'Do you think it's as simple as that? Do you really believe that if we fail, that son of a bitch Valera won't make certain that I take the largest portion of the blame? You're acting like you're still important – but what you were before the war doesn't matter a damn now. As far as most people are concerned, and that probably includes the general by now, you're nothing but a piece of godless enemy scum. Whereas I – *I* – am the head of army security, and if anyone is riding for a fall here, it is me.'

'Yes,' Paco said dryly. 'You could lose your position. All they could do with me is shoot me.'

Gómez took a deep breath. 'We shouldn't argue,' he said, doing his best to sound calm and rational. 'We need each other, you and I. Don't you understand that? We either hang together, or we hang apart.'

'Or one of us hangs and the other doesn't,' Paco countered. 'And I'm willing to bet that if one us does hang, you'll make sure it isn't you.'

The major took a packet of cigarettes out of his pocket, and offered one to Paco. 'It's been a long day, and we're both tired,' he said as he stuck the match. 'So perhaps it would be wise not to talk about it any more tonight. Things will look very different in the morning.'

'Perhaps they will,' Paco agreed, greedily sucking the soothing nicotine into his lungs.

'About the sentry . . .' Gómez said tentatively.

'I thought we weren't going to discuss the case any more tonight.'

'No, but perhaps this one matter should be cleared up, since it appears to be creating an atmosphere of suspicion between us.'

'All right,' Paco agreed.

'You suspected me of lying when I said it was a matter of whim whether I posted them or didn't post them. And you were quite correct. There is nothing random about it, but that is not to say that it had anything to do with either the death of the dog or the murder of Lieutenant Anton.'

'So what does it have to do with?'

Gómez shook his head. 'That I can't tell you. If you really want to know, you're going to have to find out for yourself.'

'You've been a great help,' Paco told him.

'It's out of my hands,' the major said apologetically. He threw his cigarette to the ground, and trod on it. 'Shall we go?'

'Go where?'

'I'll escort you back to the Calle Jose Antonio.'

'I don't need an escort.'

'You surely don't intend to walk up the Calle Belén alone, do you?' Major Gómez asked. 'Not after what happened to you earlier. It's not safe.'

'You might be right,' Paco told him. 'But without wishing to cause offence, I have to say that I'll feel safer on my own than I would with any escort who was carrying a thirty-two calibre pistol.'

Chapter Fourteen

There was a cave, burrowed deep into one of the Atlas Mountains, which still occasionally gave Paco long and troubled dreams. He'd seen it for the first and last time one day in 1921 – the day that he and his platoon had been ordered to turn their backs on the blazing sunlight and enter the dark hole in search of rebel tribesmen. To have used torches would have been to make them an easy target, and so they had groped their way through in the darkness, hoping to hear the enemy cough, or catch a glimpse of *his* lanterns.

Paco remembered everything about that seemingly endless journey. The dank coolness of the place. The fluttering of bats close to the ceiling. The sound his men's boots had made as they'd crushed tiny stones underfoot – and the way that crushing sound had echoed, and become amplified, as it bounced its way around the walls of the cavern. But most of all, he remembered the stink of fear which had seeped out through the skin of all the soldiers following him.

They were good men, he'd told himself at the time. Brave men who had not flinched in the face of an enemy attack out on open ground. It was not the enemy they might encounter, but the cave itself, which had them so scared. No man wanted to die in the blackness, the victim of a bullet fired from an unseen rifle. No man felt his life was so insignificant that it could be ended by a random shot in the dark.

The cave had proved to be empty, and later they had all joked about it, each man accusing all the others of a fear which had been wrenching at his own gut. But they had known, even then, that the memory of the cave, of the sense of desolation and oblivion they had felt while they were inside, it would haunt them for ever.

*

Sprinting along the Calle Belén, only seconds after making sure that Major Gómez had returned to his quarters, Paco found himself reliving the memory of that cave – hearing the echoes, smelling the fear which he knew was his own. Each pounded step could be taking him closer to a waiting assassin – closer to death. And yet that same assassin could equally be behind him, moving as stealthily as he had done the last time he had stalked his victim.

If only he had a gun, Paco thought, as he scanned the semi-blackness ahead for lurking shapes which might be his waiting enemy. But even a gun would be no real protection, he decided, as he strained to hear if he was being followed – because no man could guard his back from an unknown killer for ever.

He turned the sharp bend, and could see the paraffin lamps blazing brightly on Calle Mayor. Once he had reached the main street, he would be safe, he told himself. Even the most determined of murderers would not attempt to shoot him in front of so many witnesses.

He reached the end of the alley with a gasp of relief, and stopped in front of the church to regain his breath.

'What have you been doing, Señor Inspector?' asked a mocking voice. 'Investigating the murder of that officer who had his throat cut on the Plaza de Santa Teresa?'

Paco turned and saw that the speaker was the rat-faced Private Pérez. The private was sitting on the church steps, and smoking with all the care and attention of a man who is down to his last cigarette.

'So you've heard all about the murder, have you?' Paco asked.

Pérez laughed. 'Of course I've heard. There's not much goes on in this village that I don't get to know about.'

'Is that right? Then could you please tell me who it was who shot the general's dog?'

Pérez shook his head. 'No,' he admitted. 'I couldn't. That's something I haven't heard the slightest whisper about.'

Paco squatted down next to the rat-faced boy. 'Why aren't you out drinking with your mates?' he asked.

'It's one of my mates I'm waiting for now,' Pérez said sourly. 'Jiménez!' He flicked his thumb in the direction of the church door. 'He's in there. Praying to that Virgin again.'

'I got the feeling from the way you taunted him in my office, that you didn't like him very much.'

Pérez waved his hands in a gesture of dismissal. 'I neither like him nor dislike him. He's just the same as all the other country boys. They can scrub and scrub till their skin is red raw, but they still stink of the cow shit they've spent their whole lives working in. They're not even worthy of my contempt.'

'Is it such a crime to work on the land?' Paco asked. 'Do they deserve to be despised just for that?'

'No, not just for that,' Pérez said. 'But there are so many other things. They live in absolute terror of the haggard old crones half their size, who they call their mothers. They think their stinking little villages are the centre of the universe. And though they've no real idea of what all this religious mumbo-jumbo is really about, they're willing enough to fall down on their knees before a badly painted statue and stay like that for hours.'

'So if you have such a poor opinion of Private Jiménez, why are you waiting for him?'

Pérez sneered. 'I've already spent all of my day's pay – a private's wages don't buy many drinks. But Jiménez is a completely different matter. He's still got all his money, because he's been far too busy praying to that lump of wood to get around to spending his wages yet.'

'Where do you come from, Pérez?' Paco asked.

'Why do you want to know?'

'Just idle curiosity.'

Pérez had smoked the cigarette down so far that he was in danger of burning his fingertips. With a deep sigh of regret, he stubbed what was left of it out on the stone step. 'A policeman's curiosity is never idle,' he said. 'Where do *you* think I'm from?'

Paco shrugged. 'From the way you carry yourself and some of the slang you use, I'd guess you're no stranger to the back streets of Madrid,' he said.

The rat-faced soldier stared at Paco for several seconds, then shook his head wonderingly. 'You really don't remember me, do you, Inspector?' he asked. 'I thought at first that, for some reason of your own, you were only pretending not to know me, but now I think it's genuine.'

Paco took out his Celtas, stuck one in his own mouth, then, seeing the longing look in the private's eyes, offered the pack to Pérez. 'Why should I know you?' he asked.

'Perhaps because you once arrested me.'

'For what?' Paco said, striking a match and holding it out in his cupped hands under Pérez's cigarette.

'What did you arrest me for?' the rat-faced private repeated, taking in a lungful of smoke. 'Why, for murder of course!'

'Remind me of the case,' Paco told him.

'I was running four or five whores on a street down by the Puerta de Toledo. Country girls, they were.' Pérez sniggered. 'Big cow-like things. Any one of them could easily have been Jiménez's sister. Anyway, one of my girls disappeared, and when she turned up again she was floating in the river with her throat cut. So naturally, the first thing you did was to arrest her pimp.'

It was all coming back to Paco now. 'Your name wasn't Pérez back then, was it?' he asked.

The private shook his head. 'No, I was calling myself Pepe Delgado at the time. I've had a number of different names over the years.'

Pepe Delgado! Yes, now Paco could remember the case quite clearly. 'We had to let you go in the end, didn't we?' he said.

'That's right. She was one of my whores, and I never denied that fact, but there was no hard evidence to link me with her murder. And as a matter of fact, I didn't kill the girl.'

'They all say that.'

'True,' Pérez agreed. 'But why should I bother to lie to you about it now? Even if I confessed to the crime, there'd be nothing you could do about it out here, is there?'

'You don't seem to hold a grudge over the fact that I arrested you,' Paco said, intrigued. 'Why is that?'

Pérez shrugged. 'I'm a businessman, and it's not good for business to waste your time holding a grudge. After a couple of days, I was released, and as far as I'm concerned, that's the whole matter over and done with. Besides,' he added, slightly self-consciously, 'you treated me a damn sight better than most of the cops who've ever taken me in. You didn't hit me once.'

'What I don't understand is what a "businessman" like you is doing in the army,' Paco said. 'I can't quite figure out what your angle is.'

'I haven't got an angle,' the soldier told him. 'I was in hot water, and the military seemed a convenient place to disappear to for a while. But if I'd known that war was about to break out, you'd never have got me anywhere near the recruitment office.'

Paco reached into his pocket, and pulled out a couple of the one-peseta notes which Major Gómez had so reluctantly handed over to him. 'You want these?' he asked.

Pérez eyed the money hungrily, yet there was also a look of suspicion in his pinched features. 'Nobody gives money away as easily as that,' he said. 'What do you want in return?'

'Very little,' Paco assured him. 'Just tell me what you know about your officers.'

'Why should you be interested in hearing about them?' Pérez asked guardedly.

'Why shouldn't I be interested?' Paco responded, rustling the notes between his fingers.

'There was a day when I'd have laughed in your face if you'd been insulting enough to offer me a miserly two pesetas,' Pérez said sadly. 'But times change, don't they?'

'Indeed they do,' Paco agreed. 'Why don't you start by telling me about the general?'

'From what I've heard, he's never been a very good soldier, but now he's no use at all.'

'Why should that be?'

'Because he's so obsessed with that pretty wife of his that he leaves most of the real work to Colonel Valera, and spends his time shopping for things for her to wear. It's my belief that's the only way he can get his thrills – dressing her and undressing her as if she was some kind of china doll.'

Paco grinned. 'You're just guessing now,' he said.

'You wouldn't say that if you'd seen some of the underwear he's bought her,' Pérez replied, sounding stung.

'How would you know about the underwear he's bought her?' Paco asked sharply.

It was Pérez's turn to grin. 'Even a fine lady's underwear gets dirty sometimes. And when it does, it has to be washed, doesn't it? And once it's been washed, it's hung out to dry. A lot of the boys get a kick out of seeing it hanging out on the line.'

'And do you?'

Pérez shook his head. 'No. One way or another, sex has been my business since I was around thirteen years old. Where there is no money to be made out of it, I'm not interested. But that doesn't mean to say I don't hear the others talking about what they've seen.'

'And how about the general's wife. Is she as obsessed with him as he seems to be with her?'

The private laughed. 'You've seen him with your own eyes. What do you think?'

'So why did she marry him?'

'Because he's rich. I used to run whores just like her – girls willing to do anything with any man as long as it gave them the money to buy artificial silk drawers and cheap jewellery.'

Paco lit a second cigarette from the stub of his first, and again handed the pack across to Private Pérez. 'Keep it,' he said. 'I've got some more in my other pocket.'

'Oh, to be rich again,' the private said, quickly palming the cigarettes into the folds of his cheap uniform.

'What do you think about the rest of the officers billeted in this village?' Paco asked.

Pérez pulled a face. 'They make me sick – the whole bloody pack of them. Look at the difference between the way they live and the way we live. They stay in nice houses and sleep between clean sheets, while we have to make do with tents, sleeping head to toe. They have their fine mistresses, and we're forced to settle for poxridden whores. I tell you, things were different in the old days. Back then I had a motorbike and *three* good suits.'

'Does Colonel Valera have a mistress?' Paco asked, remembering the naked woman's foot he had seen disappear round the corner of the stairs only half an hour earlier.

'Most of the people I've talked to seem to think he has, but if it's true, he's certainly very discreet about it – so nobody really knows for sure.'

'And Major Gómez?'

Pérez laughed. 'He'd like to have one, but he can't afford the luxury. He's not from a rich family like the general is, you know. His father's a baker in Valladolid – spends his days up to the elbows in dough – so for all his airs and graces, the major's no better than the rest of us.'

But he wanted to be, Paco thought. Major Gómez had a burning ambition which shone as brightly as the noonday sun – an ambition so compelling that he was probably prepared to risk everything he already had in order to gain more. The first stage of his plan was to step into the colonel's position, and then perhaps into the general's. By the time this awful war was over, he could be one of the most powerful men in the country – and if he had to kill an ex-inspector of police on the way, it wouldn't bother him at all.

'Tell me about the general's dog,' Paco said to Pérez.

Pérez's eyes narrowed. 'What about it?'

Paco took a deep drag on his cigarette. 'I'm only interested in finding out who killed the animal,' he said. 'Whatever you did with the collar is your business and no concern of mine.'

'I've told you before – we never even touched the bloody collar,' Pérez protested.

Paco shook his head disbelievingly. 'Of course you did. You did more than simply touch it. You lifted it over what was left of the dog's head and slipped it into your pocket, just as you did with my cigarettes just now.'

'Not true!' Pérez said obstinately.

'A man like you – a man who got used to the finer things in life, like having a motorbike and three good suits – isn't going to pass up the chance to grab a small fortune when fate suddenly lets it fall right into his hands. But as I said before, I don't give a damn about the collar. What I'd be interested to find out is *why* the dog was killed.'

'Well there's no point in asking me,' Pérez told him. '*I've* no idea why the brute was shot. But I'll tell you one thing I've learned in my life – no man stirs up a pond unless he has something to gain from making it murky.'

Perhaps that *was* it, Paco thought. Pickpockets on the Puerta del Sol often worked in teams of two – one creating some kind of scene to attract attention, while the other went around the square lifting the spectators' wallets from inside their jackets. Was it possible, then, that the killing of the dog had been much along the same lines – had it been nothing more than a clever stunt aimed at shifting the focus away from what was really important?

He handed the one-peseta notes to Pérez. 'Keep your eyes and ears open, will you?' he said. 'If you hear anything that might help me, I'll pay well for the information.'

The church door opened, and Private Jiménez stepped out. He seemed surprised to see Paco there – almost frightened – but then these country boys were always intimidated by anyone wearing a suit.

'So you've finally stopped talking to God, have you?' Pérez said contemptuously.

'I . . . um . . .' Jiménez mumbled, then fell silent.

Pérez stood up, his hand in his trouser pocket, his fingers touching the two peseta notes Paco had given him. 'Well, come on!' he said to the big, slow peasant. 'Let's go and have a drink. But remember, Jiménez, you're buying tonight – because I haven't got any money.'

Paco watched the two young men walk towards the nearest bar, then pushed the heavy door open and entered the church. It was much cooler inside than it was out on the street. Much quieter, too, without the incessant noise of the carousing soldiers. And though he had long ago lost his own faith, he still felt the soothing effect of the centuries of belief and certainty which pervaded the building.

He walked up to the statue of the Virgin. The wooden tears which she cried over the death of her beloved son had not moved even a fraction of a centimetre since the moment they'd been carved – but the world which surrounded the church had changed immeasurably in just a few days.

'They're killing your priests, Madonna,' he said softly to the statue. 'Did you know that?'

It was true. The priesthood was so closely associated with the old order – with the landlords and the bosses – that the backlash had been ferocious. Priests and nuns had been murdered all over the Republican-held territory. Paco himself knew of one case in Madrid where the priest had been shot by the militia for no other reason than that while he always took care to wear a clean collar when he was officiating at a rich man's funeral mass, he had considered a soiled one good enough when the deceased was poor.

The Virgin looked down on him with the fixed expression of piety and grief she had held since the master craftsman had finished his work – and was silent.

'But none of it would ever have happened if the Army hadn't risen,' Paco told her. 'There is blood on everyone's hands now, but it has stained some more than others.'

He turned, and walked down the aisle to the door. Once out on the street again, he lit a cigarette, and looked around him. He could see big slow Jiménez and wily little Pérez leaning against a barrel-turned-table, and drinking away what was left of the country boy's pay.

He understood now why Pérez had felt it necessary to insult Jiménez's mother. And from that insight, it was no great trick to reconstruct the heated conversation he'd seen them having outside his office.

I had to say something, Pérez would have explained to the slow-witted Jiménez. *If I hadn't, you'd have been bound to give the game away.*

'*You said very bad things about my mother*, Jiménez would have whined in reply.

Yes, I know I did, Pérez would have countered, doing his best to keep the exasperation out of his voice. *But I didn't mean it. You know that. It was the only thing I could think of to shut you up.*

The two young soldiers drained their glasses, and left the bar. Paco watched them until they had been swallowed up by the crowd, then turned his mind back to his more pressing problems. He needed to get his hands on some weapons, he told himself. Not just guns – though he would feel a great deal safer if he had one in a snug shoulder holster under his armpit. No, what he really needed were psychological weapons – levers which he could use to exert pressure on the people who mattered: a threat he could employ against Major Gómez; a secret of Valera's he could threaten to expose unless the colonel agreed to co-operate with him. It was only through the skilful manipulation of such instruments that he and his darling Cindy had any chance of surviving.

A few minutes earlier he had felt as if he were facing an impossible task, but now he was experiencing the faintest pulse of hope. He finally had one of the weapons he needed. True, it was only a tiny one – a penknife, when what he would have preferred was a machine-gun – but at least it was a start. He had finally discovered what had happened to the dead dog's collar.

Chapter Fifteen

The smell of freshly brewing coffee had always been enough to wake Paco from even the deepest sleep, and the morning after the attempt on his life was no exception. His first instinctive reaction was to groan, and wonder if he could get back to sleep again. His second reaction, a more recently acquired one, was to reach across for Cindy Walker, only to find that she wasn't there.

'Of course she's not here,' he told himself irritably, as he threw off the sheet and swung himself out of bed. 'Coffee doesn't make itself, does it?'

He put on the overcoat he'd been using as a dressing-gown, and made his way downstairs. Cindy was wearing nothing more than one of his shirts. He let his eyes play on her long, slim legs, and marvelled that anyone could be so totally unselfconscious as this blonde *Yanqui* seemed to be.

She heard his footsteps on the stairs, and turned to face him. 'Just in time,' she said with a smile. 'The bread's still hot, and whatever jelly they've brought with it smells just delicious.'

She looked tired, he thought, but it was a tiredness born more out of an emotional exhaustion than anything else. In a way, he was having a much easier time of it than she was. Certainly, he had to venture out on the streets, never sure when someone would take a pot shot at him. But at least he was investigating both the case and their possibilities of escape, while she was confined to the house all day, with nothing to occupy her mind but worries about their future.

'What happened last night?' Cindy asked. 'The last thing I remember was sitting in the chair, waiting for you to come back. Then it was morning, and I woke up in bed.'

Paco kissed her lightly on the lips. 'You were asleep when I got back,' he said. 'I carried you upstairs.' He grinned. 'You're getting fat. Did you know that? It's time you went on a diet.'

'The hell I am! And the hell I will!' Cindy replied. 'So what did you do yesterday, Ruiz?'

Paco sat down at the table and spread some *mermelada* on the bread. Cindy had been right, he thought. It did smell delicious. 'I don't want you

106

to get too worked up about this,' he said, 'but last night, someone tried to kill me.'

Cindy took a deep breath, and he knew she was making a tremendous effort not to scream – or at least burst into tears. 'Well, I suppose you'd better tell me about it,' she said in a shaky voice.

He described his confrontation with the assassin on the Calle Belén, leaving nothing out except the depth of his own fear. 'But that's awful,' she said when he finished. 'You're a sitting target.'

'Not quite that,' Paco said, unconvincingly. 'Besides, getting shot at is an occupational hazard. People are always trying to kill me – and not one of them has succeeded even once.'

But Cindy refused to treat the matter lightly. 'I feel so useless,' she told him. 'If only I could be out there with you. Or if only there was some other way I could help.'

'There is,' Paco assured her. 'After last night, I'm not sure I can trust Major Gómez any more, which means that if anyone's going to take Fat Felipe's place, it'll have to be you.'

'What an honour,' Cindy said, regaining something of her fighting spirit. 'OK, Ruiz, give me the low-down.'

He described the murder of Lieutenant Anton, the interview he'd had with Colonel Valera, and his argument on the square with Major Gómez. He told her about his conversation with Private Pérez, and his sudden insight into what had happened to the dog's collar. She listened seriously; her chin tilted forward, her eyes set deep in concentration.

'But can you be absolutely sure that the murderer is an officer?' she asked, when he finished.

'He took Anton's gun,' Paco reminded her. 'What else can he be if he did that?'

Cindy frowned. 'Say that instead of an officer, he was one of the enlisted men or a villager,' she argued. 'Someone with a pistol which can't be traced. Someone like your Private Pérez, for example.'

'Pérez had nothing to do with it,' Paco said firmly.

'You can't be sure of that,' Cindy countered. 'So say it's Pérez who follows you up the alley, gets into the fight and loses his weapon in the process. It doesn't bother him, as he's running back to the Plaza de Santa Teresa, that he's had to abandon his pistol. Why should it? It's never going to be connected with him.'

'But . . .?' Paco said.

'But then he sees this Lieutenant Anton standing near the fountain, and he comes up with a brilliant idea.'

'And what idea is that?'

'That if he kills the lieutenant and takes his weapon, you'll reach the very conclusion you have – that the man who tried to murder you was an officer. In other words, he kills Lieutenant Anton not because he wants the pistol, but to make you think he wants it.'

It was certainly an interesting theory, Paco decided. A very interesting theory. And he found himself wondering why Major Gómez, who was always trying to deflect his attention away from the officers, hadn't come up with something similar the night before.

*

The Calle Belén did not hold the same terror for him in the morning sun as it had under the cover of darkness, and the Plaza de Santa Teresa, which had seemed so sinister in the bobbing light of the two dozen officers' lanterns, was once again nothing more than a pleasant residential square.

Paco walked over to the fountain in the centre of the plaza. The bloodstains were still clearly visible in the dirt. He examined the ground, and sighed with disgust. From the way the body had been lying, he could work out where the killer must have stood when he committed the act. And given that he would have been bracing himself to hold his struggling victim in a tight grip, there should have been footprints in the dirt. And there were! Far, far too many of them!

Like the amateur that he was, Colonel Valera had turned the place into a circus the night before, and instead of sealing off the square the moment he'd been told about the discovery of the body, he'd allowed his officers to trample all over it. If any of the policemen who'd worked for him back in Madrid had handled the initial stages of a murder case in such a ham-fisted way as this, Paco thought, he'd have seen to it that the man was instantly dismissed from the Force.

He ran Cindy's theory through his mind again. Anton had only been killed to make him think he was looking for an officer, she'd suggested. As theories went, it was a tempting one, but it was also altogether too complicated for real life.

As he saw it, there were three distinct circles in the village – three sets of inter-relationships. The villagers themselves were in the first: whether rich or poor, they had known each other for all their lives. Next there was the circle made up by enlisted men like Pérez – the cannon fodder who normally had no plans beyond their next drink. And finally there were the officers: Anton, Gómez, Valera, General Castro, and, by extension, the general's dog – which had worn a collar worth more than most of the agricultural labourers would earn from ten years' backbreaking work. And the point about these circles was whilst they might briefly touch, they were, in fact, completely independent of each other. If a peasant killed, it would be another peasant he murdered. If a common soldier took a life, it would be from one of his own. And if the general's dog and a fresh-faced lieutenant were murdered, then the chances were that an officer was behind the crime.

Paco looked at the house across the square. Now, when it was totally unnecessary, there was a sentry posted there. He lit up a Celtas. He didn't like what he was going to have to force himself to do next, but there was no choice in the matter. If he was to make any progress in the case at all, he admitted to himself, it would first be necessary to talk to Colonel Valera again.

*

It was mid-morning, and already casualties from the front line were arriving back at the village and being dealt with – as well as the primitive conditions allowed – in what, until recently, had been the *ayuntamiento*, the centre of local government. Perhaps some of the six young soldiers who had found the dead dog in the Calle Belén would be killed that day, Paco thought. Perhaps, indeed, they would all be killed – and he would then be the only person in the whole world who knew the secret of the dog's precious collar.

He looked down at the man sitting behind the desk – the man who was gazing self-importantly at a stack of documents in front of him, and making the occasional leisurely notation on one of them with his pen. Colonel Valera had kept him standing at full attention for over ten minutes, but then that was what people like Valera always did.

The colonel finally lifted his head from his work. 'Well, Ruiz, have you made any progress with your investigation into the death of Lieutenant Anton?' he demanded.

'It's only a few hours since the murder was committed, sir, and I'm working almost entirely alone,' Paco said. 'Even in Madrid, with the facilities of the entire police-department to back me up, I would not have expected, at this early point, to have—'

'In other words, you've made absolutely no progress at all,' the colonel interrupted him. 'So what are you doing here now, wasting my time as well as your own?'

Paco took a deep breath. 'I shall need your permission to talk to your officers,' he said.

The colonel slammed his pen down on the desk, and gave Paco a look which could have burned holes in sheet metal. 'What!' he demanded. 'Are you daring to suggest, even for a second, that one of my officers might be behind this ghastly crime?'

'No, sir,' Paco lied. 'Not at all. But they are billeted around the square where the murder took place. It's possible, even though they may not realize it themselves, that they saw or heard something of significance. If I could talk to them, I might be able to—'

'I could never permit any of my officers to be questioned by one of the enemy,' the colonel said disdainfully. 'Especially by a common militiaman like yourself.'

'Until just a few days ago, I was, in fact, an inspector of police,' Paco pointed out.

'An inspector with, no doubt, strongly republican sympathies,' the colonel countered.

'A professional policeman who has never let politics get in the way of his investigations,' Paco said firmly. 'And it's because I am a professional that I can assure you that without questioning witnesses, there is almost no chance of bringing the lieutenant's killer to justice.'

Valera frowned, but was clearly beginning to waver. 'Perhaps your dear friend Captain Gómez could talk to them,' he said finally. 'Since he is head of security, I could see no objection to that.'

'And would it be possible for me to be present while he is conducting these interviews?'

'Present?' Valera repeated, as if he had no idea what Paco was talking about. 'Do you mean, sitting next to him?'

'That's what I had in mind,' the ex-policeman admitted.

The colonel shook his head. 'That simply wouldn't do. It wouldn't do at all. It would seem to the officers being questioned as if Major Gómez were no more than a puppet, and that you, a man who they have every right to hate, were the one actually pulling the strings.'

'So what—?'

'We will have the meeting in the church,' the colonel said decisively. 'Gómez can convene it as soon as the men return from the front line. You will stay by the door. That way, you can hear what's being said without making any of the officers feel uncomfortable.'

It wasn't a very good deal at all, Paco thought, but it was probably the best that Colonel Valera was ever going to be prepared to offer him. 'Thank you, sir,' he said.

'I don't want your thanks,' the colonel said tartly. 'What I want is this whole matter cleared up – one way or the other.'

There was a knock on the door behind him, followed by the sound of the door swinging open. The colonel gazed with something which was very close to horror at whoever had entered the room. Paco, seeing Valera's attention was focused elsewhere, risked a quick glance over his shoulder.

The woman standing in the doorway was dressed from head to foot in black, like all the other peasant women in the village. She was, at first brief glance, somewhere around thirty years old, and though the beauty of her youth had long since faded away, she was still nothing less than a strikingly handsome woman.

Was this the mistress whom Private Pérez had talked about outside the church the previous evening? Paco wondered. She certainly didn't dress at all like a kept woman, but if Valera was deliberately being very discreet about his affair, as the private claimed he was, then wasn't it the best possible disguise to wear the same clothes as everyone else?

'What, in God's name, are you doing here *now*?' the colonel screamed at the new arrival.

'I'm . . . I'm sorry,' the woman stuttered. 'I . . . I didn't know that you were busy.'

'Get out!' the colonel shouted. 'Get out, and don't come back again until I send for you!'

Paco could hear the woman's hasty retreat and the sound of the door closing behind her. Valera was still looking visibly shaken. Half a dozen questions ran through Paco's quick mind. Who was this woman who had had such a dramatic effect on the colonel? Had it been her bare foot which he'd seen disappearing around the corner of the stairs the night before? Could she really be Valera's mistress? And if she was, and lived with him, why had he been so shocked when she appeared? Could it be that she had become an embarrassment to him – that he was ashamed to admit that he was still enthralled by a woman who was already past her best?

'These peasants!' Valera said, with a disgust which Paco was almost sure he was faking. 'They have absolutely no idea of time at all, do they? I asked her to come and do some work for me yesterday afternoon, but did she arrive when she was supposed to do? Of course she didn't! Instead she turns up now, right in the middle of a busy working morning. Is it any wonder that we need the army to run the country, when we constantly have to deal with people like that?'

Paco heard the faint, but distinct, click of the front door. The peasant woman – if that was what she really was – had left the house, and would be crossing the Plaza de Santa Teresa by now. He wondered what his chances would be of catching her up, and whether he'd dare take the risk of talking to her if he did. 'Could I go now, sir?' he asked.

The words seemed to remind Valera whom he was talking to. The vestiges of shock drained from his face and were replaced by his normal expression of haughty disdain. 'Do you fully understand my instructions of how to behave while Captain Gómez talks to the officers?' he asked.

'Yes,' Paco said.

'Then repeat them to me.'

Paco, who was itching to be out on the street, chasing the woman, suppressed a sigh. 'I'm to be allowed in the church, but I must stand at the back and not talk to any of the officers.'

'And do you think you'll be able to communicate those instructions to Major Gómez?'

'Yes,' Paco said, but he was thinking: This is deliberate. The son of a bitch is keeping me here until he's sure the woman has got clean away.

'What did your father do for a living?' the colonel asked.

'He had a small farm,' Paco replied.

'In other words, he was a peasant,' the colonel said. 'Then I'm not surprised that you get on so well with Gómez. His father's a baker, you know.' He flicked his hand dismissively. 'You can get out now.'

He really hates Gómez with a passion, Paco thought, but then at least the feeling is mutual. He clicked his heels in the approved military fashion, turned, and marched out of the room. Valera was already studying his papers again by the time he closed the door.

Once he was out on the Plaza de Santa Teresa again, Paco quickly scanned the area. There were several black-clothed peasant women around, but there was absolutely no sign of the one who had disturbed Colonel Valera by walking in unannounced. Paco strode rapidly across the square.

112

He couldn't see the woman on the Calle Belén, but perhaps she'd already rounded the bend. Or perhaps she hadn't gone up Belén at all, but had instead chosen the Calle Cristo Rey. He considered asking the sentry outside Valera's house which way she had gone, then quickly dismissed the idea. The last thing he wanted was to alert anyone connected with Valera to the fact that he had an interest in the woman.

He had to make a choice which way to go. He selected the Calle Belén, and once he was out of the sentry's line of vision, his walk turned into a sprint.

By the time he had reached the main street, he was forced to admit to himself that he had taken the wrong decision and that, at least for the moment, he had lost the woman. Still, even knowing of her existence was a marked advantage. It was possible – even probable – that she was simply the secret mistress Pérez had told him about, and therefore had nothing to do with either the death of the dog or the murder of Lieutenant Anton. But Valera's reaction to her had certainly shown a weakness – an Achilles heel. And if Paco could find a way to use that, he just might be able to transform the colonel from being an enemy into a very reluctant ally.

Chapter Sixteen

The last rays of a dying sun filtered in through the church windows, throwing bars of pale gold and purple across the flagstone floor. Paraffin lamps had already been lit in anticipation of the darkness which would soon follow, and these burned in the alcoves, casting a glowing light over the plaster saints who normally had the space to themselves. The officers of the rebel army sat close together in the front few pews of the church, and Major Gómez, with his back to the altar, was gazing down on them like an officiating priest.

Paco, standing at the back of the church, did a rapid head-count. These were not all the officers serving under the general – only the ones billeted on the Plaza de Santa Teresa – but they still formed a large enough group of potential suspects to give him a headache just thinking about it. He wished that he could be standing right next to Gómez, watching the officers' faces as they answered the head of security's questions, but he knew that, in this one case at least, Colonel Valera had probably been right, and the men would have resented his presence so much that they would have said nothing at all.

Gómez surveyed his audience with all the confidence of a natural commander of men.

'Lieutenant Luis Anton was a brother officer,' he said solemnly, 'and whoever is responsible for his death must be found at all costs. That is why we are having this meeting. I'm going to ask all of you to account for your movements last night, not because I suspect any of you of having anything to do with this cowardly crime, but merely to establish whether or not you were close enough to the incident to be of any value as a witness.'

Gómez was good, Paco thought. Perhaps even better than good. Yet he couldn't bring himself to shake off the uneasy feeling that something wasn't quite right about the major's presentation. He closed his eyes, and replayed Gómez's words in his head. He had said all the right things at the right time, yet there was an air of unreality about it all. It was almost as if the man were simply going through the motions – pretending to want to catch the murderer, while in fact being more intent on playing some game which was entirely his own.

Gómez stretched out his arm and pointed to the officer who was sitting at the end of the first row of pews. 'You, Lieutenant Martinez,' he said. 'Can you please tell me exactly where you were last night?'

The lieutenant, who, like the dead Lieutenant Anton, was little more than a boy, stood up and came to attention. 'I was playing cards with three of my colleagues, Major,' he said.

Gómez smiled in an indulgent, almost fatherly, way. 'What game were you playing?'

'*Mus*, sir.'

'And where, exactly were you playing your game?'

'In my room, sir.'

Major Gómez stroked his chin, reflectively. 'Does your room face on to the square, Lieutenant?' he asked.

'No, sir, it doesn't. It's located at the back of the house. It overlooks the mountains.'

Gómez nodded, as if that had been what he'd expected the young man to say.

'Did you see, or hear, anything which might help us to get to the bottom of this dreadful affair?'

Lieutenant Martinez shook his head. 'No, sir, I'm afraid I didn't. It was quite a lively game, you see, and I imagine we were making a fair amount of noise between us.'

'So when was the first time you realized anything was wrong?'

'I didn't know anything out of the ordinary had happened until someone battered on my door and shouted that poor Anton was dead.'

Gómez nodded again. 'Could the other members of the *mus* card school stand up, please.'

Three other officers – all of them lieutenants like Martinez – rose quickly to their feet.

'Did any of you lads hear or see anything suspicious last night?' Gómez asked.

'No, sir,' the three men replied in unison.

'I'm going to suggest to you that perhaps you *did* see something,' Gómez said, speaking in such a way as to give the impression that he was addressing one particular man. 'I'm going to suggest that during a break in the game of *mus*, you went outside, either to have a piss or just to clear your head. You saw something unusual on the square, but you thought nothing of it at the time, and returned to your game. But later, after you'd heard about the murder, you understood the implications of what you'd seen, and realized that if you'd perhaps acted differently, you might have saved Anton's life. Now you feel ashamed of yourself, and you're afraid to tell me what you know.'

At the back of the church, Paco shook his head admiringly. As the veteran of a hundred interrogations himself, he recognized when someone else was doing an excellent job.

'Don't feel ashamed,' Gómez continued, still talking to the one particular unknown man who just might have seen something on the square. 'Don't be afraid. We all make mistakes, and my objective here is not to punish anyone, but to find a killer.' He spread out his hands in supplication. 'So I'll ask you again. Did any of you see anything?'

'No, sir,' the four young officers said.

Mistake, Paco wanted to scream from the back of the church. Bloody big mistake!

Gómez had handled it all perfectly until the last two sentences. But he should never have asked them if they'd seen anything a second time. By getting them to publicly deny it twice, he was making it doubly difficult for any of them who *was* holding back to see him later in private.

Paco felt a sudden chill run through his body. Had it been a mistake at all, he wondered. Or was what he'd just witnessed Gómez's deliberate attempt to sabotage his own investigation!

'Very well, gentlemen,' the major said. 'Since you have now been eliminated from the inquiry, you may go.'

As simple as that? Paco thought. Did you see anything? No. Fine, you're eliminated.

The four young officers made their way down the aisle to the door. They were looking straight ahead, and there was no acknowledgement in their eyes that they even saw him standing there. It was almost as if he were invisible, and in a way, he supposed, he was. They lived in a closed world, a world which had its own rules and standards, which offered both a sense of direction and a sense of safety. Now an outsider had come to threaten that world – to turn its values upside down. How else could he expect them to act than by pretending that he didn't exist?

At the front of the church, Major Gómez had already turned his attention to the next man on the front row of the pews. 'Where were you at the time of the murder, Captain Ortega?' he asked.

'I was with my friend Captain Hernández.'

'In your room?'

'No. We went for a walk.'

'Around the village?'

'No, again. We left the village and walked towards the front line. We were discussing what strategy we thought it would be best to adopt when we begin the push towards Madrid.'

'Can you confirm that, Captain Hemández?' Gómez asked.

'Indeed I can, Major.'

'So, of course, you saw nothing either.'

'Naturally.'

The pattern which had started to emerge continued throughout the rest of questioning. None of the officers in the church had been alone at the time when Lieutenant Anton met his end. None of the groups of officers had seen or heard anything. The meeting lasted for almost an hour, and at the end of it Paco was no wiser than he had been at the beginning.

*

Paco and Major Gómez sat at a table outside what had become firmly established as the officers' bar on the Calle Mayor. To their left, a couple of military policemen were in the process of breaking up a fight. On their right, a group of drunken soldiers had filled a bucket with beer, and were unsuccessfully attempting to persuade a tethered donkey to drink from it.

'So tell me, Inspector, do you still think there's a chance that I might be your murderer?' Major Gómez asked, and tonight the notion seemed to amuse rather than anger him.

'I don't know what to think,' Paco confessed. 'Were you surprised by the answers you were given in the church?'

'Not really,' Gómez replied.

'Well, I was,' Paco told him. 'I've interviewed hundreds of men in my time, and even the ones who've led the most sociable of lives have never been able to produce an alibi which satisfactorily covers every minute of their time. "I was on a bus, travelling to my mother's house," one will say. "I didn't know any of the other passengers." Or another might tell me, "I stopped for a couple of drinks in a bar I've never been to before. The barman might recognize me, I suppose, but he was so busy I don't think he

117 of the other passengers.

117

even looked me in the face." And the fact that they haven't got alibis doesn't automatically make them guilty! The first man may really have been on a bus, the second could be telling the truth when he says he was alone in a strange bar. These things happen.'

'What exactly is the point you're trying to make?' Major Gómez asked guardedly.

'I would have expected some of the officers you questioned to have had alibis,' Paco said. 'But not *all* of them.'

'In war, men are often too afraid to be in their own company for long,' Gómez replied.

'And did you notice that it was the officers with quarters looking out over the mountains who were at home when Anton was killed,' Paco continued, ignoring the major's comment, 'while the ones whose rooms had a view of the square were invariably out?'

A look of rage suddenly filled Gómez's face. 'Are you suggesting what I think you're suggesting?' he demanded. 'Because if you are, then you're deliberately insulting almost the whole officer corps of this regiment, and that is something I cannot allow to happen.'

'You can put on a good act when you have to,' Paco said, 'but you don't fool me. You were the man who didn't mind me calling his general a butcher, remember. Besides, you're far too intelligent not to have noticed the same things I did – and to have drawn the same conclusions. So why don't you drop the act, and tell me what you really think?'

The anger drained from the major's face almost as quickly as it had appeared. He took a reflective sip of his wine. 'You're right. I have reached the same conclusions. There will have been officers without alibis, so some of those men were obviously lying. But it was not, as you seem to be starting to think, a deliberate attempt to block your investigation.'

'You're saying we might both have seen the same thing, but you understood what was going on in there better than I did?'

'Naturally. I'm one of them. I know how they think. You're nothing but an outsider.'

'And, of course, you can't explain to me how they think,' Paco said caustically. 'It's like the business of when you post a sentry outside Valera's house all over again. If I want to know the logic behind it, I'll have to find out for myself.'

118

Gómez sighed. 'You're not going to let go of this, are you, Inspector?' he asked. 'Unless I explain to you exactly what you've witnessed, you're going to keep coming back to it like a dog worrying a dead sheep.'

'Probably,' Paco agreed.

'Very well, I'll give you your explanation,' Gómez said. 'But before I do that, I want to make it quite clear to you that I do not think that any of the men in the church was capable of killing Lieutenant Anton.'

'Understood.'

'There is a certain spirit in the army – a spirit which is born out of the fact that we all depend on each other. You may have felt a little of it yourself during your military service, but let me assure you, you will only have got the slightest whiff of the real thing.'

He looked at Paco as if he expected some reaction. 'I'm still listening,' the ex-policeman said, deadpan.

'The phrase "brother officer" is not as meaningless as most phrases of that nature are,' Gómez continued. 'In battle, we rely on each other absolutely – trust each other without reservation. And, as a result, we will do anything we can to protect each other anywhere the need arises. That's what you've just seen demonstrated in the church. If it is a conspiracy, as you seem to have decided it is, then it's nothing more than a conspiracy of men who believe in the integrity of their comrades-in-arms, and will do anything to preserve it.'

'Even if it means shielding a murderer.'

Gómez shook his head exasperatedly. 'Don't you understand what I've just said? It is impossible for any of those men to imagine that a brother officer could be a murderer. Besides,' he hesitated for a second, 'as well as personal loyalty, there is the honour of the regiment to consider.'

'What do you mean by that?'

'I mean that since a dishonourable action by the one reflects on the rest, it is perhaps best that the dishonourable action does not come to light. Which means, in its turn, that any man who betrays a brother officer is shunned from then on – both by his equals and his superiors.'

'So we're back to the fact that they'd willingly shield a murderer,' Paco said stubbornly.

'No!' Gómez replied sharply. 'We would never shield a murderer – that would only be to protect one living brother officer at the expense of a dead one. We would deal with the killer – but we would deal with him in our way.'

'I've heard some self-serving bullshit in my time,' Paco said, 'but I really think that takes the prize.'

Gómez shook his head. 'You really don't understand, do you?' he asked. 'You have absolutely no idea of the way we think or of our approach to life. Shall I tell you what I would do if I discovered that Lieutenant Anton's killer was a brother officer?'

Paco shrugged. 'Why not? I might even believe you.'

'The very next day, I would arrange for him to be sent into the thick of the battle. He might well return that evening – many men do – but if he did, then the day which followed I would send him out there again. And the day after that. He could not survive for ever. Every man's luck runs out in the end, and eventually, he would be one of those who was posted as dead.'

Paco looked first up, then down, the street. The military policemen were dragging away a couple of swaying, handcuffed privates, and the soldiers who had tried to get the donkey drunk were now clearly regretting the fact that they had wasted money which could more wisely have been spent on wine.

'What you've just said is very interesting, Major,' he told Gómez, 'but when you examine it carefully, it doesn't really hold water. You claim you would send the guilty man out to the front, but since you're totally incapable of believing your brother officers to be guilty of murder in the first place, that would never, in fact, happen.'

'I said that the officers I spoke to in the church were incapable of believing their comrades-in-arms would commit a murder,' Gómez countered. 'I never claimed to be naïve myself.'

'Yet you've already told me that you're sure none of the men in the church killed Anton.'

'That is correct. I don't think they were involved.'

There was a code behind his words, Paco thought – a code which he obviously expected an ex-policeman to be able to understand. 'So what are you saying?' he asked. 'That while those particular men had nothing to do with the murder, that doesn't rule out all the officers stationed in the village?'

'I'm not the detective, Inspector Ruiz,' Gómez said. 'It's your role to investigate. Mine is to do no more than see to it that you're allowed to do the work you've been trained to do without undue hindrance.'

'You'd never have said what you have if you weren't toying with some kind of theory,' Paco insisted. 'Why don't you tell me what that theory is?'

Major Gómez stood up, produced some coins from his pocket, and uncharacteristically threw them on the table without even counting them. 'It's getting late,' he said. 'I think it's about time I returned to my quarters.'

'Do *you* have an alibi for the time Lieutenant Anton was murdered?' Paco asked.

Gómez smiled, and Paco got the distinct impression that he had been expecting the question – had perhaps even been manoeuvring the conversation in such a direction that it was bound to be asked.

'No, I don't have an alibi,' the major said. 'I'm like all the men in those old cases of yours which you talked about earlier. I was walking around the village entirely alone. It's possible that some of the soldiers might have seen me, but the state most of them were in, I doubt they will remember. Do you have any more questions before I go?'

Paco leant back in his chair, and took a measured sip of his wine. 'Do you think that Colonel Valera will have an alibi?' he asked – and the moment he had put the question he realized that that was what Gómez had been steering him towards all along.

'Colonel Valera!' the major repeated. 'You're aiming high, my friend. Perhaps far too high.'

'Isn't that what you want me to do?' Paco asked. 'And you still haven't answered the question. Do you think Valera's got an alibi?'

'I believe that the colonel will have one,' Gómez said. 'But whether he would ever be willing to produce it is quite another matter.'

Chapter Seventeen

Morning. The military trucks rumbled across the main square under a sky of the deepest Castilian blue. It was going to be another beautiful day – a day which would seem to have no other aim than to show to the people of the mountains how wonderful it was to be alive. But before the sun finally set again, Paco thought, as he crossed the Plaza Mayor, many young men would already have died under that perfect sky.

He stopped by the fountain and lit a cigarette. Enough of thinking of the young men who would be slaughtered like cattle, he told himself. He had problems enough of his own.

He was desperately worried about Cindy Walker. Throughout the whole of her ordeal, she'd shown a courage and resilience which had almost taken his breath away. But even for someone with her magnificent spirit, the strain of being locked up all day – and under virtual sentence of death – had eventually begun to tell.

He had to find a way to get her back behind Republican lines soon. Private Pérez would help him – the rat-faced young man didn't have any choice – but Pérez, for all his cunning, wasn't enough. What Paco really needed was someone more powerful on his side. And there the choice seemed to be restricted to either the devious Major Gómez or the vicious Colonel Valera.

The first thing he saw as he left the square and turned on to the Calle Mayor, was a group of black-clad women huddled together around the doorway of one of the humbler houses. Some of the women were weeping loudly. Others were talking in low, urgent voices. Even from a distance, it was obvious that such a scene could only mean there had been a death.

Paco felt the hairs on the back of his neck prickle. People could – and did – die all the time. There was absolutely nothing to say that this particular death had anything to do with his case. Yet his instinct, backed by the experience of years of investigating violent crime, told him that this *wasn't* an ordinary death – that, like the murder of Lieutenant Anton, it would never have occurred if he hadn't happened to be in the village.

He reached the edge of the small crowd. The women were so wrapped up in their blanket of grief that they didn't even notice his arrival. He laid his hand gently on the shoulder of one of them. The woman looked up to see who had touched her. She had a wrinkled face and nut-brown skin, and though she must have seen many deaths in her time, her eyes still glistened with tears.

'Who died?' Paco asked softly.

'It was C . . . Carmen Sanchez,' the old woman blubbered. 'Her mother's a cousin of mine.'

'So she wasn't a very *old* lady?'

'Old? No! She was barely more than a girl.'

Paco eased his way through the crowd to the front door, brushed aside the bead curtain, and entered the house. He found himself in a single large room, which had a kitchen with a wood-burning range at the back of it. In the centre of the room was a rough wooden table, and at it sat an old woman with her head in her hands – almost definitely the cousin of the mourner outside. Another woman, probably not more than forty herself, sat at the old woman's left, and was whispering earnestly into her ear. A white-haired parish priest, who plainly felt useless in this women's world of sorrow, stood awkwardly in the corner.

The younger of the two women looked up when she heard Paco's footsteps. 'I recognize you,' she said dully. 'You're that detective from Madrid. What are you doing here?'

'I've come to find out what's happened,' Paco replied sympathetically. 'Who are you?'

'I'm Isabel Cordobés.'

'A relative?'

'No. Not a relative. A neighbour. I'm just here to offer Rosa what comfort I can.'

The older woman lifted her hands from her face. 'There can be no comfort for me!' she wailed. 'My poor, misguided daughter has taken her own life, and now she will burn in hell for all eternity.'

Paco looked across at the parish priest, who merely shrugged at him as if to say, 'What can I tell you? The poor woman is quite right.'

'When did this happen?' Paco asked.

'I don't know for sure,' Isabel Cordobés told him.

'Of course you don't,' Paco agreed. 'But we should be able to pin it down roughly. When was the dead woman last seen alive?'

'She was fine when her mother and I went to the church at eight o'clock,' Isabel told him. 'She said she'd have some coffee waiting for us when we got back. But there was no coffee and we . . . we found her hanging from the ham hook in the bedroom.'

'The ham hook?' Paco repeated, mystified.

'Rosa has a great fear of thieves,' Isabel said, stroking the old woman. 'When she's draining a ham, she always does it upstairs.'

It made sense, Paco thought. A leg of *jamon serano* was probably the greatest luxury that a peasant woman would ever indulge herself in. What better place to keep it at night than in the security of her bedroom?

'It's all my fault,' the dead woman's mother moaned. 'If the hook hadn't been there, she'd never have done it.'

'Did she leave a note?' Paco asked.

Isabel shrugged. 'I don't know whether she did or not. We didn't look. What does it matter, anyway?'

'Can I see her, please?' Paco asked.

'Why should you want to do that?' Isabel asked, suddenly suspicious of this stranger.

Paco was not sure he even knew the answer to that question himself – except that he couldn't throw off the feeling that this death was somehow connected to those of Anton and the dog. 'I'd just like to pay my respects,' he said.

The younger woman looked questioningly at the older one, who nodded her head apathetically.

'She's upstairs on her mother's bed,' Isabel said. 'Do you want me to come with you?'

'That won't be necessary,' Paco told her. 'Which room is it? The one on the left of the stairs, or the one on the right?'

'The one on the left.'

Paco climbed the wooden stairs and opened the left-hand door. The room he entered had whitewashed walls, and was furnished only with an iron bed, a washstand, an old wardrobe and a stool which was lying on its side. A mirror was mounted on the wall facing the bed, and over the bed itself hung a large crucifix.

The woman lying on the bed was dressed in black, and had been in her early thirties. Even someone who was seeing her for the first time would have been able to guess that though she was past her best, she'd been very pretty in life. But Paco wasn't seeing her for the first time. He'd caught a glimpse of her once before – when she was standing in the doorway of Colonel Valera's office.

Why would a woman who had seemed perfectly normal the day before choose to hang herself at around half past eight on this beautiful summer morning, he asked himself. Why would a woman who'd promised to have the coffee made for her mother's return suddenly decide, instead, to greet the old woman with her own lifeless body?

He looked up at the wooden beam which ran the length of the bedroom ceiling. The ham hook, made from a single piece of what was probably steel, was firmly embedded in the centre of the beam, and hanging from the hook was part of the twisted bed sheet which Carmen had used to strangle herself.

Paco searched around for the rest of the sheet, and found it on the floor beside the bed. He took it over to the window, so he could examine it in better light. The noose was tied in a very professional way, he noted. But what did that prove? All peasants began to learn how to tie knots as soon as they could walk, and Carmen Sanchez would have been no exception.

It was because his police training had taught him to be methodical, rather than for any other reason, that he decided to examine the part of the sheet which was still draped around the hook. Since it was obvious he wasn't going to be able to reach the hook without standing on something, he looked around, and saw the upturned stool. That, he thought, would do nicely.

Even standing on the stool, he found he had to stretch a little to loosen the knot which secured one end of the bed sheet to the hook, but less than a minute later he was examining this piece of evidence, too, in the light which streamed in from the window.

The second knot was as professional as the first. Paco tried to reconcile two conflicting images in his mind. One was of a woman so desperate to end her life that she had no thought of the distress she could cause for her ageing mother when she came home. The other was of a woman who, despite that desperation, had taken the time to make knots which were so neat in their execution they could almost have been military.

You're being an idiot, he told himself angrily. You're only now starting to realize something which should have been more than obvious to you at least two minutes ago.

He dropped the sheet and stood on the stool again, once more stretching slightly to get his finger completely over the hook. He nodded his head, as if he had just confirmed what he'd already strongly suspected. 'You bastard!' he hissed. 'You evil son of a bitch.'

Paco walked over to the bed, and looked down at the dead woman. Her eyes had been closed – probably by Isabel Cordobés, the neighbour – but it was a simple enough matter to peel back one of the eyelids. The eye which stared lifelessly up at him hardly bulged at all, nor did the woman's face have the bloated look which was common in most cases of hanging. He lifted her head a few centimetres off the pillow with his left hand. Then he ran the fingers of his right hand slowly across the back of the dead woman's head. Without experiencing any feeling of triumph, he found exactly what he'd been expecting to find.

*

Downstairs in that house of sorrow, nothing had changed. The white-haired priest still stood helplessly in the corner, the neighbour continued to speak soft, soothing words to the bereaved mother. Paco crossed the room and opened the back door. An alley ran behind the house – an alley which was deserted then and had probably been deserted at half past eight that morning. Of course! That was the way it would have to have been.

He re-entered the house, and sat down at the table opposite Isabel. 'I know this is a difficult time, señora, but would you mind if I asked you a few questions?' he said.

The woman looked up at him. 'Questions?' she repeated. 'What kind of questions?'

'You were with Carmen's mother when she found her daughter, weren't you?'

'That's right. Like I said, we had just come back from the church. It was our day to clean it.'

'And what exactly happened?'

'We expected Carmen to be waiting here for us. When she wasn't, Rosa called out her name, but . . . but, of course, she didn't answer.'

'Go on,' Paco said encouragingly.

'Rosa wasn't really worried then. She made a joke about the idle girl probably having fallen asleep on her bed and went upstairs to look for her. She'd been gone for less than a minute when I heard her scream. I ran straight up the stairs myself, and saw Carmen hanging there. Rosa was in a terrible state. She didn't seem to be able to move, but she couldn't stop screaming either. I knew we had to do something. I came downstairs again to look for a knife. You know – to cut her down.'

'I understand.'

'I went back to the bedroom. Rosa was a little better by then. While she held Carmen so she wouldn't fall, I cut through the sheet. We laid her on the bed and I felt her neck for a pulse. But there wasn't one.'

'Think very carefully about your next answer, señora,' Paco said. 'Was there any furniture in the room at the time which has since been removed?'

'Furniture?'

'A chair? A blanket-chest? Something of that nature?'

'No,' Isabel said firmly. 'There was nothing there then that isn't still there now.'

Paco turned his attention to the grieving mother. 'Listen to me, Señora Sanchez,' he said softly, 'you don't have to worry about your daughter's immortal soul any more. She won't go to hell.'

'Not go to hell!' said the white-haired priest, speaking for the first time. 'But she killed herself and that is a mor—'

'She didn't kill herself,' Paco interrupted, 'although that's what you were all meant to think. I'm positive that she was murdered.'

'How can you be so sure?' the priest demanded.

'The sheet was carefully knotted around the hook,' Paco explained. 'Standing on the stool, I could just about have done the job myself, but Carmen was shorter than I am. She couldn't have reached the hook, which means she couldn't have tied that knot, which, in turn, means that someone much taller than her did the job.'

'Perhaps some wicked person assisted her?' the priest suggested.

'No! What some wicked person *did* do was to hit her on the head before he strung her up. There's a huge contusion on the back of her skull.' Paco turned his attention back to the mother. 'She didn't suffer much, Señora Sanchez,' he said. 'By the time the noose was put around her neck, she was probably already dead.'

Chapter Eighteen

Though the women did their grieving out in the streets, the men found it hard to express their sorrow without a glass of wine in front of them. So it had always been in Spanish villages, and when Paco entered the bar closest to the murdered woman's house – a slightly shabby place with cracked wall tiles and faded bull-fighting posters – the room was already full of customers eulogizing about the life of poor Carmen Sanchez.

The ex-policeman ordered a red wine at the counter, then, with a deceptively casual air, he looked around him for a potential source of information. All the men in the bar were late middle-aged at least, he noted. But then that was hardly a surprise. When the army took over the village all the younger men would either have fled, been conscripted – or ended up in front of a firing squad.

He finally settled on three ancient drinkers who were sitting at a rickety table in the corner of the bar. They had been watching him with interest since he arrived, and seemed just the sort of garrulous old souls who would tell him all he wanted to know – and probably much more. He made his way over to their table, and asked if he could join them.

'You're that policeman from Madrid, aren't you?' said the man who was probably the oldest of the ancient trio.

'That's right,' Paco agreed.

'And you've seen her? Carmen, I mean?'

'Yes, I have.'

The old man pushed a stool from under the table in Paco's direction. 'Take a seat, and tell us all about it,' he said.

Paying the price for information he'd already known he'd have to pay, Paco described the hook, the knotted sheet, and how it had all led to the conclusion that Carmen Sanchez had been murdered. The old men listened to his narrative with a mixture of sorrow, amazement and morbid curiosity. When he'd finished, one of them removed his beret, scratched his bald head and said, 'But who would have done such a terrible thing?'

'I have no idea,' Paco said. 'Did she have any enemies in the village that you know of?'

'Enemies? Why would Carmen have had enemies? She was a very quiet young woman.'

'Nobody gets through life without acquiring enemies,' Paco told him. 'She could, for example, have had a boyfriend who found out she was seeing someone else, and killed her in a jealous rage.'

The old man shook his head. 'Carmen never had a boyfriend in San Fernando. Never even had the chance to find one.'

'Why was that?'

'She left the village just after her twelfth birthday, and from that day to this, she's only come back for her holidays. She wouldn't still have been here now if the war hadn't cut off the road to Madrid.'

She left the village when she was twelve, Paco repeated thoughtfully to himself. For what reason? Had she, perhaps, met a young army officer who was passing through the village, and fallen in love with him? And had that same army officer been so captivated by her that, despite her age, he'd persuaded her to abandon her family and live as his mistress? If that was what had happened, then it was Valera's presence in San Fernando, and not the outbreak of war, which had kept her there.

'Why did she leave?' he said aloud. 'And where did she go?'

'She left because she got a job in Miraflores through her mother's second cousin. A very good job, it was, too. She worked for some rich people who had a house so big it was almost a palace. She told me all about it. They had stables, and baths with gold taps and dozens of servants to wait on them hand and foot. She was sitting pretty.'

Perhaps she was, Paco thought. Or perhaps the story of the big house with dozens of servants was nothing more than that – a story.

'Did anyone from San Fernando ever go visit Carmen in Miraflores?' he asked.

The old man looked at him as if he were deranged. 'Why would they want to do that?'

Paco forced himself to suppress a smile. He was dealing with peasants here, he reminded himself. For them, the world consisted of a distance from their own village which could comfortably be reached on foot, or on the back of a donkey. Miraflores, which was over thirty kilometres away, was so distant to them that even if Carmen had never set foot in the place, it would still have been quite safe for her to have claimed to be living there.

'Yes, she did really well for herself,' the old man continued. 'Didn't have to scrub the floors or polish the furniture like a lot of girls who go into service do. She learned a trade, you see, and you can't go wrong if you've learned a trade.'

'No, you can't,' Paco agreed.

But he was already picturing Carmen Sanchez living in a series of lodging houses, moving when the army moved, and spending most of her time yearning for the moment when her dashing officer could find the time to visit her.

'And she was good at her trade,' the old man continued. 'She brought some of the things she'd made back to the village to show us. Wonderful work, it was. Pillow cases with fine embroidery on them. Handkerchiefs it was almost a shame to use. The people she worked for even let her make clothes for them – though, God knows, they could easily have afforded to pay shop prices if they'd wanted to. That's how good she was.'

There came a moment in many of his cases when Paco had an insight which almost took his breath away – a moment which changed his whole perspective. When that happened, he always felt as if, up to that point in the investigation, he'd been like a man groping around in a dark room and occasionally banging into the furniture. The insights, on the other hand, were like a light being turned on – a light which enabled him to see each piece of furniture, and to comprehend how they all fitted together to make a whole. And as he sat in that shabby bar, drinking with the three old men, he was suddenly gripped by one of those insights of his. He knew now why Carmen Sanchez had had to die, why the dog had had to die, and why Colonel Valera had been so discreet about his mistress.

'Are you all right, señor?' one of the old men asked him. 'You've gone very pale all of a sudden.'

'A seamstress!' Paco exclaimed excitedly. 'Carmen Sanchez was a bloody seamstress!'

*

The sun was high over the Plaza Mayor as Paco crossed it for the second time that day, and the dogs who spent their mornings scavenging had already taken shelter in the shady arcades. Outside one of the bars, two whores were arguing with a large man who was probably their pimp, and over at the fountain a donkey which didn't have the sense to get out of the heat was thirstily lapping up water.

Paco checked his watch. It was just after two o'clock. Cindy would be expecting him for lunch, and he couldn't wait to see her. He felt like a conquering hero coming home from the wars weighed down with the spoils of victory. And what spoils they were! They were more precious than gold, worth more than a whole sackful of diamonds. The spoils were knowledge – a knowledge which he just might be able to use to save both their lives.

As usual, there were sentries posted outside the small house on Calle Jose Antonio. Paco recognized one of them as the corporal he'd threatened to kill if the man ever again called Cindy a whore, but he was feeling so elated that even the reminder of that unpleasant confrontation didn't really get to him.

The sentries had been standing on either side of the door, but now that they saw him coming they shifted position so they were actually blocking it.

Something's gone wrong, Paco told himself, as he felt a ball of fear start to form in the pit of his stomach. Something's gone very badly wrong. He came to a halt in front of the two guards. 'Would you step aside, please? I want to go inside the house,' he said to them.

The corporal sneered at him. 'And I want to shag the general's wife from supper right through to breakfast time,' he said. 'But we can't always get what we want.'

The ball of fear in Paco's stomach was growing by the second, but it was not fear for himself – it was for Cindy. 'Have you forgotten I'm working on an investigation for Major Gómez?' he asked. 'He's given orders that I'm to have fullest co-operation.'

The corporal's sneer widened. 'Major Gómez?' he mused. 'Well, Major Gómez is a very important man around here, there's no disputing that fact. But I think that even you will have to agree that he's still not *quite* as important as General Castro.'

'What are you trying to say?' Paco demanded.

'The general's orders are that, apart from Major Gómez, nobody's to be allowed to enter this house. And nobody is to be allowed to leave it.'

The fear had grown so great that Paco had to force himself not to vomit. 'Is Cindy . . . is Señorita Walker . . .?' he gasped.

'Is she what?' the corporal asked, enjoying Paco's obvious distress. 'Is she still inside? Is she still unharmed? Yes, to both those things. All in accordance with the general's orders. But who's to say when the situation might change? At the best of times, General Castro is an unpredictable man,' he leered, 'and I, for one have hopes of eventually getting lucky.'

It would be so easy to kill the son of a bitch, Paco thought. A single blow with the heel of his hand would wipe away that lascivious smile for ever. But the corporal's death would swiftly be followed by his own – and who would be left to protect Cindy then?

'I didn't mention the fact that the general wants to see you, did I?' the corporal asked.

'You know you didn't,' Paco replied.

'Wants to see you *urgently*,' the corporal said. 'He's had men out looking for you for the past fifteen minutes.'

Chapter Nineteen

Paco stood with his back to the wall, looking across the courtyard which had been filled with the general's furniture on his last visit, but was now completely empty. On another occasion, he might have speculated about what life had been like in the old days, when fine coaches had driven through the large double doors, so that the aristocrats inside them would not have to walk more than a few metres to reach their rooms. But this was no time for thoughts of that nature – it was a time to concentrate all his efforts on surviving for the next hour, so that he might have a chance of surviving the hour after that.

His earlier nausea had all but gone, but his fears for Cindy were still with him, and would stay with him until he knew that she was safely back in Madrid. He had been a fool to feel so cocky earlier, he told himself. It was true he had uncovered some very deep secrets, but of what value was that if he never got a chance to put them to use?

There was a sound of clicking heels on the stairs. The general's wife! His enemy! Paco kept his gaze fixed firmly on a spot high on the opposite wall.

The nature of the clicking changed as the woman crossed the courtyard, then stopped altogether. 'What's this bastard doing here again?' the general's wife shrieked at one of the two soldiers who were serving as Paco's escort.

'He's here because the general says he wants to see him, señora,' the soldier replied.

'Does he?' the woman demanded. 'Does he, indeed? Well, we'll soon see about that!'

Without knocking, she flung open the door of the general's office, and stormed inside. 'Did you issue orders for that son of a bitch militiaman from Madrid to be brought here?' Paco heard her demand loudly the second she was through the door.

'Well, yes, my dear, I did,' the little general squeaked back. 'You see, we have not yet found the man who killed Principe—'

'Nor will you, as long as that incompetent fool is conducting the investigation,' his wife retorted. 'You should have had him shot days ago. If you ask me, he's nothing but a spy.'

'He can't be a spy, my love,' the general said weakly. 'He was captured in the fighting out on the sierra.'

'That's what he wants you to think,' his wife countered. 'But I wouldn't be in the least surprised if he arranged to be captured. Why don't you have him shot while you still have the chance?'

The general coughed nervously. 'You're looking exceptionally beautiful today, my dear. Isn't that the dress I bought you for your birthday that you're wearing?'

His wife gave a loud sigh of exasperation. 'You know it is. You know because you always remember everything you've ever bought for me. But tell me, do you really think I'm such an empty-headed woman that you can divert me from my purpose with flattery?'

'No, my dear,' the general said contritely. 'Of course not. I'm very sorry, my dear.'

'Don't you know what we're doing here?' his wife demanded. 'We are engaged in a holy crusade. We have been entrusted by God – by *God* – with the duty of purging our beloved Spain of the atheists and the Communists, and all those who reject the station given to them in life by divine decree.'

A minor actress from a humble background, and she talked that way, Paco thought. But, of course, it was mainly *because* of her background that she did. No one is more afraid of slipping down the social scale than the people who have had to painfully claw their way up it.

'Purifying the Fatherland will be a bloody business, yet it must be done,' the general's wife continued. 'And you, my husband, could be at the forefront of it.' Her voice dropped, but not so low that Paco couldn't still hear it. 'When this war is over, when right and justice have triumphed, the country will be looking for new leaders. And who do you think those new leaders will be?'

'Perhaps Mola and Franco,' the general suggested tentatively. 'They have been the ones who—'

'The new leaders will be the men who fulfilled their duty with the utmost zeal!' his wife interrupted him. 'The men who have dispatched the most of the enemy to eternal hellfire.'

'I'm sure you're right, my dear,' the general said. 'And I'll make sure to do just as you say. But listen, I've taught Reina to do a new trick today. She can roll over and play dead. Would you like to see her do it?'

'There's only one death I'm concerned with at the moment,' his wife said relentlessly. 'I want to see that Communist scum of a militiaman outside this door taken down to the Plaza Mayor and executed!'

'All in good time, my dear,' the general assured her soothingly. 'All in good time.'

'Oh, you're impossible!' the general's wife screamed. 'You have an ideal opportunity in this war to really make your name for yourself, and all you seem to be concerned about is teaching the dog to fetch and roll over. Sometimes I wish you were more like Major Gómez.'

'Gómez is a good officer—' the general began.

'Gómez is nothing more than a scheming snake,' his wife cut in. 'In fact, I would sooner trust any snake than trust him. But one day – perhaps sooner than you think – he will be a general in his own right. And then where will *you* be?'

A renewed clicking of her heels – angrier than it had been before – told Paco that she was leaving the office again. He braced himself for the worst. The woman closed the door after her. Paco was aware that she was standing directly in front of him, but he continued to stare at a spot on the opposite wall, high above her head.

'Look at me!' the general's wife commanded. 'Look at me, you godless bastard.'

Paco lowered his own eyes until they met hers, which were flashing with the deepest kind of hatred. 'Did you hear what I've just been telling my husband?' she asked.

'No, señora.'

'Liar!' she screamed, slapping him hard across the face. 'Bloody liar! You heard every word of it. And you heard what he said to me – that he will keep you alive for the moment, but when the right time comes, he'll have you executed. So now you know you're a dead man whatever you do.' She stepped back a little so he could get the full effect of her haughty expression. 'A real man wouldn't just wait around until the firing squad came for him,' she hissed. 'He would try to make his escape whenever he saw his opportunity. But then you aren't a real man, are you? You're lower than a guttersnipe.'

She had had her say, and now she turned and walked away. Paco lifted his hand up to his stinging face. It was interesting that she had left the door open while she'd ranted at the general, he thought – and even more interesting that she had closed it before talking to him.

*

The fat little general sat behind his huge desk, and glared at Paco. 'Do you know why I've had you brought here?' he asked.

'No, sir.'

'I had you brought here because it has been drawn to my attention that you've been spreading a vicious rumour around the village that a woman who hanged herself this morning was, in fact, murdered. And what I want to know is this – exactly what was your purpose in telling such fantastic lies?'

'They weren't lies,' Paco replied. 'Someone knocked her out, and then strung her up. There was a bruise on the back of her head. Anyway, she wasn't tall enough to have tied the bed-sheet to the hook she was hanging from herself'

The general slowly absorbed this new information. 'Then what you are saying is that there have been *two* murders since you began your investigation into poor Principe's death?'

'Yes, señor.'

The general's already piggy eyes narrowed even further. 'How do I know that you were not involved in the murders yourself?' he asked.

'If I killed Carmen Sanchez, then surely I would have been a fool to go around telling the people who had already accepted it as a suicide that it was, in fact, a murder,' Paco pointed out.

'True,' the general agreed, nodding his round little head. He sighed. 'This is a very sorry state of affairs indeed. I'm expecting to be leading part of the big push on Madrid within the next couple of days, and I need this unfortunate matter cleaning up by then. That is why it is imperative that you find the killer of my poor little dog – and, of course, the murderer of my officer and that unfortunate peasant woman – within the next twenty-four hours.'

For a second, Paco considered trying to trade the name of the killer for a safe passage out of the village. But that wouldn't work, because the truth he'd have to deliver to the general would be so unpalatable that Castro would probably have him shot anyway, whatever he'd promised beforehand. No, the only way to escape would be to threaten, rather than negotiate – and he had nothing he could threaten the general with.

'Haven't you anything to say for yourself?' the general demanded. 'No whining excuse for why you have failed to complete the task I set you?'

'You have to understand my position, sir,' Paco replied. 'If I were back in Madrid, I would have access to the forensic lab, a team of other officers whom I could use to check out—'

The general dismissed his argument with an impatient wave of his podgy hand. 'You are making difficulties where none exists,' he said. 'If I had the time, I could find the man myself – and I am a soldier, not a policeman.'

'You could find him?' Paco asked, before he could stop himself.

'Of course,' the general replied. 'The murderer must obviously be someone from the other side of the front line . . .'

'We have no evidence of that.'

'. . . because no one but a godless Republican would commit such terrible deeds. And once we have grasped that one simple idea, it should be very easy to spot the guilty party, shouldn't it?'

'I'm afraid that I don't understand your line of reasoning, sir,' Paco confessed.

The general sighed at the ex-policeman's obvious stupidity. 'Even if he is in disguise – as I expect he is – surely the man capable of such wickedness will show it in the very way he carries himself,' he said.

He had swallowed his own rhetoric – or rather his wife's rhetoric – Paco realized with utter astonishment. As far as the general was concerned, all Republicans were nothing more than shifty-eyed, nun-raping devils, while the Nationalists were all straight and true and virtuous.

'In fact,' the general continued, 'the more I think about this matter, the more convinced I become that you have already discovered the guilty party, but, for reasons of your own, are conspiring to keep him hidden.'

He was getting too close to the truth – far too close to it. 'I have some good leads,' Paco said. 'If you'll just give me a little more time—'

'Silence!' the general squeaked. 'It is obvious to me that you need a stronger incentive to make you carry out your work diligently. Very well then, I'll give you one. If the guilty party is not brought to me by eight o'clock tomorrow morning at the very latest, I will have this woman of yours handed over to my officers for their amusement. When they are bored with her, she'll be passed on to the enlisted men, and when even they've finished with her, I'll have her shot.'

He couldn't mean it, Paco thought, horrified. Even a man like the general couldn't be contemplating such a monstrous deed. But deep down inside himself, he knew that the general could. It didn't matter if his men raped Cindy, because she was from the Republican side, and hence a whore already. It didn't matter if he had her shot, either – since she was little more than vermin in his eyes.

'Let her go!' Paco pleaded. 'Let her go, and I promise you on my honour as a Spaniard that I will have the case solved by morning.'

'Your honour as a Spaniard,' the general said contemptuously. 'You have no honour, or you would be fighting on our side. I've already told you what will happen if you don't bring me the results I require. Now get out of my sight!'

*

Out on the street once more, Paco took in a lungful of the fresh mountain air, and tried to will his racing heart to slow down. Though he had killed in the past, he had never actively wanted to kill anyone before he came to this village. Now he had a list which was growing by the hour, and the little general had just placed himself right at the top of it.

He took another breath of air in an attempt to clear from his body the foetid atmosphere of corruption and bigotry which existed in Castro's office. After the gloom inside the *palacio*, the bright sunlight on the Calle Mayor was almost blinding. Paco shaded his eyes, and looked down the street. There were a few soldiers around, but most of them had gone out to the front line which the general confidently expected to start advancing towards Madrid within the next two days. He wondered again how many of the boys who had left for battle that morning would come back in the evening. He prayed, fervently, that Private Pérez would be one of those who returned – because he would need the rat-faced soldier if the desperate plan he had still only half formulated was to have even the slightest chance of working.

Chapter Twenty

Darkness fell over the sierra, and with it came another day's lull in the fighting – another chance for the men who knew just how expendable they were to drown their fears in alcohol for a few short hours. For Paco, the arrival of the evening had a very different significance. It offered him his one and only chance to see his plan through to success, and it served as a painful reminder that if the plan didn't succeed, Cindy would be handed over to the soldiers soon after the light had returned.

He threaded his way through the crowd along the Calle Mayor. Drunken soldiers, hardly aware of where they were, stumbled into him. Prostitutes, attracted by the fact that he was wearing a suit, propositioned him every few metres, their voices crooning hoarsely, their breaths smelling of cheap brandy, as they offered him forbidden pleasures at bargain prices.

He reached the church steps and was more than relieved to see Private Pérez sitting there, smoking a cigarette with his usual care.

'What are you doing here?' he asked the soldier. 'Waiting for Jiménez to stop praying, so the two of you can spend his wages?'

'Something like that,' the rat-faced soldier agreed.

'You're a liar,' Paco told him pleasantly. 'We both know that Jiménez isn't here to pray.'

Pérez held up his cigarette, and examined its glowing end against the night sky. 'If Jiménez's not here to pray, then why is he here?'

'Because he's the one with the reputation for being religious – so he's the one you can send to check up without anyone getting suspicious.'

Pérez's eyes narrowed. 'Check up?' he said. 'Check up on what?'

'On whether they're still there, of course.'

'I don't know what you're talking about.'

'Let's go inside,' Paco suggested.

Pérez shook his head. 'I've told you before, I don't hold with none of that religion.'

'But you like money,' Paco pointed out. 'And you place a considerable value on that miserable skin of yours. So bearing those two things in mind, perhaps it would be wise to do as I say.'

Reluctantly, the private rose to his feet, and stood aside to let the ex-policeman enter the church.

'Oh no!' Paco said. 'After you.'

Private Jiménez was kneeling down in his customary pew near to the Virgin. Paco walked down the aisle, only coming to a halt when he was standing directly over the country boy. 'Listen, lad, there's no need to keep up that pretence any longer,' he told him.

Jiménez lifted his head, and Paco could see the puzzled expression on his face. 'I beg your pardon, señor?' the young peasant said.

Perhaps it wasn't pretence at all, Paco thought. There was no reason why the private couldn't be both praying to the God his mother had drummed into him and doing the job that Pérez had sent him in to do.

Pérez! his brain screamed. The rat-faced soldier should have been right there beside him – and he wasn't. Paco looked quickly around the church. There was no sign of the man he'd once arrested for murder.

He cursed himself for being so careless. 'There's no need for games, Pérez,' he said loudly. 'If I'd meant to do you any harm, I'd never have been so foolish as to come here alone.'

His words echoed around the high rafters over his head. 'Alone . . . alone . . . alone . . .'

There was a slight noise from somewhere near the back of the church – almost a scuttling sound. Perez was on his hands and knees, a rat-faced soldier who could actually move like a rat when he needed to.

'Have you got a knife on you, Private Pérez?' Paco asked. 'Your sort usually does have one. Or do you prefer to use a razor? Whichever it is, you won't be needing it tonight. I'm here to help you. Why don't you come out of hiding so we can talk about it?'

'*You* talk about it, then *I'll* decide whether or not I'm coming out,' Pérez said.

The sound of his voice had pinned him down more accurately than his scuttling had done, but he would be long gone from that spot by the time Paco reached it. Besides, if he could not win Pérez's co-operation with words, he could not win it with anything.

Paco walked towards the altar, then turned round again slowly, so as to make it obvious that he wasn't playing a trick on Pérez. 'The soldiers who searched the village were looking for a dog's collar,' he said. 'They shouldn't have been. What they should really have been looking for were the things which gave the collar its value – the jewels which were set in it. What did you do with the collar once you'd taken those jewels out, Pérez?'

'I've no idea what you're talking about,' the private said – and now his voice sounded much closer than it had before.

'It doesn't really matter what you did with it,' Paco said. 'A strip of leather and a buckle would have been easy enough to destroy. But you still had the problem of the gemstones on your hands, didn't you? Where could you hide them? I expect it was Jiménez who gave you the idea.'

'You're still not making any sense to me.'

Paco turned his attention to the still-kneeling Private Jiménez. 'Do you ever tell your drinking friends in the Calle Mayor about the village you come from, son?' he asked.

'Sometimes,' the boy admitted.

Of course he would. What else would someone like him – a peasant with little imagination – have to talk about? 'And what, exactly, do you tell them?'

Words were not the country boy's forte, and he had to struggle hard to find the right ones. 'I . . . I tell them about how the sun shines on the houses, and the wind blows in from the mountains,' he said finally. 'I tell them how, when it rains, the water can soak right through to the bones.'

'Anything else?'

'I talk about the livestock we have at our little farm, and the crops that my family grow . . .'

'And you tell them about your village Virgin, don't you?' Paco interrupted. 'About how your Virgin is so beautiful that, though the people of the villages around yours would never admit it, they envy you.'

Jiménez bowed his head, and was silent.

'*Don't you?*' Paco insisted.

'Yes,' Jiménez confessed.

Naturally he did. Even non-believers took pride in their village Virgin and considered her far above any of her local rivals. 'What did you say about her?' Paco asked.

'That she has the most wonderful expression on her face. That she has as much gold paint on her cloak as any Virgin from the big town . . .'

'And that her jewellery looks almost real?'

'Yes.'

Pérez had heard the country boy's words and – when they were standing over the murdered dog with its expensive collar still around its neck – that had been the inspiration for his plan.

'Look at this Virgin, Private Jiménez,' Paco said. 'Infinite care has been taken over the carving and the painting – except with the jewellery. There, the craftsman was as clumsy as a beginner. The pattern's irregular. The shape – the flow of the whole statue – is destroyed by the way he's placed the jewels. Now why do you think that should be?'

'You tell us,' said Private Pérez – and now he seemed altogether too close for comfort.

'Because while some of the stones are merely carved and painted, some of them are the real things,' Paco said. He ran his finger over one of them, removing the layer of dust which had been artfully placed there, and even in the dim light of the church, it sparkled. 'How did you fix the jewels on to the statue, Pérez?' he asked. 'With glue?'

'I didn't want to do it!' Private Jiménez blubbered. 'I said it was wrong from the very start. But Pérez told me that the Virgin only helps those who help themselves.'

'Shut up!' the rat-faced soldier said viciously.

But the country boy was not to be silenced. 'I prayed to her every day to see if she minded us using her like that,' he sobbed. 'Every day! But she never gave me an answer.'

'There are two of us – and only one of you,' Pérez said, from somewhere not far from Paco's right shoulder. 'We could kill you here and now, and nobody would ever be the wiser.'

'If you think Jiménez would go along with that plan, you're very much mistaken,' Paco said, glancing quickly down at the bowed and still-sobbing country boy.

'Then I'll do the job myself,' the rat-faced private told him. 'I've taken on bigger men than you before, and like you said, I'm the one with the knife.'

'But how can you be sure that killing me will solve all your problems?' Paco asked. 'What if I've written a letter to the general, to be handed over in the event of my death, which explains exactly what you did with the collar?'

'By the time he gets it, the jewels will be gone,' Pérez argued. 'So there'll be no proof that we had anything to do with the theft.'

Paco threw back his head and laughed. 'Are you forgetting what sort of times we're living in?' he asked. 'Don't you realize just how cheap life has become? If I tell the general in my letter that you shot his dog, he will believe it without question because—'

'But we didn't shoot the dog!'

'He will believe it because it is what he *wants* to believe – because that will be easier for him than accepting the truth.'

'The truth?' Pérez repeated. 'Are you saying that you know who shot the dog?'

'Oh yes,' Paco replied. 'I know who killed the dog, and how I can use that information to escape. But I'm going to need some assistance. You told me you'd like to get out of here if you could, Pérez. Well, I can get you out – you *and* your jewels. But first you're going to have to learn to trust me.'

He had made his pitch, and there was nothing more he could say to persuade Pérez to join him. So now the matter was in the hands of the man with the knife, who was hiding somewhere within striking distance. If the rat-faced private decided to take him at his word, there was still a chance his plan would work. If not, he was as good as dead.

It would not take a quick mind like Pérez's long to make his choice, Paco thought. Ten seconds at the most. He started to count slowly. One . . . two . . . three . . . four . . . five . . .

He had reached nine when Pérez suddenly emerged from a pew frighteningly close to him. 'I always said that you were a lot straighter than most of the cops I've come across in Madrid,' the private said. 'But if you do try to double-cross me on this—'

'I won't,' Paco interrupted. He glanced down at Jiménez, who had remained on his knees during the whole confrontation. 'Let's go somewhere we can talk privately, shall we?' he suggested.

'Why not?' Pérez agreed. 'Do you want me to lead the way, like I did when we came in?'

'No,' Paco said. 'I've got to start trusting you some time, and it might as well be now.'

He turned and walked down the aisle. Pérez fell in step just behind him, and Paco's heart began to beat a little faster because, despite what he'd said about trusting the rat-faced private, he would not have been entirely surprised if he'd suddenly felt a searing pain in his back.

'That's far enough,' Pérez said, when they'd almost reached the church door. 'Jiménez can't hear us from this distance, and I'd rather be here than out on the street when I decide whether or not I like what you've got to tell me.'

'There are really three main things that I'm going to need you for—' Paco began.

'Just a minute,' Pérez interrupted. 'You keep saying "you" like it was only me you're talking about.'

'It is.'

'Then there's no deal,' Pérez said firmly.

'Oh, for God's sake!' Paco protested. 'Things are going to be difficult enough as it is. If you want to take your whole gang out with you, they'll be bloody impossible.'

'No, not my whole gang,' Pérez told him. He made a stabbing gesture over his left shoulder with his thumb. 'I just want to take Jiménez.'

'Jiménez?' Paco repeated, incredulously. 'Why him?'

Pérez shrugged awkwardly, as if the conversation were taking a turn which he was starting to find uncomfortable. 'Jiménez would be lost without me to look after him,' he said. 'So that's the deal. It's both of us, or neither of us.'

He meant it, Paco thought. He'd rather stay behind himself than leave without the dull-witted country boy. Jiménez's muscle might come in useful at some point in the operation,' he conceded. 'All right, he can come with us.'

Pérez grinned. 'Hey, Jiménez!' he shouted across the rows of pews. 'I've some good news for you. This policeman here thinks we need you for this job we're about to pull. I tried convincing him you'll be a liability, but he just won't listen. So it looks like you're in.' He turned back to Paco. 'Let's get down to brass tacks. How do we get out of the village, and what do I have to do to earn a place for Jiménez and me?'

'We'll get out of the village because we'll already have created a diversion which should keep the sentries busy,' Paco told him. 'But before we get to that stage, there's a couple of other little jobs we'll have to do.'

'And what might they be?'

'The first one will be to break into a house on the Plaza de Santa Teresa,' Paco said.

'That's no problem,' Pérez told him. 'When I was kid, my old man used to take me out on burglaries with him. I was small, you see, so I could get through the windows people thought weren't big enough to bother putting bars on.'

'Can you pick a lock?'

'Sure. My old man was at the top of his profession, and he taught me all he knew. I can even crack a safe, if I have to.'

'I don't think that what we'll be looking for will be in a safe,' Paco said.

'What's the second thing?' Pérez asked.

'The second thing?'

'You said there were a couple of little jobs we'd have to do. The first one seems like a piece of cake, which has got me thinking that the second one probably isn't quite so easy.'

He was right, Paco thought. The second job would require more nerve than breaking into a house – more nerve, perhaps, than even the hardened little criminal from Madrid possessed.

'Well, what is it?' Pérez demanded. 'Come on! Spit it out!'

'Again, it's only something small,' Paco said. 'Something that will only take a minute or two at the most.'

'And what might that small thing be?'

'All I want you to do,' Paco said, slowly and deliberately, 'is to threaten to take the life of a high-ranking officer.'

Chapter Twenty-One

The sentry standing on guard duty outside Colonel Valera's house on the Plaza de Santa Teresa was, by turns, apprehensive, bored and resentful. The apprehension came from the knowledge that only two nights earlier, an officer had been killed on this very square – and if an officer was not safe, then a humble private certainly wasn't. The boredom was natural enough, considering that, apart from the occasional officer making his way to his billet, the square had been deserted for the last two hours. But perhaps it was the resentment which the sentry felt the strongest. All the other lads were out having a good time, and here he was standing outside an empty house, his rifle in his hand. And for what? Was it likely that the Republicans were suddenly about to appear, and attempt to steal his officer's pots and pans? Hell, everybody knew they were on the run – so why was he wasting his time?

The sight of the two men emerging from the bottom of the Calle Belén and heading straight for his post brought his feelings of apprehension to the fore again. He studied the men carefully. One of them moved with the slow, ponderous gait of a peasant who knows better than to waste his energy when it is not really necessary. The other, while doing no more than keeping pace with his big, awkward friend, seemed much quicker and stealthier in his step.

As they got ever closer to him, the sentry started to relax. He could see now that they were just a couple of privates. He thought he even remembered talking to the smaller of the two at a bar on the Calle Mayor.

The privates drew level with the door, and stopped. 'What have we found ourselves here, Jiménez?' asked the smaller, quicker one. 'Why, it's a man condemned to stand on guard alone. A man friendless in a world where, without friends, he has nothing.'

They were very drunk, the sentry realized, and he wished that he were in a similar state himself. 'Go on about your business, the pair of you,' he said, trying to sound stern – and not quite making it.

'We have no business,' the small private said, waving his hands about wildly in the night air. 'No business at all.'

146

'If you don't move on immediately, then you leave me no choice but to take your names,' the sentry threatened, again half-heartedly.

The smaller soldier either didn't hear, or didn't care. 'I wonder if we can do anything to comfort this poor, solitary soldier?' he asked his larger companion. He reached into his pocket and, with all the flourish of a magician pulling a rabbit out of his hat, produced a bottle of cheap brandy. 'Might this help take away the loneliness?' he suggested, offering it to the sentry.

'I'm not supposed to drink anything when I'm on duty.'

The little man shrugged. 'So don't take the bottle, then. It'll mean all the more for us.'

The sentry licked his lips nervously, and looked quickly around the empty square. 'I shouldn't,' he said.

'Well, I'm not going to force you.'

The sentry hesitated for another second or two, then reached out for the bottle with his right hand. His fingertips were almost touching it when the big peasant swung the electric torch he was carrying and caught him a blow on the back of head. The sentry's knees buckled underneath him, and he fell in a heap.

The instant the man was on the ground, Paco stepped out of the shadows. 'You didn't hit him too hard, did you, Jiménez?' he asked.

The country boy shook his head. 'I've stunned animals like that,' he said. 'He shouldn't be out for more than half an hour.'

Pérez reached into his pocket again and pulled out a set of skeleton keys which he'd probably had since the days he worked with his father. He slid the first one into the keyhole, and cursed softly when the lock didn't immediately click open. 'I should never have let you talk me into this,' he complained, as he stabbed at the lock with a second key. 'We could be shot for what we've just done.'

He's panicking, Paco thought. We're only at the beginning, and already the little bugger's losing his nerve!

Yet who could blame Pérez? Hadn't he the right to panic when they were standing there – with an unconscious sentry at their feet – in full view of any officer who decided to enter the square.

The second key was as ineffective as the first, but when Pérez turned the third in the lock there was a muted click, and the door swung open. Paco and Pérez quickly stepped into the hallway. Jiménez followed, dragging the sentry behind him. Once Paco had closed the door behind them the country boy lowered the unconscious soldier to the floor, pulled a short length of rope out of his pocket, and set to work tying the man up.

'How long have we got to search the place?' Pérez asked, the panic still evident in his voice.

'I don't know,' Paco admitted. 'Colonel Valera doesn't keep me posted on his movements.'

'What if he comes back while we're still here?'

'Then we'll have to kill him.'

'And if he's not alone? If he brings some of his mates back with him for a game of cards?'

'Then we'll probably be the ones who die,' Paco told him. 'Listen, Pérez, I told you this was risky. But it's no more risky than marching out to the front line every day, and having some man you've never even met try to kill you.'

Pérez's fear – which had almost succeeded in getting Paco in its grip – had had no effect on Jiménez. The big peasant had continued to work slowly and methodically throughout the exchange. Now he took a handkerchief out of his pocket, and gagged the unconscious man. 'Good knots,' he said, admiring his own handiwork. 'Vine knots. He won't get out of that in a hurry.'

Pérez shook his head in amazement. 'Sometimes I wonder whether it's him who's crazy or me,' he said to Paco. He turned to his comrade. 'Do you have any idea – any idea *at all* – what we're doing here, Jiménez?'

'We're breaking into the house,' Jiménez said. 'We're going to steal something.'

'But what exactly is it that we're going to steal? And why are we going to steal it?'

The big peasant scratched his head. 'I don't remember,' he confessed.

'He doesn't remember,' Pérez said to Paco. 'There are times when I think we come from different worlds.'

'You do,' Paco said, silently thanking whatever gods were on his side that some of Jiménez's peasant placidity seemed to have rubbed off on Pérez, and the rat-faced private was once again back on an even keel. 'You know what you're looking for,' he continued. 'And remember, when you're searching, keep your torches low to the ground.'

Pérez grinned. 'You're trying to teach your grandmother to suck eggs now. I've broken into more houses than you've had hot dinners. Mind you, I've never actually done it with a policeman as a partner before.'

'You check the downstairs rooms, and I'll go through the top floor,' Paco told the two privates.

He climbed the stairs and turned the same bend around which he had seen a naked female foot disappear two nights earlier. He thought about how wrong he had been then – how little he had known about what had really gone on in the village since the death of the dog. He had reached the landing. Four doors faced him, and since all were equally unknown, he chose the first.

It was a large room, overlooking the Plaza de Santa Teresa – and was obviously the colonel's bedroom. Apart from the bed, there was a wardrobe, a chair, and a chest of drawers. Paco went over to the window to check that the square was still deserted, then he opened the wardrobe. It contained a spare everyday uniform, a more formal dress uniform, a riding habit and a couple of civilian suits. There was no sign of any of Colonel Valera's mistress's outfits – but, of course, he'd never expected to find even one of them.

He went through the chest of drawers. Underwear, socks and shirts. He knelt down and shone his torch under the bed – and found only the fluff which the maid had missed.

There was nothing left to search in this room but still Paco was reluctant to leave. 'It should have been here,' he said softly to himself. 'If it was going to be anywhere, it should have been here.'

The second and third bedrooms overlooked the back street, and were shuttered, so there was no need to take care with the torch. Not that there was much to see in the full beam of light. Though both these rooms, like the first, contained a chest of drawers, a bed and a wardrobe, there were no clothes, or anything else to be found in them.

He entered the fourth room, which was next door to the master bedroom, and so also had a view out on to the main square. The shutters were open. So was the window – and through that window came the sound of several pairs of footsteps, and voices raised in animated conversation about wild-boar hunting.

Paco dropped quickly to the floor, just as the footsteps stopped. 'That's strange!' one of the men below said loudly. 'Bloody strange!'

'What is?' asked a second man.

'There's no guard on duty outside the colonel's door.'

There were four of them out there on the square, Paco estimated. Four officers, each of them armed with a pistol – while he and his fellow

149

burglars only had one knife and one rifle between them. It didn't seem like very good odds.

'So what if there isn't a sentry on duty?' asked the second officer. 'Does it really matter?'

'Of course it matters. After what happened to poor Julio Anton, I'd have thought Major Gómez would have made it his business to see to it that there was always a man on guard.'

Paco's breaths started to come louder and faster – so fast and so loud that he was surprised the men below in the square couldn't hear them. Any second now, one of the officers was going to suggest raising the alarm – and then his chances of rescuing his darling Cindy would be gone for ever.

'Are you laughing?' the first officer demanded suddenly. 'You are, aren't you? Well, I don't see what's so funny about Anton's death.'

'That's not what's funny,' the other officer told him between giggles. 'It's funny that you've forgotten why Gómez withdrew the sentry in the first place.'

'Oh, you mean . . .?'

'Exactly. And we've no reason to think that particular situation has changed, now have we?'

'But there are no lights on,' the first officer said, as if he were reluctant to give up the thesis that something was wrong without a fight.

'Would you need the lights on?' his companion asked, half-stifling another chortle.

'I suppose not,' the first officer admitted. 'Do you know, I think I've had too much to drink.'

'We've *all* had too much to drink,' the other man said. 'Why wouldn't any man who had to face what we do tomorrow have too much to drink? And we've not finished yet. I've got a bottle in my room.'

The footsteps started up again, and soon began to recede into the distance. Paco lifted his eyes cautiously above the level of the window-sill, and watched the officers cross the square and enter a house opposite.

Snatches of the officers' conversation quickly replayed themselves in Paco's mind:

It's funny that you've forgotten why Gómez withdrew the sentry in the first place, one had said.

The officers had known for a long time what he himself had only discovered that morning. But now, finally, he did know the truth – and that truth was that though Gómez had been the man who'd told the sentries to stand down, he'd never been the one who'd decided when that would happen.

And we've no reason to think that particular situation has changed, have we? the second officer had said, giggling.

Paco prayed it hadn't – prayed, too, that there was still a chance of finding the one piece of vital evidence he needed.

He raised his torch cautiously. He appeared to be in a sort of lumber-room which contained the colonel's trunk, his saddle, a broken chair and a brace of hunting shotguns.

Paco opened the trunk. What he was looking for had to be there, he told himself – because if it wasn't, he had no idea where else it might be. Of course, it was possible the colonel had already returned it to its owner but, given the circumstances, he didn't see how Valera would have had the opportunity.

There were thick wool blankets at the top of the trunk, vital in winter but totally superfluous in the summer heat which even invaded the high sierra. He lifted them out and threw them on the floor. Next he found several spare shirts which stank of mothballs. He discarded them, too.

'It has to be somewhere in here!' he told himself desperately. 'It simply *has* to be.'

Had to be, because without it his case crumbled to dust – and even though he knew he was right about what happened on the night the dog died, he would have absolutely no way of proving it.

A military topcoat was on the next layer. Like the shirts, it smelled strongly of mothballs. Stripping that away, Paco uncovered two pairs of the colonel's riding jodhpurs.

He had almost reached the bottom of the trunk – and the end of his tether when he came across an article wrapped in thin tissue paper. He took it out almost reverently, carefully opened the tissue paper, and spread the article out on the floor. It was a petticoat, but not such a petticoat as his wife – or even his liberated Cindy – would have worn. It was designed to be seen. It was designed to excite. And it must have cost more than many women spent on their entire wardrobe.

A room overlooking the square wasn't the place to examine his prize properly – there was far too much danger of his torch beam being spotted by an officer returning to his quarters. Paco retreated to the landing, and closed the lumber-room door quietly behind him.

Back in comparative safety, he ran the petticoat through his fingers, and felt the richness of the pure, shot silk. He examined the intricate embroidery – the swirls and the flowers which subtly – but inevitably – focused the eyes of the observer on one central area. He had not necessarily been expecting it to be a petticoat that he found – though he was not surprised that that was what it had turned out to be. Yet even the garment itself wouldn't provide him with the proof he needed unless it had the exact modifications he was looking for.

He held the petticoat up, and shone his torch on it. It was perfect! Bloody perfect!

'Oh shit!' he groaned.

Could he have been *so* wrong? he wondered. Could he have so disastrously misread all the clues that instead of moving closer to the solution of the case, he'd merely been running up a blind alley? Was it possible this petticoat had nothing to do with the investigation at all?

He ran the torch over the petticoat once more – and gasped with relief. The old man in the bar had told him that Carmen Sanchez had been a good seamstress, and now he saw that it was true. She had been better than good – she'd been one of the best. But despite her skill with invisible mending, the two zigzag tears were just visible under the strong light of the torch.

Paco folded the petticoat back in its tissue paper, put it under his arm and made his way downstairs. Pérez and Jiménez, their own hands empty, were waiting expectantly for him in the hallway.

'You've got it, haven't you!' Pérez said, looking at the parcel.

'Yes, I've got it,' Paco replied.

The rat-faced private grinned. 'So what do we do now?'

'Now, Jiménez goes and tells the man who can get us out of here that I want to see him.'

'Just you?' Pérez asked. 'Not the two of us?'

'Just me,' Paco confirmed.

Chapter Twenty-Two

The sound of the drinkers and revellers on the brightly lit Calle Mayor drifted down the dark, narrow Calle Belén like some rumour of another life. Standing alone in the darkness, Paco shivered. It had been on this street that the general's dog had lost his life. Here, too, was the spot where he had almost been killed himself – not for what he knew, but for what his would-be assassin had been afraid he might find out. The killer had emerged from this street and slit Lieutenant Anton's throat. Carmen Sanchez, the seamstress, had probably gone home for the very last time along this route. And now the final phase of Paco's investigation into the death of the dog would be acted out here, too.

A black shape appeared at the bottom of the street, and began to walk briskly towards him. Paco felt himself tense. Cindy's future and his own would be determined by what happened in the next few minutes. He had to get it right.

The black shape stopped about four metres away from him. 'Isn't this all rather melodramatic, Inspector Ruiz?' asked a voice which Paco recognized as belonging to Major Gómez.

'Is it?' Paco asked.

The major moved a few steps closer, so that Paco could almost – but not quite – distinguish his features. 'That's certainly what I'd call it,' he said. 'Why have our meeting on a deserted street in the middle of the night, when we could just as easily have held it in the comfort of my quarters?'

'Because in the comfort of your quarters, I'd have been caught like a rat in a trap,' Paco told him. 'And I wouldn't have been just at *your* mercy. I'd also have been at the mercy of your "brother officers", who would have supported you in whatever action you chose to take against me, because that's what brother officers do.'

'Am I to understand from the tone of what you've just said that this isn't going to be a friendly discussion?' the major asked.

'That's entirely up to you,' Paco replied. 'Would you like to come a little closer?'

'I can hear perfectly well from here,' Gómez told him. 'Say what it is that you have to say.'

'Do you know who killed the general's dog?' Paco asked.

'I have my suspicions.'

'And they're probably exactly the same as mine. But the more interesting question is, do you really *care* who killed the dog?'

'As I think I've explained to you before, if the culprit is uncovered, the general will be grateful to me – and that will certainly not do my chances of promotion any harm.'

'But your chances of promotion would be even greater if I made another, much more significant discovery, wouldn't they?' Paco asked. 'If, for example, I uncovered a certain secret – even though that secret was already known to most of the officers in this village?'

'I don't know what you're talking about,' Gómez said, lying just as Private Pérez had done earlier in the church.

'When you warned me off investigating the officers – as you did on several occasions – did you really think that I'd take your advice?'

Gómez laughed softly in the darkness. 'No, quite the reverse. I told you I was a good judge of men, and from the very first moment we spoke to one another I've had you marked down as a man who will do exactly the opposite of anything someone in authority tells him to do.'

Yes, you're right, Paco thought. That's always been my problem. 'I should have known what game you were playing from the moment we exhumed the dog,' he told the major.

'You're still not making sense,' Gómez said, lying again.

'I expect you were waiting for *me* to suggest that we dug it up,' Paco continued, 'but I didn't. You see, I was only pretending to be interested in the case at that point, and I wasn't really thinking like a policeman. Anyway, it soon became plain to you that I was going to do what you'd expected, so you were forced to make the suggestion yourself.'

'And what was my motive for that, pray tell?'

'If your suspicions about the killer were correct, you knew we'd find a pistol bullet in the animal. That would point the finger of suspicion squarely at one of the officers. And once I started investigating them, there was more than a fair chance I'd stumble across Colonel Valera's secret.'

'His secret?' Gómez repeated.

'His mistress!' Paco said exasperatedly. 'You wanted me to find out about his bloody mistress!'

'Why should I have wanted you to do that?'

'Because she's not exactly like the ordinary run-of-the-mill mistresses officers tend to keep, is she? If I'd told the general what I'd discovered about her, Colonel Valera would certainly have been ruined, and you, as the next in line, would have got his place.'

Even in the dark, Paco caught the movement of Major Gómez's hand as it moved slightly closer to his holster. 'Assuming this knowledge would, in fact, ruin the colonel, why didn't I just take the information to the general myself?' the major asked.

It was Paco's turn to laugh. 'Oh, you'd have liked to do that,' he said. 'You were aching to do it. But that would have ruined you, too, because you'd have broken the officers' code of loyalty by ratting on a brother officer. You might have got this one promotion from the general, but you'd have gone no higher than that. You'd have been a pariah, despised by the whole officer corps.'

'Very interesting theory,' Gómez said, noncommittally.

'You probably thought of denouncing Valera in an anonymous letter,' Paco continued, 'but even that avenue was closed to you, because, as the main beneficiary of his fall, you would have automatically come under suspicion. But if an outsider – a man not even supposed to be involved in this particular issue – gave the information to the general in an attempt to save his own life, as I thought about doing this morning, you'd have been completely in the clear.'

The major's hand moved a few centimetres closer to his weapon. 'You're not telling me this without a reason,' he said, and Paco was struck once again by how little difference there was between this high-ranking officer and a petty criminal like Private Perez. 'You're going to offer me some kind of deal, aren't you?'

'Obviously,' Paco agreed.

'Give me the details.'

'I'll destroy Colonel Valera for you—' Paco began.

'And for yourself,' Major Gómez interrupted. 'Or at least for the Republicans.'

'True,' Paco conceded. 'Without Valera, the general's army won't be half as effective as it's been so far. But that's not the point, is it? However Valera's removal affects the running of the war, you'll get what *you* want.'

'And what do *you* want in return?'

This was going to be the difficult part to sell. Paco took a deep breath. 'I want you to help me and three other people to escape from the village.'

'When?'

'Tonight.'

'And if I refuse?'

'Consider the alternative to helping me escape,' Paco said. 'I could let it be known to the other officers in the village that you've been pointing me in the direction of the colonel all the time. I might even exaggerate what you've said a little. You'd be ruined.'

'Do you seriously think my brother officers would ever take your word against mine?' Gómez asked.

'Maybe not at first,' Paco conceded. 'But once they've tasted the poison, it will gradually seep through their entire systems. By the end of the week, there won't be a man amongst them who doesn't have some serious doubts about you. By this time next month, it will be taken as established fact that you did all you could to sabotage the career – and jeopardize the life – of a comrade-in-arms.'

For another second or two, Gómez's hand hovered over his pistol, then he lifted it up slowly, and scratched his ear in an almost leisurely manner. 'Perhaps you're right,' Gómez agreed. 'In which case, I don't have much choice but to help you to escape, do I?'

It had all been too easy, Paco thought. Far too easy. Instead of agreeing to assist in an escape which could only reflect badly on himself as head of security, he should have been putting forward other alternatives. He could have argued that it would be better to postpone the escape until the ideal opportunity presented itself. He could have said he was sure that, given time, he could persuade the general to grant them safe passage back to Madrid. There were a hundred things a clever man like him could have suggested – and instead he'd folded like a house of cards. But of course, he didn't yet know *how* Paco planned to get out of the village. It would certainly take more arm-twisting to get him to agree to that.

Paco took a deep breath. 'The village is surrounded by sentries,' he said. 'We'll never get past them unless we've created a diversion first. And as far as I can see, the only diversion which will work is—'

'If I'm to have any part of this, then I'll do the planning,' Gómez interrupted. 'You're quite right about the need to divert the sentries, and I know just how to accomplish it.'

'You do? How?

'I'm told that in San Fernando, the fiestas usually take place in September. This year, we're going to have to advance them a little.'

Paco gasped. That was his own plan – the one he'd intended to use every threat he could muster to pressure Gómez into agreeing to. It would never have occurred to him, even in his wildest dreams, that the general's head of security would suggest it himself. 'You . . . you do realize that you'll get the blame for it, don't you?' he said.

Gómez shrugged. 'Perhaps. But I'll soon talk my way out of it. I'll say all the damage was caused by a crack unit of Republican militiamen who somehow managed to infiltrate the village. No one, not even the general, could hold me responsible in such circumstances.'

Not hold him responsible? Of course he would be held responsible, Paco thought – and whatever he says, he must know that as well as I do.

He felt sweat forming on his brow. What game was Gómez playing this time? What cunning twist did he intend to add to what, on the face of it, was a straightforward plan? And at which stage of the plan would the major's double-cross come?

Gómez took a couple of steps forward and held out his hand, 'Do we have a deal?' he asked.

'We have a deal,' Paco agreed, shaking the hand and feeling a cold chill run through his entire body as he did so.

'You took a risk meeting me here,' Gómez said. 'I could have shot you, you know. For a while, I was considering doing just that.'

'Take your pistol out of its holster and point it at me,' Paco said.

'Why should I do that?'

'Just humour me.'

Gómez shrugged. 'All right. If that's what you want.'

He unclipped the flap and took out the pistol. He had not even raised it to chest height when he felt an arm wrapping around his chest – and a knife pressing against his throat.

'You can let him go now, Pérez,' Paco said.

The rat-face private released the major and took a couple of steps backwards.

'What was that little demonstration meant to prove?' Gómez demanded, brushing off the sleeves of his jacket as if contact with the private soldier had contaminated him.

'It was meant to show you that I had Pérez watching my back,' Paco said. 'And I will always have Pérez watching my back. You'd do well to remember that.'

'You're very smart, Ruiz,' the major said. 'But then, so am I. Only time will tell which of us is the smarter.'

Chapter Twenty-Three

The house outside which the two sentries were posted was slightly bigger than its immediate neighbours, but was otherwise unremarkable. Standing in the shadows, watching the sentries smoking their cigarettes and occasionally hearing a snatch of their conversation carried to him on the breeze, Paco was beginning to feel deeply troubled.

'Why are there only two of them?' he asked Major Gómez, in a suspicious whisper.

'Two of what?' the major answered.

'Two sentries on guard. Considering what you've got stored in there, I should have thought you'd have posted at least half a dozen.'

'We're at least ten kilometres behind the front line in a village which is surrounded by a chain of roadblocks and mobile patrols,' Gómez said. 'It doesn't need more guards – because only a madman would think of attacking it.'

What *was* his game, Paco asked himself for the hundredth time since they'd shaken hands on the Calle Belén. How could the major possibly turn what was about to happen to his advantage? And when the double-cross finally came, what form would it take?

'Who lives in the houses on each side of it?' he asked, wondering if Gómez's counter-strike would come from there.

'Nobody,' the major replied. 'We're using them as offices. Look, there's your man now.'

Paco stuck his head out the shadows for a second. Private Pérez had appeared at the other end of the street. He was lurching, and was clearly holding a bottle in his hand.

'He plays the drunk well,' Gómez said.

'In his line of work, he's had the chance to study a great many of them,' Paco replied.

Pérez drew level with the two guards, waved his bottle defiantly at them, and then keeled over. 'They'll wait for half a minute,' Gómez whispered. 'A minute at the most.'

But it was not even that long before one of the guards stepped forward, prodded Pérez with his foot, then bent down and picked up the bottle.

'When they come round, they'll both swear they were overrun by a huge force and that they fought like demons,' Gómez said dryly. 'And I, of course, will pretend to believe them.'

The sentry who had stolen the bottle from Pérez took a generous swig, then handed it over to his companion.

'How long will it take?' Paco asked.

'Not long at all. I was very liberal with the dosage.'

The first guard to take a drink was already starting to wobble. The second looked at him questioningly before starting to sway himself. Then they were both sprawling on the ground, just as Pérez was climbing to his feet.

Was now the time for betrayal? Paco wondered. Would they be surrounded by soldiers the moment they stepped out on to the street? But how could Gómez have alerted his security men? They had been together every second since their meeting on the Calle Belén.

'Shall we make our move?' the major asked.

'Yes, let's go,' Paco replied, making a promise to himself that if Gómez *had* double-crossed him, the final thing he would do before he died himself was to kill the major.

They stepped out into the street, and walked rapidly towards Pérez, who was kicking the unconscious men as hard as he could.

'Leave them alone!' Paco said.

'They stole my bottle from me,' Pérez told him, as he slammed his boot into the groin of one of the fallen guards.

'We wanted them to steal your bottle,' Paco pointed out. 'The plan wouldn't have worked if they hadn't.'

'They didn't know that,' Pérez said, delivering one last kick before walking away in disgust. 'I'm a thief myself, but I'd never sink so low as to steal from my own kind.'

Gómez had produced a set of keys, and was opening the first of several padlocks which were attached to the door.

'And how will you explain this away?' Paco wondered aloud.

'I imagine I'll say that the raiding party from the other side of the lines must have had a skilled locksmith with them,' Gómez replied.

Too glib, Paco thought. Much too glib! How could the major continue to act as though what they were doing wouldn't damage his career, when it was so obvious that it would?

There was the sound of rattling wheels just behind them. Paco spun round and saw it was only Private Jiménez, placidly pushing an old wooden handcart in front of him.

The country boy came to a halt next to the unconscious sentries, bent down and lifted the first one effortlessly into the cart. 'Dump them somewhere they're not likely to be found for a while,' Paco said, and the big peasant nodded to show that he had understood.

Major Gómez unhooked the last of the padlocks, and swung the door open. Was this the moment, Paco asked himself. Would he be shot as he stepped into the building? If only he knew what Gómez's angle was, he'd have more of an idea what to expect.

The two men entered the house and closed the door quickly behind them. Paco shone his torch around the room. Before the army had taken it over, it would have contained tables and chairs, pots and pans. Now it was filled with stacked rifles and boxes of cartridges.

He found what he looking for in one corner – several wooden boxes labelled DINAMITA.

'Are you quite sure you know how to use this stuff?' Gómez asked, and for the first time since they'd begun their desperate gamble, there was a hint of real anxiety in his voice.

'When I was with the Army of Africa, we built a road through the mountains,' Paco told him. 'For more than half its length, we had to blast our way through solid rock. So don't worry, major, there's nothing you can teach me about creating mayhem.'

*

Alone in the little house on the Calle Jose Antonio, Cindy was remembering the letter she had been writing to her parents when she was kidnapped – and wondering what letter she would write if she had the same opportunity now.

Dear Mom and Dad, she composed in her mind, *I've been taken prisoner, and I'm now behind enemy lines. I've been treated very well so far, but I don't know how long that's going to last. The guards were somehow different today. They didn't glare at me, like they usually do. There was a strange look in their eyes. I couldn't exactly put a name to it, but if you pressed me, I guess I'd have to say it was 'expectation'. As if they knew what was going to happen to me! As if they were looking forward to it!*

She lit a cigarette, and felt the smoke curling around her lungs. Women back in her home town never smoked, but then she'd done so many things that women in her home town never did.

I'm very worried about Paco, she composed. *He always comes back to the little prison which we've made our home together every lunchtime, but today he didn't. I keep trying to tell myself that nothing has happened to him – that it's in Major Gómez's own interest to keep him safe. . . .*

She stopped, realizing that her parents would have no knowledge of the major, or of what his interest was in keeping Paco safe. But that didn't really matter, did it? This wasn't really an imaginary letter to her mom and dad. If anything, she was writing it to herself.

I don't think we are going to get out of here alive, she continued. *I really don't. If anyone could make it work, it would be my Paco, but the odds are stacked just too heavily against him, and even if you're a good bluffer, you still can't win at poker when all you're holding is ten high.*

Can't win at poker when all you're holding is ten high? she repeated to herself What am I turning into – some kind of backwoods poet? Jesus, I'd be embarrassed if I was really putting this down on paper.

Don't be sad when you hear about my death, she ploughed on. *It's true I've not had a very long life, but it's been a good one. You were the best parents a girl could ever have. And then there's Paco. He's given me more happiness – and worry and frustration and downright exasperation – than most women ever get to experience. I feel as if I was born to be with him, and if it was only for a short time, well, I guess those are the breaks.*

Am I that brave? she wondered. Can I really face death so calmly? With so few regrets?

And she was amazed to discover that she was, and that she could.

*

Paco stood on the corner of the Plaza Mayor, a small brown canvas bag held carefully in his right hand, and watched Major Gómez walk confidently down the Calle Jose Antonio. He was giving Gómez yet another chance to betray him, he thought, yet another chance to set the trap which would sooner or later clamp its sharp steel jaws around him. But what choice did he have? Cindy had to be told what was about to happen, and using the major was the only way he had to get that message through to her.

Gómez had reached the house, and was talking to the sentries. But what was he saying to them? That he wished to see the prisoner? Or that he wanted them to inform his security people that it was nearly time to swoop?

'Damn you, Gómez,' he said softly. 'I wish I knew why you were so sure you're going to come out of this thing on top!'

*

The three young lieutenants drinking with Colonel Valera at the bar on the Calle Mayor were beginning to realize that the colonel was, quite uncharacteristically, a little drunk.

'This war will bring men of true ability to prominence,' Valera said, stabbing his finger in the air to punctuate each word. 'But it will also show up other men for the med . . . mediocrities they really are.'

The other officers nodded in agreement because what he said was undoubtedly true – and anyway, it was not wise to disagree with someone as high-ranking as the colonel.

Valera took a large slug from the brandy-glass in front of him. 'I have been under considerable strain for the last few days,' the colonel continued. 'But has it affected my performance in any way? No, of course it hasn't! Because I am a professional. I have nerves of steel.'

He signalled the waiter for another round of drinks. 'It is at times like this, gentlemen, when it is easy to see the difference between the wheat and the chaff – when it is possible to spot the real headless chickens. There is a certain major right here in this very village – I name no names, but you all know who I mean – who has proved beyond a shadow of a doubt that he is not worthy of his position. And believe me, gentlemen, steps have already been taken to ensure he does not have that position much longer.'

The waiter placed the drinks on the table, and Valera drained his in three rapid gulps. 'And now, if you'll excuse me, gentlemen, I must return to my quarters to see if the sentry, which that same major assigned to me, is doing his job.'

He fumbled in his pocket for change. 'We'll take care of the bill, sir,' one of the lieutenants said.

'Very kind of you,' the colonel replied. He rose to his feet and, swaying slightly, headed off in the direction of the Plaza de Santa Teresa.

'By God, the Old Man's really got it in for Major Gómez, hasn't he?' one of the lieutenants said when Valera was out of earshot.

'You can say that again,' a second agreed. 'To tell you the truth, I don't think the major's going to be with us much longer. By this time next week, he'll be lucky if he's got the job of counting paper clips back in Burgos.'

*

Gómez emerged from the house on the Calle Jose Antonio, spoke briefly to the sentries, then began to walk back up towards the Plaza Myor. What had the major told the guards? Paco wondered. That in five minutes time one of them should be in the alley behind the house, with his rifle at the ready? But was even that necessary? He still had his pistol. If any killing had to be done, it would be easy enough for him to do it himself.

The major reached the spot where Paco was waiting for him.

'I've explained to your woman exactly what she has to do,' he said. 'She should be quite safe if you're anything like as good with explosives as you claim you are.'

'What's that supposed to mean?' Paco demanded angrily. 'That you think I'll make a mess of it? That you don't believe me when I say I've worked with explosives before?'

Gómez was taken aback by the sudden outburst. 'No,' he said. 'I didn't mean that at all.'

'I'll do my job,' Paco said, almost shouting now. 'Just you make bloody sure you do yours.'

'You've lost your nerve, haven't you?' Gómez said, as realization dawned. 'You're scared.'

'Of course I'm scared!' Paco said, and though the anger was still in his voice, Gómez thought he could now detect the fear which underlay it. 'I'm shitting myself. Why aren't you? Don't you know just how many things could have already gone wrong?'

'If you can manage to keep control of yourself for another few minutes, it will all—'

'Keep control?' Paco interrupted. 'How can I keep control when, for all I know, they've found the sentry in Valera's house by now and have men out looking for me?'

'You're only worried because you feel exposed out here in the open,' Gómez said soothingly. 'It's a little earlier than we planned, but why don't we go to the alley straight away? You'll be safe there.'

'Safe?' Paco said. 'How the hell can I feel safe anywhere in this bloody village?'

But when Gómez set off in the direction of the alley, he followed obediently at the major's heel.

*

The only lighting in the alley shone through the back windows of houses on the Calle Jose Antonio, but though both the major and Paco were carrying torches, they thought it safer not to use them.

They were about half-way to their destination when Paco came to an abrupt halt.

'Is something the matter?' Gómez asked.

'My bloody shoelace has come undone,' Paco said petulantly. 'That's all I bloody needed.'

He laid the brown canvas bag carefully on the ground, and bent over. But only for a second. When he straightened again, it was to twirl Gómez round, slam him hard against the wall, and twist his right arm as far up his back as it would go without snapping.

'Struggle, and I'll break it!' he threatened.

'What the hell are you doing?' the major gasped. 'Have you gone completely off your head?'

'We needed to talk,' Paco told him, 'and I just thought I'd make sure I had the advantage when we did.'

'You seem to have got your nerve back,' Gómez said grimly. 'I should have known a man like you wouldn't suddenly go to pieces like that. So what's this all about?'

'Tell me about the double-cross!' Paco demanded roughly.

'Double-cross? What double-cross?'

'The one you've only a few more minutes to pull off. I want to know where it will happen, and what it will be.'

'There *is* no double-cross,' Major Gómez protested. 'Why should you think there would be?'

'Because, as head of security in the village, you're going to take a lot of shit if we actually do what we've been planning to do.'

Despite the uncomfortable position he found himself in, the major laughed softly. 'You've got it all wrong, my friend,' he said. 'It's Colonel Valera who's going to take a lot of shit.'

'Valera?'

'That's what I said. For some time now, the colonel has not been at all happy about the way I have been carrying out my duties as security officer.

165

As from this evening, I have been relieved of my post, and it is now the sole responsibility of the colonel.'

It almost made sense, Paco thought. But not quite. 'You've already got enough on Valera to ruin him,' he said. 'Why run all this risk just to get some more on him?'

'The colonel has many powerful friends back in the army central command in Burgos,' Gómez explained. 'It was always possible that with their help he could survive the scandal of his mistress, whatever the general might want. But after we've finished our night's work, nothing – not even powerful friends – will be able to save him.'

Paco shook his head, though he was not entirely sure whether it was in admiration or disgust. 'You're right,' he admitted. 'After tonight, nothing's going to save the colonel.'

'And there's an additional bonus in all this for me,' Gómez continued. 'We're about to create a living hell, and in conditions like that even strong men can sometimes go into shock. And it's at such moments, when everyone else is losing his head, that a natural leader emerges – the one man who can take control and forge all the shell-shocked into an effective force again.'

'And the natural leader on this occasion will have the advantage that the explosions won't come as a surprise to him.'

'Exactly,' Gómez agreed. 'I shall be in the thick of it, directing operations. And once calm is restored, you can be sure I'll make certain that the people who have the power to secure my advancement learn all about the crucial role I've played.' He paused. 'So now we've cleared up that small misunderstanding, would you mind letting me go.'

Paco released his grip and stepped back. The major turned around and dusted off his jacket.

'You're a devious bastard, aren't you?' Paco said.

'Am I the only one?' Gómez asked.

'What do you mean by that?'

'It's true I was the one who suggested this particular method of escape,' Gómez said, 'but can you honestly say that you weren't about to come up with a similar scheme yourself?'

Paco grinned. 'No, I can't. My plan was almost exactly the same as yours.'

'So out of all the alternatives open to you, you'd already chosen the one which was designed to inflict maximum damage on your enemies. Why don't you admit it? This isn't just an attempt to save your own skin – this is an act of war.'

Paco's grin widened. 'For a few days, you've had me thinking like the detective I used to be,' he said. 'But that's all over. Now I'm a Republican militiaman again.'

The village clock above the town hall struck the hour.

'Five minutes before Private Pérez does his part of the job,' Major Gómez said.

'Five minutes,' Paco agreed, opening up the canvas bag.

Chapter Twenty-Four

One moment there were only the normal noises of the village – the clinking of glasses, the loud voices of the soldiers, the howling of the dogs – and the next all hell broke loose as the explosion rocked the buildings on the Plaza Mayor, and filled the night sky over the armoury with a bright crimson cloud.

'We're under attack!' men shouted to each other. 'The enemy are in the village!'

Some of the unarmed soldiers on the square stood frozen to the spot. Some started to run blindly, elbowing their comrades aside, and inevitably crashing into other men who were running, just as aimlessly, in the other direction. Bar tables were overturned. Men who had been knocked over, or had fallen down, sprawled on the ground and were trampled into the dirt. Prostitutes screamed with terror. Donkeys brayed loudly, and lashed out with their hind legs at the empty air. It had taken only seconds to turn a well-ordered village into a maelstrom of panic.

The boom of the initial explosion died away, and was replaced by thousands of smaller ones as the cartridge boxes in the armoury caught fire. By the checkpoints at the edge of the village, sentries who did not know whether to stay at their posts or head towards the attack argued between themselves in loud, hysterical voices. In the officers' billets all around the Plaza de Santa Teresa, lieutenants and captains tried desperately to recall what they'd learned during their training in the military academy in Zaragoza. And in the general's *palacio*, the general himself was bawling rapid, contradictory instructions to anyone who would listen to him.

*

When he'd visited the house on Calle Jose Antonio a few minutes earlier, the first thing Major Gómez had done was to upend the dining-table and place it by the window, with its top pointing towards the back wall.

'Get behind that,' he'd told Cindy. 'And *stay* behind it until you're told it's safe to come out.'

'I don't understand what's going on,' Cindy had said.

'You don't need to. Just do as you're told.'

'Why won't you explain to me what's happening?' Cindy had pleaded. 'Why won't you tell me what to expect?'

Gómez had merely smiled, as if he were really enjoying having the power of knowing something she didn't. 'Isn't it obvious what's happening?' he asked. 'Your knight in a shiny old suit is on his way to rescue you.'

She'd been crouched behind the dining-table for about ten minutes when she heard the explosion which was soon to cause complete pandemonium on the main square.

'Paco?' she mouthed silently.

Almost immediately, there was a second explosion – much louder and much closer than the first. She felt a shock run through the floor on which was kneeling, and heard the groaning of the masonry as it crumbled. Cindy's ears were ringing, and the air was suddenly thick with plaster dust, which rapidly found its way into her throat and set her off coughing uncontrollably.

She raised her head above the edge of the table. Through the cloud of plaster, she could see a dark finger crossing the room towards her.

'Paco?' she croaked.

'Are you all right?' he spluttered.

She nodded, because that was easier than talking, and climbed from behind the table. He threw his arms around her, hugged her tightly for the briefest of moments, then led her towards the gaping hole where, seconds earlier, there had been a solid back wall.

It was easier to breathe outside. Paco took Cindy's hand, and half dragging her, started to run down the alley, away from the Plaza Mayor.

'Where are we going?' Cindy gasped.

'Car,' Paco replied. 'Just ahead of us.'

The beaten-up old Peugeot had its engine running, and Pérez and Jiménez were already sitting in the back seat. Paco got in through the driver's door, and once Cindy was safely inside, slipped the car into gear and eased it forward.

'Christ, but wasn't that a big bang?' Pérez said, high on excitement and destruction. 'Old Jiménez here was really crapping himself, but I thought it was wonderful.'

They had almost reached the end of the alley, and the checkpoint at the village's edge loomed up in front of them. Three sentries, who had been arguing fiercely about what they should do next, turned to face the oncoming Peugeot, and one of them, a corporal, stood in the middle of the street, holding up his hand to order the car to come to a halt.

'Why are they still there?' Paco muttered, through gritted teeth. 'Why in God's name haven't they gone to see what's happening in the village – like they were supposed to?'

'What are we going to do now?' Pérez asked. 'Try and bluff our way through?'

Paco shook his head. 'No. It wouldn't work. I'm too well known around the village for that.'

'So what *are* we going to do?'

'This!' Paco told him, slamming his foot down hard on the Peugeot's accelerator.

The tyres screeched like banshees, pebbles from beneath the wheels flew in the air with the speed of bullets, and the big car suddenly shot forward. The corporal in the middle of the road hesitated for a split second, then flung himself to one side. The other two soldiers were already raising their rifle butts to their shoulders. Paco, his foot pressing the accelerator into the floorboards, wished he were driving a faster car.

The Peugeot hit the barrier at almost its top speed. The pole disintegrated. Wood chips flew into the air, then fell to earth again as a powdery rain. As the car plunged on into the darkness of the sierra there was the distant sound of at least two rifle shots. Then the car was clear of the village, climbing as fast as it could up a narrow, twisting road flanked on one side by dark pine trees, and on the other by a stomach-churning drop.

'We've done it!' Pérez shouted jubilantly. 'We've bloody done it. We're in the clear!'

Paco shook his head doubtingly. It couldn't be that simple. Nothing in his life ever was. Though he didn't know what else could go wrong, he was willing to bet that *something* would.

They were less than a kilometre out of the village when the trouble started. At first Paco told himself that it was the change in the road surface which was making the ride increasingly bumpy, but after a while – when there was not even a moment's relief from the jarring, and as steering the Peugeot became more difficult with every second which passed – he was forced to acknowledge the truth of the situation.

He pulled into the side of the road. 'We've got a flat tyre,' he told his passengers.

'You don't say?' Pérez replied sourly.

They all climbed out of the car, and Paco quickly made his way round the side towards the boot.

'What are you doing?' Pérez asked.

'Getting the tools to change the wheel.'

'You!' Pérez said contemptuously. 'Are you a motor mechanic as well as a cop?'

'I've changed wheels before,' Paco told him.

'And how long did it take you?' Perez countered. 'I used to *steal* wheels for a living – and you can be sure I learned to do it quickly. Better leave this job to me and Jiménez.'

Paco walked to the other side of the road. From where he was standing, he could look down on the village in which he had done so much damage. The explosion was still having an effect. The fire in the armoury was not burning as fiercely as it had earlier, but now it had spread to the buildings on either side of it. At that very moment Major Gómez would be demonstrating his cool leadership by organizing men to contain the blaze, Paco thought.

But not everyone in San Fernando was concentrating their efforts on the fire! On the road along which the Peugeot had so recently travelled, he could see the headlights of a speeding car!

'Hurry up, for God's sake!' he shouted to Pérez, who was bent over one of the back wheels while Jiménez stood bovinely by his side, shining the torch. 'They're after us.'

'I'm working as quickly as I can,' the rat-faced private screamed back over his shoulder. 'But it's not as easy as I thought it would be. Some of these bloody bolts are rusted on.'

The car below was making good time – better than the Peugeot had. Paco wondered who had sent it. Was it Gómez, finally playing the double-cross he'd been expecting for so long? Or was it Valera, trying to save his own reputation by capturing the people who had caused all the destruction?

It doesn't really matter which of them is behind it, he told himself.

Because whether it was Colonel Valera or Major Gómez – or even the general – the plain fact was that a car full of armed soldiers was approaching them at an alarming rate.

'How much longer are you going to take?' he called to Pérez.

'Nearly there.'

But so was the other car! There were several sharp bends separating the two vehicles, but even if they had to keep slowing down, it would not take the pursuers long to reach the Peugeot.

'Finished!' Pérez shouted.

Paco sprinted across the road, and got behind the wheel. As he pulled away from the side of the road, the headlights of the other car appeared round the bend behind them.

'Shit!' Pérez said.

'Shit!' Paco echoed. The pursuers were in a new Renault which was much more powerful than the old banger he was driving. The Renault probably couldn't overtake them on this narrow strip of road, but it would have no difficulty keeping up with them until it *did* have the chance. And then? And then the four of them – with no weapons other than Pérez's knife – would be at the mercy of five or six armed soldiers. He wrenched hard on the wheel, and the Peugeot screeched round yet another bend at fifteen or twenty kilometres an hour more than was remotely safe.

They had reached a straight stretch of road, and through his side window, Paco could see another village – San Ignacio – deep in the valley below them. The twinkling lights in the houses seemed so comforting – seemed almost to offer security and salvation. He remembered visiting the village in happier days, when, after a long, invigorating walk in the mountains, he would call in at the *taverna* for a glass of wine and a plate of mountain ham. But times had changed. Now the village would be full of men in uniforms who would see him as just one more enemy to be eliminated as quickly as possible.

The Renault was gaining on them with every metre both cars travelled. In his mirror, Paco could now see the white blobs which were the faces of the driver and the front-seat passenger.

The Peugeot jolted as the Renault smashed into its back bumper. Paco's head was filled with noises. The crash of metal against metal. A gasp from Cindy as she was thrown forward in her seat. A loud cry of 'Jesus Christ!' which he thought may have come from himself. And suddenly the lights of the village of San Ignacio were no longer to the side – but straight ahead of them!

His stomach heaving, Paco wrenched on the steering wheel with all his might. The Peugeot shook and rattled in protest, but turned away from the edge – away from the long dark plunge into oblivion.

As the Peugeot turned the next bend, the rear window suddenly exploded, showering Pérez and Jiménez with glass.

'Are you all right?' Cindy screamed.

Jiménez grunted that he was.

'What about you, Pérez?'

'I'm cut, but I've had worse!' the rat-faced private bawled back.

They'd had a narrow escape, but their luck couldn't last for ever, Paco thought. The next bullet could well be more accurate – might burst one of the tyres and send them into an uncontrollable skid.

The opposition had fire-power, and a faster car. Those were their strengths. But a good fighter didn't concentrate on the enemy's strengths, Paco reminded himself – he sought out its weaknesses. He knew this road. They probably didn't. There had to be a way to turn that to his advantage.

He visualized the stretch of road which lay immediately ahead of them. There was a bend to the right, followed by one to the left, then another straight stretch. And on the straight stretch some of the trees had been cut down and the embankment carved out in order to make a picnic area!

Another bullet thudded into the side of the old Peugeot as Paco negotiated the first of the two bends. The men behind wouldn't even have to shoot out a tyre, he thought – if they managed to hit the petrol tank, the whole bloody car would go up in a tower of flame.

He was on the straight stretch now, rapidly approaching the picnic area. The Renault was accelerating, ready to ram him again.

The timing has to be exactly right, he told himself – because if it's out by even a second, we'll all be dead.

He began his countdown. Three . . . two . . . one. The Peugeot was level with the picnic area now. He twisted the wheel fiercely to the left, and stamped down hard on the brake pedal.

The tyres screamed. The car rocked and shuddered. But he had stopped exactly where he'd intended it to – slewed across the road at an angle, the boot of the car very close to the edge, the bonnet almost in the picnic area.

'Get to the right-hand edge of the seat, Pérez!' Paco shouted. 'Sit on Jiménez's bloody knee if you can.'

The driver of the Renault slammed on his brakes – but it was too late! Paco felt the impact of the other car smashing against his back door at the very moment he pressed his foot down on the accelerator. The Peugeot struggled between the opposing forces – the collision with the Renault impelling it further down the road, the drive shaft straining to go forward into the picnic area. The vehicle wobbled its rear like a demented mambo dancer, then lurched towards the gap in the trees.

The Renault, deflected to the right, was already off the edge, flying through space. For an instant, it was hard to imagine it had ever been on the road at all. Then there was a flash of light rising from below the lip of the road, followed by the roar of an explosion as deep and angry as the cry of a dying god.

Chapter Twenty-Five

Paco and Private Pérez stood at the edge of the road, looking down at the smouldering wreckage of the Renault below. Though they seemed to have been celebrating their escape from death for at least a hundred years, it could not have been much more than a minute since the car took its fatal plunge.

'So what do we do now, *jefe*?' the rat-faced private asked.

'The first thing is to dump the car—'

'Dump it?' Pérez interrupted. 'Abandon the car and walk – when with it we could ride in style? Why the hell should we want to do that?'

Paco took out a packet of cigarettes, lit two, and handed one over to the private.

'In the first place, we don't even know that the Peugeot will get very far after the battering it's had,' he said.

Pérez inhaled the smoke from his cigarette hungrily. 'Even if it only makes a short way before it gives up on us, that's still a bloody sight better than nothing,' he said.

'And in the second place, they'll have heard the explosion in San Ignacio,' Paco continued, pointing with his cigarette to towards the village down below them, 'and they'll already have sent people out to investigate it. So if you and your friend Jiménez want to take the car and drive straight into the arms of a military patrol, then that's entirely up to you. But I'm going deep into the woods. And I'm taking Cindy with me.'

'So we have to walk back to Madrid, do we?' Pérez said, sulkily. 'That could take all day.'

'It'll take much longer than that,' Paco told him. 'The army will be out looking for us, so we can't afford to run into them. And you're wearing a rebel uniform, so we don't want to meet any Republican militiamen either. Which means that we only travel at night and during the first couple of hours of daylight before the fighting starts.'

'We can't stay hidden for ever,' Pérez pointed out.

'No, we can't,' Paco agreed. 'Once we're well behind Republican lines, Cindy will find some way to get us three boiler suits, then we'll be able to just blend into the background.'

'Might work,' Pérez said grudgingly. 'Well, what are we waiting for? Let's get started.'

'Not quite yet. There's one more thing we have to do before we leave,' Paco said.

'What's that?'

'We have to push the Peugeot over the edge, close to where the Renault went off.'

Pérez snorted in disgust. 'Why, in God's name, should we waste our time doing that?'

'Because it will take very little of our time, but a great deal of the army's,' Paco explained. 'The officer in charge of the first unit to arrive at the scene will send men down to investigate the wreckage. They'll find charred bodies in one car, but no sign of the occupants of the other. That will puzzle him. He'll order his men to search for more bodies, and it should take him at least half an hour to come to the conclusion that the Peugeot was empty when it went over the edge. By that time, we could be a couple of kilometres away.'

Pérez laughed. '*Joder*, but you're a smart one,' he said. 'Do you know something? If you'd ever put your mind to it, you could have made a fortune out of crime.'

They put the battered Peugeot into neutral, then pushed it out of the picnic area on to the road.

'I still can't believe I'm doing this,' Pérez grunted as he put his weight behind the vehicle. 'I know it might be not much more than a wreck, but I could still have found somebody stupid enough to pay me quite a lot of money for this car back in Madrid.'

'You could have found someone in the old days,' Paco said. 'The Madrid you're going back to is not the one you knew.'

'Bollocks!' Pérez said. 'There was crime there before I was born, there'll be crime there long after I'm dead, and whatever you say about the recent changes, there'll be crime there right now.'

They reached the edge of the road, and pushed the car over. It bounced a few times down the steep slope, then burst into flames.

His new plan was a good one, Paco thought, as he watched the Peugeot burn. It had none of the complexities he'd been forced into adopting back in the village – none of the delicate balancing of threats and promises, none of the split-second timing, none of the reliance on others.

Yes, it was a good plan because it was a very simple one – and he had no reason on earth to think that within a few hours it would come completely unravelled before his very eyes.

*

Even with the help of their torches, they made slow progress through the woods that night. Tree roots lurked in the shadows, then snaked out to trip them when they drew level. Holes in the ground cunningly covered themselves with leaves, to form traps for unwary ankles. And small nocturnal creatures scuttered through the undergrowth, making as much noise as the platoon of enemy soldiers which the four fugitives were sometimes convinced was lying in wait for them.

Private Pérez led the way, his wiry body tense, yet his movements always fluid. Private Jiménez brought up the rear, crashing through the forest like a bumbling ox. And in between them were Paco and Cindy, holding hands when the terrain made it possible, and walking in single file whenever it didn't.

'You know who killed the dog now, don't you?' Cindy asked, when they'd been on the move for about an hour.

'Yes, I know,' Paco replied.

'And who killed the lieutenant?'

'I know that, too. And I also know who murdered the poor bloody seamstress.'

'But I've never heard you mention anything about a seamstress!' Cindy protested.

No, she wouldn't have, Paco realized. With all that had gone on the day before, it already seemed an age since he had examined the body of Carmen Sanchez. But now that he thought about it, it was probably no more than fifteen or sixteen hours since he'd entered the modest house on the Calle Mayor and seen the knotted sheet hanging from the ham hook.

'Do you know *why* they were all killed?' Cindy asked.

'Yes. They all had to die for the same reason – to cover up a guilty, dangerous secret.'

'Then tell me about it. Give me all the details.'

'Not now,' Paco said tiredly. 'When we're back in our own apartment in Calle Hortaleza, sipping copas of brandy, I'll explain the whole thing to you. But right at this moment, it's as much as I can do to keep my eyes open and place one foot in front of the other.'

*

By three o'clock in the morning the stars by which Paco was navigating seemed to him to be bouncing around the heavens like fireflies. By four o'clock he had all but given up trying to estimate exactly how much ground they'd covered since they'd left the road.

His legs ached, his back creaked with every step he took, lead weights had somehow been attached to his arms, and his tongue had swollen up so much that it seemed to fill his entire mouth. The others were starting to show the strain, too. Cindy's athletic strides had lost most of their bounce. Pérez no longer darted between the trees like a wary rodent. Only Jiménez seemed unaffected. He continued to lumber along behind them much as he had from the beginning.

Dawn broke, but by then they were so exhausted that even with the light to assist them, they were slowing down. They found a stream and Paco ordered a halt. They lapped up the cool mountain water, and that seemed to help a little.

'When I get back to Madrid, I'm going to order myself the biggest steak I can find,' Pérez said, as they squatted on the bank of the stream. 'And when I've eaten that, I'm going to order another one.'

Paco put his last cigarette in his mouth, and regretfully threw the pack away. 'We're going to have to look for somewhere to go to ground soon,' he told the rat-faced private.

'Hell, there's no need for that. There's nobody around for miles and miles, and like I said, I want that steak.'

'You do it my way, or you're on your own,' Paco said sharply.

Pérez grinned. 'I can learn my way round a town in a couple of hours,' he said, 'but I'm so useless with bloody nature that I could be wandering around in it till doomsday.'

'So what are you saying?'

'I'm saying that you're the boss.'

Paco took a drag on his cigarette, and painfully stood up. He had no idea how big the blisters on his feet were, but he was sure they had set some kind of record.

'Another half an hour,' he said. 'Another half an hour and then we stay put until nightfall.'

*

They had only been walking for five minutes when a faint smell wafting through the air alerted Paco to the fact that something was wrong. It was an odour which blended with that of the pine needles, yet at the same time was quite distinct from it. He couldn't pin it down at first, and by the time he had correctly identified it as freshly brewing coffee, a big Republican militiaman had already stepped out from behind the tree which was serving as his hiding place.

He was a broad man, with broken teeth and the expression of a natural bully – the sort of minor thug Paco had been used to arresting on a Saturday night when he'd been a patrolman. He had a leer on his face, and his rifle was pointing squarely at Pérez's chest. 'Well, just look what we've gone and caught ourselves here, lads,' he said.

From the corner of his eye, Paco could see more shapes emerging from behind other trees. 'This isn't how it looks,' he said. 'I can explain everything if you'll just give me the chance.'

'You can explain *nothing*,' the big militiaman told him, 'because nothing needs to be explained. What we've bagged here, comrades, is a couple of rebel soldiers, a filthy capitalist on the run, and a woman who, I've no doubt, is the capitalist's fancy piece.'

'You're right about that, Mauricio,' someone else called out. 'That's exactly what they are.'

There were ten of the militiamen – each of them armed with a rifle. Paco's quick gaze swept their faces, looking for an expression on one of them which might suggest the man was open to reason – but they all gazed back at him with the same hatred as he had seen in the eyes of the soldiers back at the village. They wouldn't listen because they didn't want to listen. But he still had to try.

'My name's Ruiz,' he said. 'I know I'm not dressed like one, but I'm a militiaman from the central district. Maybe you know some of my comrades. Ramón Valdes, who's secretary of the local union branch? Pedro Dos Barrio—'

'You'll say anything to protect your worthless skin,' Mauricio interrupted. 'But I'm not fooled. If you're a militiaman, why aren't you with your comrades right now?'

'I was captured and—'

'And instead of shooting you, like they've shot so many others, the rebels decided to dress you up in a fine suit, did they?' Mauricio scoffed – and all the men around him laughed.

'He was a famous police detective before the war broke out,' Pérez said, with a hint of desperation creeping into his voice. 'Inspector Ruiz. You must have heard of him. The man who solved that murder in Atocha. That's why the army spared him because they wanted him to investigate a crime. And that's why they gave him the suit.'

'Wanted him to investigate a crime,' Mauricio repeated, slowly and thoughtfully. 'And what crime would that be?'

'Someone shot the general's dog,' Pérez said. Then he paused and shook his head, as if he'd just realized that with every word he said, he was digging them all into a deeper hole. 'But it only started out like that,' he pressed on valiantly. 'There were other murders—'

'Cats and pet rabbits, no doubt,' the big militiaman interrupted, getting another laugh from his companions. 'You see now what lying scum all these rebels are, comrades?'

There was a general muttering of approval at his words. 'The woman has nothing whatever to do with all this,' Paco said. 'Take us prisoner if you like, but let her go.'

'No!' Cindy gasped. 'I won't leave you! Whatever happens, I won't leave you!'

'Please!' Paco begged her.

'If she's with you, then she's just as much our enemy as you are,' Mauricio told him.

'What shall we do, Mauricio?' one of the other militiamen asked. 'Shoot them now?'

The big man shook his head. 'No, we'll take them back to camp, and let the rest of the lads have a look at them. Then we'll try them in front of a proper people's tribunal. Tie their hands up, comrades.'

Someone standing behind Paco pulled his arms roughly backwards, and forced his hands together. Try them in front of a proper people's tribunal, he repeated to himself, as he felt the rope start to bite into his wrists. Well, there was no doubt what its verdict would be. After all the effort he had gone to, all the risks he had taken, he had still not been able to protect Cindy – and she was about to be shot by his own side. He felt a heavy guilt settle on his shoulders, and shuddered as remorse began to eat away at his insides.

*

The camp was in a clearing not far from the spot where they'd been ambushed. There were around fifty militiamen in total, Paco calculated.

Most of them were sitting on their blankets, drinking steaming coffee from enamel mugs, smoking their first cigarettes of the morning, and taking the occasional swig of anis from a bottle which was being passed among them.

Mauricio paraded his prisoners across the clearing, only bringing them to a halt when they'd reached the centre. 'Look what I've brought you, comrades,' he announced dramatically. 'Four Fascist scum! Four *we* won't have to worry about for much longer.'

A man with a huge backside had been bending over the open fire brewing more coffee, but now he turned around, and Paco could see that he had a huge belly as well – a belly which had looked more at home propped up against the zinc counter in the Cabo de Trafalgar.

'Paco!' Nacho the barman said. 'What are you doing here? And why are your hands tied behind your back like that?'

'What are *you* doing here?' Paco replied.

Nacho's big body seemed to swell further with pride. 'I'm the official cook to this militia,' he said. 'They'd starve to death if it wasn't for my tortillas and bean stews.'

'Do you know the prisoner?' Mauricio demanded.

'Know him?' Nacho repeated. 'Hasn't he been one of my best customers for the last ten years?'

'And is he really on our side, as he claims?'

'The last time I saw him, he was wearing a boiler suit and travelling out to the front with the rest of the lads. So why don't you just cut him free, then I can give him a cup of coffee?'

The other militiamen looked to Mauricio for guidance. The big man shook his head. 'I don't like this,' he said. 'I don't like it at all. He may have been on our side once – I'll take Nacho's word for that – but if he isn't a turncoat, why has he got two rebel soldiers with him?'

'They helped us escape,' Cindy said. 'They wanted to desert so they could fight on the side of the Republic.'

'Still seems more likely they're spies to me,' Mauricio said, reluctant to see his victorious capture of four of the enemy turn out to be nothing more than a mistake. 'I say we hold a trial to establish their guilt or innocence.'

Several of the militiamen nodded their heads, and others muttered their agreement.

'That's only fair,' one of them said.

'I don't really buy this story of him being saved from the firing squad just so he could investigate the death of a dog,' another muttered.

A look of triumph spread across Mauricio's ugly face. 'Very well, comrades,' he said. 'I will act as prosecutor, and as for the defence – well, if the prisoners have one, they present it themselves.'

Nacho moved his heavy body into the centre of the circle. 'If there's a trial, they'll be found guilty,' he said.

'How can you be so sure of that?' Mauricio asked.

'Because I've heard the way you've been talking before the trial's even begun,' Nacho answered. 'Besides, the people you've tried always *are* found guilty, now aren't they?'

'The people's justice is the only fair form of justice,' Mauricio told him.

Nacho put his ham-like hands on his heavy hips. 'Is it, indeed?' he said. 'Well, let me tell you something for nothing. If you decide to shoot these innocent people, I'm packing up my pots and pans, and going straight back to Madrid.'

'We can't let a cook tell us how to conduct our affairs, can we?' Mauricio protested.

'No,' several of the militiamen called back. 'Of course we can't.'

'Please yourselves,' Nacho said, walking back to the fire. Slowly and deliberately, he picked up the coffee-pot and poured its contents on to the ground. 'Yes, you must do entirely what is in the interest of justice.'

'That was a waste of good coffee,' one of the militiamen protested.

'Well, you can always make yourself some more,' Nacho told him.

'Not as good as yours,' the militiaman said.

'True. Very true,' Nacho agreed.

'I shall start the proceedings with my opening remarks,' Mauricio said in a loud voice. 'The prisoners were found in the woods, earlier this morning. They could offer no satisfactory explanation for their . . . for their. . . .'

He trailed off. Most of the militiamen were not listening to him, but were watching the cook collect his pans together.

'Nacho's a good chap,' one of the militiamen said. 'He's never given us any reason to think he's a liar, and if he says these people are all right, I think we should believe him.'

'And then there's the woman,' said the man next to him. 'I've never shot one before, and I'm not about to start now.'

The grumbling increased until almost every man in the clearing was expressing a belief that a tribunal would not be necessary. Mauricio raised his arms in the air. 'All right!' he shouted. 'Listen to me!'

The other militiamen turned in his direction. Mauricio took a deep breath. 'I've been giving the matter some thought,' he said. 'And on this occasion I think we should accept Comrade Nacho's assurance that they're all right, and let the prisoners go free.'

Paco let out a huge sigh of relief, and then permitted himself one tiny smile of genuine amusement. A general or a mayor could not have saved them from a firing squad, because men like these no longer had any respect for generals and mayors. But a cook – especially a cook as excellent as Nacho was – did have that power. For the moment – in the topsy-turvy society which the revolution had created – the hand that stirred the paella dish could rule the world.

Chapter Twenty-Six

The old open lorry coughed and spluttered its way up the Gran Via, finally coming to a halt at the corner of the Calle Hortaleza. The driver climbed out and walked around to the back of the vehicle.

'Is this close enough to home for you?' he asked the four people he'd brought down from the sierra.

'It's fine,' Paco said.

'Anywhere will suit us,' Private Pérez told him.

The driver lowered the tailboard. Paco jumped to the ground and held out his hand for Cindy. The woman shook her head. 'I appreciate the gallantry, Ruiz,' she said, 'but I'm a farm girl, and I've been climbing in and out of trucks by myself ever since I learned to walk.'

Paco stood back and admired the grace with which the woman he loved managed even such a mundane task as getting out of a lorry. Pérez followed her – lithe and coiled – as if he expected some kind of ambush, and finally Jiménez lowered his bulky body on to the pavement.

The ex-policeman looked around him – up the Gran Via towards Plaza de Callao, down the same road towards Alcala. The hot summer streets of Madrid were as full – and as animated – as they'd been in the days before the bloody conflict broke out. True, there were fewer men to be seen around now that the militias were finally starting to get properly organized, and true, most of the men who *were* there wore blue boiler-suits. Yet for all that, the city had an air of pre-war normality about it.

The *madrileños* were still not taking this struggle for survival seriously enough, Paco thought. But they would – and very soon – because the well-trained military machine he had seen up in the mountains was not to be stopped by a group of poorly armed, poorly trained militiamen – however much those militiamen might be willing to fight and die for their cause.

Paco turned his attention to the two men standing next to him. Jiménez looked far from comfortable in a boiler suit which was a couple of sizes too small for him, but Pérez somehow managed to wear his *mono* with some style – almost as if it were one of the flashy suits he'd owned when he'd been working as a pimp down by the Manzanares.

184

'What will you do now?' Paco asked the wiry young man. 'Join one of the militias?'

Pérez laughed. 'What? Jump right out of the frying-pan straight into the fire?' He shook his head. 'This isn't my war, Inspector. I've no intention of giving up my life for God or the Republic or any other nonsense.'

He'd been wrong to think of Pérez as a rat, Paco thought. The private was much more like an urban fox – cunning and watchful, grabbing whatever he could when the opportunity presented itself, and obeying no rules but his own.

'Without a union or party card, it'll be very difficult to get anything to eat,' he warned.

Pérez shrugged. 'I'll get by somehow.'

'And what about him?' Paco asked, glancing across at the bulky Jiménez, who was studying the busy street with a mixture of what was probably wonder and incomprehension.

'I'll see he gets by, too.'

Yes, Paco thought, he probably would. Because for all his sneering comments, the city fox seemed to have become attached to the lumbering country bear. 'If you need any help—' he began.

'Thanks, but that won't be necessary,' Pérez interrupted. 'We've still got the jewels, and when we've used them up, well, we'll soon find some other way to make a bit of cash.'

'Be careful,' Paco advised. 'Most of the tricks you used to get up to in the old days now carry an automatic death penalty.'

'They'll have to catch me first,' Pérez replied. 'Anyway, we all have to die sometime.'

There really wasn't much more to say. For a few seconds, these three men who had been through so much together, yet had absolutely nothing in common, stood in embarrassed silence. Then Paco held out his hand to Jiménez. 'Good luck to you,' he said.

'Thank you, señor,' the country boy mumbled, awkwardly taking Paco's hand in his own huge fist. 'Goodbye, señorita.'

'Goodbye,' Cindy said. 'Look after yourself.'

Paco turned back to the smaller man. 'And the best of luck to you, too, my lad.'

Pérez grinned. 'I make my own luck,' he said. 'I'll tell you what, though, Inspector. When things are back to normal, maybe I'll let you arrest me again – just to make your record look good.'

'Things will never be back to normal,' Paco told him. 'Not in our lifetimes, anyway.'

The grin disappeared from his face, and Pérez was suddenly solemn. 'You're right,' he agreed, nodding his head. Then, as if solemnity were not in his nature, he brightened again. 'What the hell!' he said. 'Normal was never that good for me anyway.'

Paco watched the two men walk down the street, big Jiménez dwarfing the wiry Pérez, and was reminded again of the bear and the fox. Perhaps they would survive the war, he thought, and perhaps they wouldn't. But that was about as much as you could say for anyone.

He put his hand on Cindy's shoulder and squeezed it softly. 'Let's go home,' he said.

*

All the fires which had raged through the night had been finally doused, most of the rubble had been cleared from the streets, and any building in danger of imminent collapse had been demolished. Twelve hours after the explosions which had rocked the village of San Fernando de la Sierra, the place had been returned to something like military order.

The general paced his office fretfully. The previous evening had been a disaster. His troops had lost most of their small arms, and all of their explosives. If reinforcements hadn't arrived from Burgos mid-morning, there would have been nothing to stop the Republicans overrunning the village. As it was, the march on Madrid would have to be delayed. And who was to take the blame for that? It would not be him, he resolved. Colonel Valera had chosen to put himself in charge of security. Very well, then, Colonel Valera would be the man who bore the responsibility for things going so badly wrong.

But where the hell *was* Valera? he wondered. No one had seen the colonel since the explosions, and it had been left up to Major Gómez to take charge of the situation.

There was a knock on the door, and one of his aides entered.

'Yes, what is it?' the general snapped irritably.

'There's a village woman outside, sir,' the aide told him. 'She says she has some important information.'

'What kind of information?'

'She wouldn't say. She told me it was so important that it was for your ears alone.'

'What can a peasant woman know which could be as important as that?' the general demanded. 'Send her to Major Gómez.'

'Major Gómez is out in the sierra, sir.'

'And what the hell's he doing there?'

'I believe he's looking for the prisoner Ruiz.'

'The prisoner Ruiz!' the general said bitterly. 'The bloody prisoner Ruiz. If I'd had him shot when my wife suggested it, we'd never have been in this mess now.' He realized what he was almost admitting to. 'Of course,' he continued hastily, 'if Colonel Valera had been doing his job properly, it wouldn't have mattered a damn whether Ruiz was alive or not.'

'Quite so,' the aide agreed diplomatically. 'What about the woman, my general? Will you see her?'

The general sighed. 'Why not? I seem to have to do everybody else's job around here – I might as well do Gómez's.'

The aide ushered the woman into the room. She was around sixty, dressed in black, and obviously intimidated to be in the presence of such an important man.

'My . . . my name is Rosa Sanchez, Your Excellency,' she stuttered.

'What of it?' the general asked brusquely.

'My daughter was Carmen . . . the seamstress . . . and . . . and. . . .'

'I'm not interested in your family history.'

'She . . . she was the one who was murdered yesterday.'

The general slammed his hand down on his desk. 'Good God, don't you know I'm fighting a war here, woman?' he demanded. 'I've no time to concern myself with individual deaths, even if they do turn out to be murder. Stop wasting my time and get out!'

For a moment, it looked as if Rosa Sanchez would faint with terror, then she bit her lip and pressed on. 'The policeman from Madrid . . .' she mumbled.

'Ruiz?'

'I don't know his name. He . . . he gave me something for you.'

'When was this?'

'Last night. About an hour before all the explosions.'

For the first time, the general noticed the brown-paper package she was holding in her hands. 'Is that what he gave you?'

'Yes, Your Excellency.'

'Then hand it over to me, woman.'

With trembling hands, Rosa Sanchez placed the package on the desk. The general picked it up and ripped it open. It contained a petticoat – a beautifully embroidered petticoat which must have cost a small fortune.

'There's . . . there's a note as well,' Rosa Sanchez told him. 'The policeman said it would explain everything.'

But even without reading the note Paco had written, the general was already beginning to guess the truth. How could he fail to, when he was holding so much of it in his hands?

Chapter Twenty-Seven

Paco could feel Cindy's body pressed against his. The bed was not really wide enough to be shared comfortably by two people who weren't in love, but they *were* in love, and they thought it just perfect.

He rolled over, expecting to find that she'd gone to sleep, but her eyes were wide open and alert.

'Well, now that you've slaked your burning lust on my poor innocent body, don't you think it's time you told me about what happened to the general's dog?' she asked.

Paco lit two cigarettes, and handed one to Cindy. 'All the indications were there from the beginning,' he said. 'I'd have spotted them right away if I'd really been thinking like a policeman, but as I was only pretending to be interested in the case at that point, I didn't put them together until much later.'

'What indications?' Cindy asked, digging him in the ribs with her finger. 'Come on, Ruiz. Let's hear all the juicy details.'

Paco smiled. 'The first time the general spoke to me in his office, two significant things happened. The first was that a soldier from the Burgos convoy arrived carrying the latest newspaper. Now, he obviously knew the general's little foibles, because instead of walking straight over to the desk as you or I would have done, he waited in the doorway for the surviving dog – Reina – to come and take it off him.'

'Is this to the point, or are you just being deliberately obscure to tease me?' Cindy demanded.

'It's very much to the point,' Paco assured her. 'You should have seen how pleased the general was when the dog took him the paper. It's pathetic that a man in command of a large military machine – a man with thousands of lives in the palm of his hand – should take so much pleasure from such childish things.'

'But then, he wasn't really in charge at all, was he?' Cindy asked.

'No, he wasn't,' Paco agreed. 'He'd probably never have been promoted to the rank of general if it hadn't been for his family's influence, and he must have realized it, because he was quite happy to let Colonel Valera issue the orders which really mattered.'

'Which left him more time to go shopping for exotic presents for that pretty wife of his.'

'Right again. Anyway, the way he'd got the dog trained should immediately have set me thinking on the right lines, but as I said, I wasn't really interested in the case then.'

Cindy propped herself up on one elbow. 'But you became interested enough in it later,' she said. 'Anyway, stop trying to show me how clever you are, and get on with the story.'

Paco grinned, sheepishly. 'If I don't put things in their proper context, you'll never see how they all fit together,' he said in his own defence. 'Now, I told you that two significant things happened while I was in the general's office with Major Gómez. The first was the delivery of the newspaper. The second was the arrival of the general's wife – several minutes later. She said that she'd come with the convoy from Burgos, too.'

'So what?'

'She didn't seem overly upset about the death of her dog – though she gave the general hell for it – but she was very angry when she was told I was going to try and find its killer. I thought at the time it was because my blue boiler-suit identified me as one of the enemy – she's very right-wing, you know. But, of course that wasn't the reason at all. What she really didn't want was a competent investigator looking into the case.'

'Then she shouldn't have been worried about having you on it,' Cindy said, teasing him.

'The second time I went to the *palacio* was interesting, too,' Paco continued, ignoring her words. 'She left the door to the general's office open while she was trying to talk him into shooting me, just to make sure I heard her. But when she spoke to me, she closed the door so *he* couldn't hear.'

'And what did she say to you?'

'She said that a real man wouldn't wait around to be executed. You see, if she couldn't have me shot, then she at least wanted me to run away.'

'What exactly are you saying, Ruiz?' Cindy asked. 'That she killed her own dog?'

'No, I'm not saying that at all.' Paco swung his legs off the bed. 'I think we both deserve a *copa* of brandy.'

'You're not wrong,' Cindy told him.

190

He padded into the kitchen, and returned with two brandy glasses almost full to the brim. He handed one to Cindy, and took a sip from the other. 'You see, my big problem was working out why anyone would want to kill the dog in the first place,' he said. 'Not only was it pointless, but it was also dangerous.'

'I know all that,' Cindy said impatiently.

'There were two additional things which helped me knit it all together,' Paco continued. 'As I told you, the general's wife left the office door open so I would fully appreciate just how hard she was working at getting me shot. What she couldn't realize was that I'd also hear something that would help me to solve the case.'

'And what was that?'

'The general said something like, "Isn't that the dress I bought you for your birthday?" And she said, "You know it is. You always remember everything you've bought for me". Which, according to Pérez was quite a lot, and usually very daring – some of the other men used to run the risk of being disciplined just to get a look at her underwear hanging on the clothes' line.'

'I'm still not getting this,' Cindy admitted. 'You said there were *two* additional things that tipped you off. What was the second one?'

'The murder of the seamstress, of course.'

'Ah yes, you were going to tell me about her.'

'She was found dead in her mother's bedroom. Hanging from a hook. The full details don't matter. The important thing is that I'd seen her in Colonel Valera's office the previous day, and that had sealed her fate. He simply couldn't take the risk that I'd talk to her, and at that particular moment it was easier for him to kill her than it was for him to kill me – although he'd already tried that, late at night on the Calle Belén.'

'You're gonna have to talk me through this, Ruiz,' Cindy said. 'You might have given me all the bits of the puzzle, but I have absolutely no idea how they fit together.'

Paco took another sip of his brandy, and tried not to look complacent. 'Let's go back to the convoy arriving from Burgos,' he said. 'Who would you think was the most important person in that convoy? The officer in charge of it?'

'I suppose so.'

Paco grinned. 'He was probably no more than a captain – a major at most – and you think he'd be more important than—'

'The general's wife!' Cindy interrupted.

'Certainly it was the general's wife. Can you imagine what it would be like escorting her? I can, because I've met her. If she wanted to go to the toilet, I've no doubt in my mind that the whole convoy came to a halt. If she decided to stop at a roadside inn for a cup of coffee, then the entire military machine would have to wait outside until she'd finished and was ready to move on again.'

'She sounds like a real bitch,' Cindy said.

'She is. But the question you have to ask yourself is why this real bitch arrived at the *palacio* considerably later than the newspaper did. Either she'd been kept waiting at the back of the convoy until some of the more routine business had been done, or—'

'Or she hadn't just come from Burgos at all!' Cindy said, with sudden realization.

'Now you're thinking.'

'She'd been in the village for some time. And the reason she was keeping her presence a secret from her husband was because she was having an affair with . . . with Colonel Valera!'

'That's right. But she knew she couldn't stay in Valera's house for ever, and she used all the confusion of the convoy's arrival to slip back home. It was risky, of course – the general might have asked to speak to whoever drove her down from Burgos. But why should he? Anyway, it's always a risky business, having an affair with your husband's second-in-command.'

'And the fact that she was in the village would explain why the dog escaped from the *palacio*!' Cindy said excitedly.

'Of course. He ran away to look for his mistress. And the fact that he knew *where* to look would suggest she'd taken him there before.' Paco looked down at his brandy glass and was surprised to find it empty. 'I think I need a refill,' he said. 'Just a small one this time.'

Cindy pulled a face. 'I'll swear you're breaking off at the crucial moment just to annoy me,' she said.

'Maybe I am,' Paco agreed. 'Is it working?'

When he returned from the kitchen, Cindy was deep in contemplation. 'I think I've got some of it figured out now,' she said. 'The dog went straight to the colonel's house. Right?'

'Right.'

'The door must have been off the latch – an easy mistake to make when you're in the throes of passion – and the dog was able to push it open and get inside. What I don't understand is why the sentry on duty didn't stop him.'

'There wasn't one.'

'How come?'

'When I asked Major Gómez why sometimes there were sentries and sometimes there weren't, he said he withdrew them to show the colonel that he wasn't as important as he thought he was. That was a lie, but it was one he had to tell in order to appear to be shielding a brother officer – even if he couldn't stand the brother officer in question.'

'So what was the truth?'

'Gómez dismissed the sentries for no other reason than that Valera told him to. You see, he didn't dare risk any of the enlisted men finding out what was going on with him and the general's wife.'

'The *enlisted* men?' Cindy repeated. 'Do you mean to say that the *officers* knew all about it?'

'Some of them, certainly, but they're bound by a code of honour. That isn't the case with the ordinary soldiers. If one of them had stumbled across the truth, news of the affair would have spread round the village like wildfire. In the end, even the general himself would probably have come to hear of it. So Valera and the general's wife knew they had to be discreet. And they were – even Private Pérez, who keeps his nose pretty close to the ground, only knew that the colonel had a mistress of *some sort*.'

'OK, so now we've got that straight, you want to hear what I think happened next?' Cindy said.

'Be my guest.'

'There was no one on the ground floor, but the dog could hear noises coming from upstairs.' Cindy giggled. 'Very interesting noises. He went to investigate. And what did he find when he got there? Why, he found Colonel Valera and the general's wife frolicking buck-naked on the colonel's bed! Well, they must have been shocked. Maybe they even shouted him. But it didn't bother the dog – he took it as part of some kind of game.'

'You're nearly there,' Paco said encouragingly.

'There was a piece of her clothing on the floor. Pants or a stocking or something.'

'It was her petticoat,' Paco supplied.

'The dog picks it up. One of the lovebirds makes a grab at it. Maybe that's when the petticoat gets the tear in it, or maybe it happens later.' She looked anxiously at Paco, as if she'd just started to wonder if she was talking a load of nonsense. 'It does get torn, doesn't it?'

'Yes, it gets torn,' Paco assured her.

'Anyway, grabbing at it only makes things worse. The dog is now convinced they're all playing a really neat game, and he runs downstairs again. There's one hell of a panic in the bedroom, with madam wailing about what's going to happen when the general finds out, and Valera getting dressed as quickly as he can. By the time the colonel's got downstairs, the dog is out in the street, and when Valera goes after him, he starts to run away.' She paused. 'What was he going to do with the petticoat? Take it to the general, just like he'd been trained to take newspapers?'

'Perhaps,' Paco said. 'Or perhaps not. It doesn't really matter one way or the other.'

'Why not?'

'Picture the scene. Valera is chasing the dog along the Calle Belén, but he's wasting his time. The animal can easily outrun him, and as long as it still thinks they're playing a game together, that's exactly what it intends to keep on doing. But as far as the colonel's concerned, things are getting desperate – because they're approaching the Calle Mayor.'

'Why is that important?'

'Because the street is full of people. That's why it doesn't matter whether or not the dog was taking the petticoat back to the general. All it would need for their secret to be out would be for someone – anyone – to see the animal coming from the general direction of the Plaza de Santa Teresa with the bloody thing in its mouth. Everyone would recognize it, you see. They all know her taste in clothes – or rather the general's taste – and she's the only woman in the village who could afford such finery. Besides, it's her dog – and everyone knows that, too.'

'So it was vital that the colonel stopped the dog before it reached the main street.'

'Precisely. He didn't want to shoot it – he knew that would only be storing up trouble for himself in the future – but he really hadn't any other choice if he was to avoid immediate exposure. So, he did shoot it. I expect he would have liked to take it away and bury it in secret – a dog which has simply disappeared is much easier to explain away than one which has been killed. But the point is, he didn't have the chance. People on the Calle Mayor had heard the shots, and were already running toward the Calle

Belén to find out what had happened. The only thing he had time for was to snatch the petticoat from the dead animal's mouth and make a run for it. Even then, he nearly got caught. Pérez and his mates didn't actually *see* him – the bend in the street ensured that – but they did hear him running away.'

'He had to get the petticoat repaired,' Cindy said.

'Naturally. The general would eventually have noticed it was missing – for all I know he made her pose in it two or three times a week – and want to know where it had gone. And how was she to answer him? Was she to say that she had thrown away a new and expensive petticoat which he had personally chosen? No, the lovers' only chance was to get it skilfully repaired and hope that in the dim light of the bedroom, the general wouldn't notice the repair. And it was that decision, plus my intervention in the case, which cost Carmen Sanchez her life.'

Cindy shook her head. 'Poor Carmen. She's the real victim in this. If she'd never learned her trade, she'd still have been alive today.' A tear ran down her cheek for the dead seamstress she'd never even met. 'I think I'd like another brandy now, Ruiz,' she said.

When Paco returned from his third trip to the kitchen, Cindy had wiped her tear away, and was smoking a fresh cigarette. 'What do you think's going to happen to Valera?' she asked.

Paco shrugged. 'The general will have the evidence of his wife's infidelity in his hands by now. He will, of course, want to have Valera shot as soon as possible. But I doubt if the colonel will have waited around to be arrested. I know that if I'd gone back to my quarters to find my sentry tied up in the hallway and a vital piece of evidence missing, I'd have left the village as quickly as I possibly could.'

'So Valera will get away with it?'

'Perhaps,' Paco admitted. 'But I very much doubt it. The general has been insulted just about as much as any man – particularly any *Spanish* man – can be insulted. And even though he's a clown, he still has a lot of influence of the rebel side of the divide. Sooner or later, he'll find Valera, and when he does, the colonel will be a dead man.'

'I hope you're right,' Cindy said, with just a trace of anxiety slipping into her voice.

Epilogue

Night cast its cloak of darkness over the city and the mountains alike, and once again the people of Castile relished their escape from debilitating summer heat.

In dozens of bars around the Puerta de Toledo, drunken militiamen alternately mourned for their lost comrades and boasted to the barely-listening whores about how many of the enemy they would kill the next day.

In one of those bars a small wiry man, his pocket stuffed with peseta notes he'd got in exchange for some semi-precious stones, ordered two more wines. 'Isn't it just like I promised, Jiménez,' he said to his much larger friend. 'I told you I'd look after you. We'll have a great time, you and me. This is the best city in the whole world for enjoying yourself.'

But the country boy, instead of sharing in the other man's enthusiasm, merely nodded vacantly, and wondered what was happening to his family's little farm.

Further north in the city, Paco Ruiz stood at his living-room window, watching the street scene below.

'What now, Paco?' asked a voice behind him.

'Now?' Paco repeated. 'Now, I suppose my detective days really are finally over, and I'm back to being a militiaman.'

Cindy laughed. 'Your detective days will never be over,' she said. 'It's in your blood. Only you could start by investigating the death of a dog, and end up uncovering a double murderer.'

Perhaps she was right, he thought. Perhaps even in war there would always be room for a trained investigator. He opened the window wider, to allow any cooling breeze that was passing by to enter the room.

There was a cool breeze in the mountains, blowing across the Plaza Mayor of the village of San Fernando de la Sierra, carrying with it the odour of cooking, of black tobacco, and of a thousand sweaty soldiers whose main aim in life was to get as drunk as possible before their money ran out. They were quieter that evening than they had been on previous ones, because what had been made plain to them the night before was that war wasn't something you could just walk away from when darkness fell – war was everywhere.

In the *palacio* just up from the square, a tearful woman knelt on the floor at her husband's feet. 'You don't know what it was like,' she sobbed. 'It's you I love, Tubby, you know that, but Valera seemed to have a strange, evil power over me. I tried to resist him, but it was no good.'

'You've made a complete fool of me,' the general whined.

'Only if that's the way you choose to look at it. Once Valera's dead, only you and I will know what's really happened.'

'But the other officers—'

'They don't suspect a thing,' the general's wife lied. She massaged her husband's knee. 'Would you like us to go upstairs?'

'I don't know. After what you've done to me, I'm not sure I ever want to go upstairs with you again.'

'But I've got some lovely clothes I could put on for you,' his wife coaxed. 'I could wear all your favourites. You'd like that, wouldn't you.'

'Yes,' the general said, nodding his head in sad resignation and rising to his feet. 'Yes, I'd like that.'

Major Gómez sat alone in his quarters, smoking a cheroot. Things had gone exceptionally well, he decided. His conduct during the 'attack' on the village had been noted, and even without the gap left by Colonel Valera on the general's staff, his promotion would be assured. It would be good to be a colonel – to be paid enough to be able to afford a new uniform, to have a house to himself instead of sharing with other officers. And there might be even one more perk to his new position. If he were careful – if he avoided the mistakes Valera had made – then he, too, might soon get to sleep with the most beautiful woman in all Spain.

Out on the high sierra, a man dressed in a cheap uniform lit a cigarette, and shivered. He had lost everything, he told himself. If he had not killed the private who'd become separated from his comrades, he would now not even have a safe identity. He ran through his plan in his mind. When it became light, he would shave off his military moustache, and his disguise would be complete. Then he would stumble into a unit where he wasn't known, and feed them some kind of story about how all his comrades had been massacred. And so he would become Private Jaime Boaz for a while. But only for a while. As soon as he saw his chance, he would cut loose and embark on his mission of punishing the men who had caused his downfall. He would kill the treacherous Major Gómez first. He would make sure it was a very slow and painful death. And when he'd finished that job, he would go after the detective from Madrid.

Printed by Amazon Italia Logistica S.r.l.
Torrazza Piemonte (TO), Italy

13774214R00114